Lazarus

SIMON FOSTER

Dedication

For the rock star in all of us.

Acknowledgments

I would like to once again thank Robert Wakeland for his cover design work.

And family and friends for their encouragement and support.

It's a long way to the shop if you wanna sausage roll.
— Oz Rock Mantra

1

I found the poor bastard just after closing time.

Anchor and I had poured the last hangers-on out the door and done our customarily cursory job of tidying up. Tossing garbage bags of empty bottles and tinnies down the basement stairs, sweeping up tons of discarded peanut shells, lifting stools onto tables to make mopping up easier for the early morning cleaning crew. I passed on Anchor's offer of a three a.m. slice at Rosario's and watched as he leapt over a puddle where we'd hosed a sheila's regurgitated peanuts off the footpath earlier in the evening. Then I lowered the shutters on the Lower East Side traffic, grabbed a six-pack of Melbourne Bitter from the fridge and climbed the internal stairs to my apartment.

"Mate, you home?" I said.

The living room was dark and a smell not quite like burnt toast hung in the air. It triggered a memory that took me back to the Queen's Birthday Weekend and fireworks season.

Gunpowder.

I hit the lights and dropped the six-pack. Shattered glass and foam sprayed across the living room floor.

I'd only ever seen one body before. The lifeless form of my mother, propped up in a coffin at a Sydney funeral home for viewing upon my return from New York, her face so wasted that she looked nothing like the person who had shaped me, her cheeks tinted orange from embalming fluid and, when I bent to kiss her, cold to the touch. Like my mother before him, this bloke was a little tough to recognize. But for less natural reasons. Vis-à-vis, he or someone not too keen on him had

1

blown off half his face. A gun rested on the floor near his outstretched right hand and an estuary of blood had gathered around his head, which was tilted back and leaning to one side. I forced myself to look again at his face, or what remained. An entry wound marked the underside of his chin. Whoever pulled the trigger must have pressed the muzzle hard against the skin, scorching a small perfect circle into his hide. The most unimaginative exercise in scarification. Four inches north, an exit wound accounted for his left eye and half his forehead. Traces of brain, blood and bone speckled the nearby wall like summer flies crowding a kitchen screen door.

Clearly, formal identification was going to take some time.

But I didn't need dental records to tell me who he was.

2

The call came through while I was out cycling. It seemed like any other call at the time.

I leaned my bike against a no parking sign on Van Brunt Street and dug my phone out of my back pocket.

"This is Luke."

"Luke Bales?" a stern voice said.

"Yeah."

"Officer Klein. Seventh Precinct."

"Gidday, Officer. And how are you on this fine, fine day?"

"You need to get your butt down here," he said, killing any talk of the weather.

"Down where?"

"Where do you think? A buddy of yours named you as his one phone call but he's in no condition to make it."

"Hold on a sec. You have some bloke at the precinct that says he knows me?"

"Correct."

"It's not Anchor, is it?" My offsider at The Billabong was a past master of finding trouble through no fault of his own. A few years back, when a sheila had gone missing from the bar, he'd quickly found his bum in the hot seat.

"Close but no cigar."

"Come again?"

I heard some papers rustle. "Says here this douchebag's name is Farmer. Barry Lionel Farmer. Goes by the name of Ajax."

"Oh," I said. "That's his stage name."

"Stage name?"

"It's a long story."

Ajax was a singer. Well, much more than a singer, actually. He was a fair dinkum Australian rock legend. Somehow he'd wandered into my bar a while back: the night after Cinco de Mayo, to be precise, the Mexican holiday that most Yanks celebrate without having a clue what they're actually celebrating. The weather had been on the right side of Spring but not far from bottoming out into another hellish New York summer, the country was still a few years away from the hope of its first black president, and, although the panic generated by 9/11 had long subsided, New York City remained wary, like a bloke who'd been mugged and would never feel safe walking down a dark alley again.

I recognized Ajax's sun-damaged mug immediately, despite last seeing him perform at a Sydney suburban beer barn with his band The Swallows over a decade earlier. As he slowly and deliberately poured beer after beer down his throat, I decided not to mention his celebrity to Anchor or anyone else. Let the man drink in peace.

And peacefully he did drink until an incident with a bride-to-be towards the end of the night. A hen's party had been drinking shots and snorting lines like it was the bride's last night of freedom, which perhaps it was. After all, she was staring down the barrel at a lifetime of commitment and all that that entailed. Sex-by-numbers, late night diaper changes, the whole kit and caboodle. Been there, done that, I thought, and reckoned the least I could do was let this sheila live it up a little. Pretty soon she was firing her wedding garter all over the joint like a lacy Exocet missile, bouncing it off lampshades, hitting blokes that took her fancy on the bum and snapping it laser-like at sheilas who didn't. Some hapless punter was probably in imminent danger of losing an eye, but I let it slide. Anyone angered by her antics soon forgave her when they saw her wedding veil.

Anyone, that is, except Ajax. When the garter inevitably ended up in his drink, he fished it out and held it up to the light.

"What. The. Fuck?" he said.

The bride-to-be hightailed it over. "That's mine."

"The hell it is," he said, raising his arm high so that the garter was just out of her reach.

"Give it back," she screeched.

"Give it to her, mate," said a stocky hipster with a lumberjack shirt and beard to match.

"I'll give it to her," Ajax said, "if she'll give it to me," then tilted his head back and slid the garter suggestively between his lips.

"O.K., enough is enough," said Joe the Bouncer, joining the fray. "Give the little lady her toy back."

Ajax smiled genially at Joe, as if to concede, then dropped the garter in his gob and swallowed hard. It went straight down his gullet. The bride screamed, leapt on him and pounded his chest. His reflex action — to this day, I don't think it was intentional — was to push her away. She toppled backwards, tripped on her high heels and struck her noggin on a corner of the pool table, opening a nasty gash on the back of her head.

The sight of blood sent the joint into a frenzy. Blokes fell on the rocker. He struggled like a Tasmanian Devil, flailing his arms and legs. But to no avail. The crowd parted as five blokes wrestled him towards the door. He looked at me, eyes pleading. But even in my lenient, everyone-deserves-a-fair-go book, mess with a sheila and you were out.

"You fucking assholes!" he yelled as they tossed him out onto the footpath. "You can't do this to me."

"We just did," said Joe the Bouncer, dusting off his hands like he'd taken out the garbage.

"Don't you know who I am?" he said, staggering to his feet as late-night pedestrians swerved to avoid him.

"The Wizard of Oz?" asked Joe.

"I'm Ajax fucking Farmer," he shouted.

"Yeah — and I'm Bon fucking Scott," someone yelled back, and everyone laughed as Joe shut the door on him.

Everyone, that is, except me.

To his credit, Ajax had returned the very next day to apologize, inviting me and my longtime girlfriend, Hannah, to his first New York gig, a low-key affair at the Living Room last night. The performance was supposed to be the first step toward getting his career back on track but instead it had gone radically off the rails. Ajax hit the stage blind drunk, barely able to perform, then got into an argument with a heckler and overturned a table of drinks before passing out.

And now, according to Officer Klein, something even worse had happened after the gig. Something serious enough to land him in jail.

"What's he done?" I asked.

"I'm not at liberty to divulge that over the phone," Klein said. "You'll need to come down to the precinct so I can explain the charges against this... this..."

"Ajax," I said.

The mere mention of his name left me a little star-struck, to be honest, as one can only be with an idol from one's teenage years. Even if said idol had fled his homeland for New York City in a bid to resurrect a career besieged by booze and drugs.

A battle that this phone call strongly suggested he wasn't winning.

I'd been riding the cobblestone streets of Red Hook in search of potential locations for a second bar so it took about twenty minutes to traverse the incline of the Manhattan Bridge, navigate Chinatown and reach the Lower East Side. After I checked in with the Seventh Precinct desk sergeant, I didn't have time to take a seat in the waiting area before a door alongside the counter swung open and a uniformed copper beckoned me forth with his index finger.

I'd studied a few years of high school German so I knew that the name on his badge meant small but there was nothing small about Officer Klein. He was a lean and lanky piece of work, his bony shoulders filling his uniform no better than a coat hanger. Blue eyes shone beneath blonde hair buzzed short; his lean face glowed with vitality. He displayed all the physical attributes of the exercise-aholic, right down to the no-nonsense digital Timex strapped to his bony left wrist, all the better to record lap times and splits. As he pointed the way to his desk, I noticed the watch's name. The Marathon. This bloke probably ran them before breakfast.

I'd not seen the inside of the Seventh Precinct squad room for several years but its vibe hadn't changed one iota. Coppers lolled at their desks reeking of dissatisfaction, mumbling into phones and prodding at computers like they were dispensing office furniture or stationery supplies rather than truth, justice and the American way. Posters proclaiming the departmental motto of "Courtesy, Professionalism, Respect" heightened the disconnect between perception and reality. At the back of the squad room, a bloke who was either drunk or deranged was banging on his holding cell door, belting out the chorus of Journey's "Don't Stop Believin'" over and over like a stuck record. Every time a copper told him to shut up, silence would descend for a moment and then he would start up again.

Klein led me to his rectangular island in a sea of rectangular islands, pulling over a chair for me before taking his seat behind the desk. One item personalized the space: a framed photo of he and his wife on their wedding day, standing on a beach waiting for whatever life threw their way. She was thin and athletic, too. They probably tied the knot while jogging hand-in-hand.

"What's this all about, Officer?" I said, taking a seat. Malone and Lirianos, two local detectives that I'd crossed paths with a few times, sat at their desks across the room. Lirianos glared at me, his eyes burrowing into my face, a wad of scar tissue on his face glowing red like a long thin strip of chewed bubble gum.

"This buddy of yours is in the shit, that's what."

"Well, I wouldn't say he's my buddy, exactly." I wondered why Ajax had nominated me as his one phone call. Probably because he had recently arrived in New York and didn't know many other people.

"What's the charge?"

Klein fixed me with Atlantic Ocean eyes. Cold and blue. "Assault."

"Assault?" I couldn't imagine Ajax bashing anything, except maybe the strings on his guitar.

"Yeah. Assault. Not just your regular assault, though."

"What's an irregular assault?"

"Take a wild guess."

"I dunno. Hitting a copper?"

"Worse. Much worse."

"Worse? Ajax did something worse than hitting a copper?"

Klein rolled his eyes at Ajax's name. "*Ajax* assaulted a woman."

"He hit a sheila?" I said, a little too loudly. Malone sniffed from the other side of the room and Lirianos smirked before picking up his phone. "I'm calling bullshit."

Klein prodded some papers on his desk. "Charge sheet never lies."

"Who?"

"One Gina Marks."

"Gina?"

"You know her?"

"Yeah." I ran my fingers over my crew cut. "Kinda."

"You can't kinda know someone," Klein said, arching an eyebrow. "You either do or you don't."

"I met her last night."

"Where?"

"At a gig…of Ajax's."

"Where was this gig?" he said, framing the last word like he'd just bitten into an onion.

"The Living Room. On Stanton." It seemed prudent not to mention how the performance had ended. I'd never seen someone so drunk attempt to perform. It had been impressive, in a full speed ahead and damn the torpedoes kind of way, but definitely not the best first step toward rebuilding a sunken career.

"Gina was there, too," I said. "Obviously. She works at the hotel where he's staying, I think. Left with him at the end of the night." My voice trailed off as I asked if she was OK.

Klein glanced at the paperwork again. "EMTs rushed her to Beth Israel for a once-over." He reached for a white mug that coffee had turned brown over the years, like nicotine seeping into a smoker's fingers. A wrinkled

Yankees logo peeled from one side. "According to the emergency room report, she had no broken bones, no concussion. No serious injuries, except for a nasty shiner that she'll carry around for a while."

"I guess that's something. Jesus, what was Ajax thinking?"

"Who knows? It's impossible to get a straight word out of him."

"He's not in a great place at the moment," I said, stating the bleeding obvious. "He just moved here from Australia and he's trying to get his act together."

"Sure going about it in a strange way."

"He is struggling a bit," I conceded.

A crashing sound from across the room interrupted my thoughts. It was Lirianos, slamming his phone back in its cradle. He stood up and stormed across the squad room. The other coppers kept working like it was nothing out of the ordinary.

"What's up with him?" I said, stealing a glance at the charge sheet as Klein's eyes flicked over to Lirianos.

Klein pointed to a crooked stack of paperwork on his desk about a foot and a half high. "Same as the rest of us. Too much to do, too little time." He took a sip of coffee. "Plus he's Homicide. They've had more than their fair share of call outs lately."

I nodded. There had been a lot of talk at the bar about the area's recent spate of drug murders. Some kind of turf war was going on, according to The Billabong's bar stool pundits, who discussed the mounting body count like fantasy football rather than the brutal ending of people's lives that it actually was. Drug dealers are pretty low on the social totem pole, and rightfully so.

"For the last time, shut the fuck up!" I heard Lirianos shout. Then, when the drunken singing started up again, there was the loud smack of flesh hitting flesh. This time, the singing stopped for good. Not so much as a murmur went through the squad room.

I swallowed and looked from the charge sheet back up to Klein's face. "This Ajax thing's not that big a deal, is it?"

"Maybe, maybe not." He tilted his wrist to check the time, ready to move on.

"Nice watch," I said, switching gears to everyone's favorite subject — themselves — to keep him talking.

"Thanks," he grunted.

"You running the marathon this year?"

"Fifth in a row." He straightened his back and for the first time looked at me as a human being.

"What's your goal?"

"Three ten."

"Nice. I probably couldn't cover it on my bike in that time."

"You'd be surprised," he said, more comfortable now that we were discussing a topic near and dear to his heart. "Just putting one foot in front of the other, that's all there is to it."

"I'm sure it's a little harder than that." I steered him back to Ajax. "So, is Ajax really in that much trouble?"

He shifted in his chair, relaxing a little. "Misdemeanor assault is a serious charge. Especially when a female is involved. He's facing a thousand dollar fine and maybe a year in jail, depending on the judge."

"Shit."

"Plus he's here on a tourist visa, right?"

I hadn't given it much thought. "I guess so."

"That's what his Homeland Security record says. ESTA Waiver. He could be deported." Klein sighed. "More paperwork."

"Deported?" Talk about an ignominious end to a mission of self-redemption. "When will we know for sure?"

"Arraignment. Sometime later today."

"That's quick."

"Has to happen within twenty-four hours of arrest. That's the law."

"Any chance I can see him before then?"

Klein shook his head. "He was moved to the Tombs just before you arrived."

"The Tombs?"

"Central Booking. Over on Centre Street, next to the courthouse. He'll sober up there for a few hours and then be moved to a holding cell prior to arraignment."

"What happens at this arraignment?" I hated even using the word. This was starting to sound pretty damn serious.

"He'll enter a plea and then the judge will decide if he should get bail or not."

"Do they usually?"

"Depends. If he pleads guilty, a judgment could be passed there and then. If not, the judge will decide whether to grant bail until the court date."

"What do you mean if he pleads guilty? Why wouldn't he? He did it, didn't he?"

"I'm not a mind reader, Bales. I'm just the arresting officer." He took another sip of coffee. "Lucky me."

"What kind of bail are we talking about?"

He shrugged his shoulders. "Five grand."

"Five grand? Sounds a little steep."

"It's standard for this kind of offence, even for first timers. Plus there's the considerable risk of flight, him not being a citizen and all."

"Seems a bit harsh when we don't even really know what happened."

Klein shrugged his shoulders. "Seems pretty open and shut to me. But be that as it may, even if you had five grand, you couldn't do anything with it until after five p.m. today."

"Why five p.m.?"

"That's when night session starts. His arraignment should come up then."

I sat there mute, nodding in agreement like one of those bobble-head dogs Dad used to have on the back ledge of our car when I was a kid. But Klein was wrong. Because I didn't have to wait till five p.m. I could get things started right now.

I reckon Ajax being my boyhood hero had something to do with my decision, but mostly it was that here was a bloke trying to get his act together and everyone was expecting him to fail. That was something I could relate to. Over the years I'd explored many paths and cocked up pretty much all of them. Even moving to New York with my successful wife hadn't changed that; at least, not until after 9/11, when Suzie chose to flee the city with our daughter Phoebe and I stayed behind to open The Billabong, the last roll of the dice to prove I could achieve something on my own. To my surprise, I had succeeded, albeit with the help of my silent partner Charlie Bertolucci, a former NYPD chief with serious political ambitions.

Clearly, Ajax deserved what we Aussies call a fair go: the chance to succeed before society consigned him to the garbage bin of history. And as far as I could tell, no one else was going to help him get it.

Of course, if I'd known how things would turn out I might have been a tad more circumspect about the matter.

3

According to Klein, I would have to wait until five p.m. that evening to bail out Ajax. But in the meantime, there was someone else I could help and maybe help out Ajax in the process.

While Lirianos' explosion at the cell block choir boy distracted Klein, I had memorized Gina's home address from the charge sheet. I left the precinct and scooted straight back to my studio apartment on Essex Street. A homeless bloke sleeping it off on the sidewalk in front of the bar complained as I crashed open the metal shutters and tossed my bike in the basement. Then I headed upstairs and plugged Gina's address into Google Maps; it told me that she lived in Sunset Park, Brooklyn, an immigrant enclave east of Red Hook and south of Park Slope. I had just ridden out to Brooklyn and wasn't keen on repeating the effort. I hoofed it to Grand Street and rode the D train out to Thirty-Sixth Street and Fourth Avenue.

Sunset Park is a hotbed of legal and illegal immigrants, mostly Latinos and Chinese, trying to latch onto their small part of the American dream. As I walked ten blocks south of the subway down Fourth Avenue, percussive Puerto Rican pop and the smell of rotisserie chicken populated the air; the mania of Brooklyn's Chinatown lay a dozen blocks east. I dropped five bucks on a bouquet of mixed flowers at a bodega then turned right onto Forty-Eighth Street. At the far end of the downhill sloping block, the Meccano-like legs of the Brooklyn-Queens Expressway partially obscured dockside warehouses and the slate grey waters of New York Harbor. Boxy, turn-of-the-century row houses refinished in cream aluminum siding lined both sides of the street. Beige iron awnings hung over their lower floor windows. You would be hard pressed to find a street with less personality, I thought, although that in itself is a personality. Each building was four floors high, two apartments per floor on either side of a common stairwell.

I found Gina's building on the northern side of the street, one in from the expressway, which probably made it considerably noisier than the rest of the buildings on her street but also considerably cheaper. Higgledy-piggledy garbage cans littered the concrete yard beside the stoop, along with a rusty propane bottle and an abandoned stroller, its cheap nylon covering shredded by the elements.

Gina's apartment number was 1A. First floor, left-hand side of the building. I climbed the stoop and peered through her front window. Bed sheets acting as makeshift curtains blocked the view.

I hit her button on the intercom.

"Hello?" a voice came back.

"Gina?"

"Yes?"

"It's me. Luke."

"Luke?"

"Luke Bales. From the gig last night. You know…with Ajax."

"Oh." There followed several seconds of silence. Then the door buzzed. I pushed it open.

The building smelled of rising damp. Somewhere, a radio blared, a stew stewed, and some wailing kid was catching almighty hell from his mother in Spanish.

Gina stood in the apartment door to the left of the stairwell wearing a faded terry-toweling bathrobe with the initials BSH monogrammed over her left breast. Blue Skies Hotel shower products presumably dominated her bathroom, too. I'd learned last night that she worked as a cleaner at the hotel where Ajax was staying. Apparently they had become mates since his arrival, although which variety of mate I didn't quite know. Relations between them had appeared purely platonic the previous night, although Ajax was admittedly so drunk that he could barely interact with anyone.

Gina's bathrobe overflowed with cleavage, bulging in all the right places. Thick, curved eyelashes saved features that may have appeared mannish on another sheila — full lips, heavy eyelids, strong nose. She was all woman all right. Or should I say senorita, because although I had grown up in the great white heartland of Australian suburbia and was therefore no expert in the ethnicities department, her olive skin suggested northern Mediterranean origins. Spain or Portugal, if I had to guess.

This morning, though, her curly black ringlets resembled the puffy wool of a merino and her one good eye was dull with sleep. The other eye's lids were fused together like she'd just stepped out of a boxing ring. It was black and bulging and fit to burst.

"Gidday." I held out the flowers as I approached her door. "I was sorry to hear about what happened."

"How do you know where I live?" she asked, ignoring the flowers.

"Oh. I…ah, the coppers told me." Not exactly a lie. After all, I had gleaned her address from official police documentation. "I wanted to check on you. Make sure that you were OK."

"I see," she said, like she didn't really see at all. She studied me for a moment and then decided to let it go. She took the flowers then stepped aside to let me in.

The apartment was run-down, its timber floor and lower walls scuffed from decades of tenants moving possessions in and out. It appeared to be a one-bedroom railroad sparsely furnished with second-hand items: a couch upholstered in black corduroy, a folding table undertaking double duty as a dining table and work bench, a twenty-four inch TV sitting atop a low pine bookshelf. The walls were bare, painted the same flat shade of white that New York City landlords default to every fourth or fifth time the tenancy turns over.

Gina walked into the open plan kitchen and lay the flowers on the counter. Cheap new pinewood cabinets clashed with an ancient gas cooker and rust-riddled fridge. Two pink polka-dot metal dishes sat on the floor, one half-full of water and the other containing a handful of cat biscuits.

Gina cinched her robe tighter around the middle, trying to make herself feel more secure in the company of a stranger. But it only served to further accentuate the curves hidden beneath. I tried in vain not to stare. Like most blokes, I had experienced love at first sight when I was too young to know any better — specifically Shona Wilder, a caramel-skinned Fijian in fifth grade — but had long since dismissed the phenomena as a symptom of immaturity. Looking at Gina now, however, I wasn't so sure.

She stretched on tiptoes to retrieve a vase from a higher shelf. The robe rose up to reveal the backs of her legs.

"Here, let me." I eased her aside and grabbed the vase.

"Thank you," she said, filling it with water.

"I shouldn't have let you get in that cab alone with him last night," I said. After Ajax had crashed and burned, Hannah and I helped Gina pour him into a taxi to get him back to the Blue Skies.

"Please. You were not to know. And you had…what was her name?"

I smiled. "Hannah."

"You had Hannah with you."

"Yeah. I did. So…how are you feeling?"

"A little shaken up but I will survive."

"That eye must hurt."

"Actually, it probably hurts more to look at." She unwrapped the flowers, took a pair of scissors from a knife block and began trimming the stems. As she finished each flower, she placed it in the vase.

"Please," she said, gesturing to a chrome stool near the kitchen counter. "Sit down."

I did as I was told, grateful that she seemed to be warming to the idea of my presence.

"So what happened?" I said. "Last thing I knew, we were helping you get Ajax into a cab. I thought you were going straight back to the hotel."

"We were. I mean, we did. The bellhop helped me get Ajax to his room. Then he would not let me leave, insisting that I drink with him. He was making a lot of noise, disturbing the other guests with his guitar playing. I tried to talk some sense into him." She fell quiet. "This was the result."

Her phrasing was strangely formal, like she'd been to language school. As bonkers as it might sound, immigrants to the United States often attend classes to master the dark art of speaking American. Perhaps I should have employed the same strategy. I remember calling to get the gas connected when we first moved into our apartment in the Village; the ConEd employee on the other end of the phone had no idea what I was talking about. Which is kind of remarkable, when you think about it, considering that we were speaking the same language.

"I can't believe he actually hit you," I said.

"He was so drunk, I am not sure he even knew who he was hitting. He kept saying the name Sharon."

"Sharon? Who's Sharon?"

"I do not have the faintest idea. One minute I was turning down the music, the next minute I was lying there on the floor amongst the liquor bottles." She shook her head. "He apologized profusely but I would not be dissuaded from calling the police." She finished trimming the last flower and carried the vase into the living room where she placed it on a coffee table in front of the sofa. She sat down and patted the cushion beside her. "Come."

I took a seat next to her, fully aware of her scent. But by scent, I don't mean perfume. I mean the smell of her. Her skin, her hair, her...well, her.

"I don't blame you for calling the coppers," I said.

"It was the only way to resolve the situation. Who knows what he might have done next."

Stray cat hairs mottled the black corduroy of the sofa and scratches scarred the legs of the coffee table. A cat was somewhere nearby, no doubt hiding from the stranger in its midst. Hopefully the same couldn't be said for a boyfriend, I thought, then guiltily remembered Hannah.

"Are you pressing charges?" I said.

Gina looked down and picked at a knot in her bathrobe cord. "A man should never strike a woman. Where I come from, it is considered cowardly."

"I think that's true of most places. And I'm not here to make excuses for what Ajax did. It is totally unacceptable. But if you go through with the charges, that'll be the end of the line for him. At best, he'll be deported. At worst, he'll end up on Riker's Island."

"What are you suggesting? That I just forget that the man hit me?"

"No. But if you drop the charges then you'll never have to think about it again. No police interviews, no courtrooms. No more seeing Ajax Farmer." I looked her in her good eye. "Gina, the bloke is trying to make a fresh start. Do you really want to be the person who brings that to a stop?"

Her good eye glared back. "I will not drop the charges."

"Fair enough," I said, taken aback by her determination. But she had every right to be indignant. After all, why should she forgive Ajax? He was the one who had screwed up. Maybe paying the consequences would teach him a lesson, calm him down a bit and set him on the right track. Lord knows he was firmly headed down the wrong one at the moment.

Gina sat silently, playing with that knot. Then she did what I least expected. She took my hand.

"You are a good friend, Luke. You are a good man."

"What do you mean?"

"Coming here, trying to defend Ajax. While I do not agree, I can admire your loyalty. I can tell that you are the kind of man who will always stand by a friend."

I could have told her that I barely knew the bloke, that I was just trying to make sure that, despite what he'd done, he didn't fall through the cracks like so many blokes before him. But instead I just gave her hand a soft squeeze and stood up to leave before I got myself into any more trouble.

How was I to know that it was far too late for that?

I scribbled down my phone number in case Gina needed any help, an ulterior motive baked in there somewhere, then headed back to the Fourth Avenue subway. On the way I called Anchor to check that he could open up The Billabong and run solo for a few hours. Then I caught the D train back to Chinatown, ducked into a Chase bank on Canal and Mulberry, then walked the few blocks crosstown to The Tombs.

The Tombs is located on Centre Street just south of Canal. Comprised of two buildings connected by an overhead walkway, its blocks of stained granite look like they've soaked up every drop of misery that the courts have trafficked in over the decades, dealing with the hand-cuffed human cargo dumped daily at the rear roller-door to meet their reckoning.

Since I was innocent — at least in the eyes of the law — I was able to wander in through the front door. I threaded my way past gloomy aged woodwork to the arraignment court. Family and friends of those awaiting judgment packed the room, as well as tourists and general nosey parkers curious to see how American justice is dispensed. I squeezed onto the end of a wooden bench beside two Japanese tourists, twenty-something sheilas with Hello Kitty handbags and stilettos with heels not much shorter than their legs. They looked at me and then giggled behind their hands to each other.

At five o'clock on the dot the sad and sorry procession of arraignments began. A parade of defendants that was almost entirely black and male, charged with offences including but not limited to possession of marijuana, breaking and entering and auto theft. Offences that hadn't upended the balance of society but crimes that, in the state's eyes, needed reckoning with none-the-less. Each offender was in court for a few brief minutes, during which time the court officer would read the docket number and defendant's name, the prosecutor and defense attorney would outline their cases, and then the judge would pronounce his bail decision and set a court date. At first the process was somewhat interesting, but after a dozen cases the spectacle of seeing someone's hopes and dreams dented grew depressingly repetitive. Then the crowd thinned as friends and family left the court after their relevant cases were settled. It wasn't long, only an hour or so, before the Japanese girls left too. They were no longer giggling.

It was a further two long hours before the court officer shouted out a docket number followed by, "People against Barry Lionel Farmer!" and two coppers led Ajax to the front of the room, leaving him to stand beside what I deduced to be the defense attorney appointed by the state. Even in a courtroom full of society's troubled, Ajax stood out like a pimple on a baby's bum. He was wearing his classic musician's garb from the previous night's gig: black t-shirt, black stovepipes. Over the t-shirt he wore a black corduroy Levis jacket sporting badges of different bands. The Jam, The Clash, The Sex Pistols. His shoulder-length hair, too uniformly black not to be dyed, was feathered LA-rock style like a young Joan Jett, softening a face whose sharp cheekbones and wan skin showed definite signs of wear and tear. Nights of partying and days of Australian sun had taken their toll — not to mention last night's shenanigans.

"Do you waive the reading?" the court officer asked the defense lawyer, just as he had for every case I'd witnessed.

"Yes," the defense lawyer replied by rote, reflecting the formality that the question apparently was.

The judge spent a few moments perusing the paperwork in front of him. Then he simply said, "Notes?"

Both the prosecutor and the defense lawyer shook their heads.

"What say the people?" the judge asked, peering over his glasses at the Assistant DA.

A young woman in a bright red pantsuit replied, "Grade 3 misdemeanor assault is a serious charge, your honor." She outlined the circumstances of the alleged crime: how Ajax, in a drunken rage, had assaulted a woman.

The judge took off his glasses and made a show of polishing them. "I can see all that in the paperwork, Ms. Haversack. I assume the state is seeking bail?"

"The defendant is an Australian citizen on a ninety-day tourist visa. As such, he's a non-citizen of the United States with no ties to the community and no means of gainful employment. In fact, he currently resides in a hotel. We think bail of five thousand dollars is appropriate."

"I see." The judge raised his eyebrows at the public defender, a pudgy bloke in a double-breasted suit and bow tie.

"We don't deny," said the defense lawyer in response, "that Mister Farmer has very little local roots, your honor."

"And how does the defendant plead?"

"Not guilty, your honor. He's not Mike Tyson. He's a musician. Bail of a thousand dollars seems more appropriate."

"Be that as it may," the judge said, "we can't have him scarpering off to Ayer's Rock, can we?" He put his glasses back on and picked up his gavel. "Bail is set at five thousand dollars. The defendant shall surrender his passport until such time as the case is resolved, and report to his nearest precinct twice weekly. The case is adjourned until June 12ᵗʰ." He rapped the gavel on a block of wood, settling Ajax's immediate fate in just a few minutes.

I rushed over to Ajax. He was in a daze, stunned by the speed and severity of the judge's decision.

"Ajax!" I whispered.

He glanced at me, then turned to his lawyer. "I thought you said bail would be a few hundred bucks."

The public defender shrugged his shoulders. "Unfortunately, this judge is not known for his leniency."

"But I don't have five grand," Ajax said, as two coppers each took one of his arms and led him away.

"No worries, mate," I said to his back. "I do."

4

I'd withdrawn ten thousand smackeroos from the Chase bank in Chinatown on the way over to The Tombs. Officer Klein had suggested that the judge might set bail at around five thousand dollars but I had doubled the amount just to be sure. The savings were earmarked as start-up funds for a new bar but I reckoned that right now I could put it to better use. Besides, I was in the early days of exploring bar options. By the time I needed the money for the deposit on a lease or to fund renovations, Ajax would have appeared in court and I'd have the dough back, minus a small processing fee, according to the surprisingly helpful city employee behind a grilled window who took my hard-earned cash.

Once I'd paid Ajax's bail, I waited beside a receiving area for his release. After two cups of vending machine coffee, the first so distinctly lacking in flavor that I returned for a second just to check that my taste buds weren't mistaken, Ajax emerged on the other side of a plexi-glass screen. I watched as he went through the rigmarole of retrieving his boots, belt and personal effects. He slipped on his black suede winkle-pickers, cinching the silver buckles tight across his feet, then he went through the laborious process of putting all his jewelry back on. He sported more rings than any bloke had a right to wear: skull ring, Celtic ring, thumb ring embossed with the word Chosen in chunky block letters. All the finger fanciness went with the several hundredweight of metal that hung from his neck and ears, not to mention his liberal use of eyeliner. Once a rock star, always a rock star.

When he was finished, he stepped through a swinging half-door and back into the wide-open world. He was a free man — at least until June 12th, when he would front court again over the charges.

He shuffled over, his shoulders slumped. "You didn't need to do that."

"But I did."

"It was my own stupid fault. You should have let me rot."

Little did we know how right he was.

I walked Ajax down Centre Street to Canal then hailed a cab back to Essex and Delancey. By this time it was about ten o'clock at night but Cosmo's, the old school diner on the corner that operated as my de facto kitchen, was still swarming with nocturnal creatures. Cosmo, a Greek widower who had recently undergone hip replacement, oversaw proceedings from behind the cash register, while his only child Maria, a once-wayward teen who had surprised everyone — maybe even herself — by stepping up to fill the void left by her father's gammy hip, scurried about servicing the dozen tables and booths. Still, flirtation is a hard habit to break. Maria put an extra waddle in her bum as she brought us the menus.

Incarceration clearly hadn't curbed Ajax's appetite. He wolfed down two cheeseburgers, a side of onion rings and a chocolate milkshake. Despite the late hour, I ate my usual: a spinach and mushroom omelet, rye toast and French fries, washed down with a Diet Coke in a small nod to caloric considerations.

I nodded at his empty plate. "A tad hungry, were we?"

"The tucker in that joint was terrible. Stale white bread baloney sandwiches." He shuddered at the thought. "Plus, you know, feed a hangover."

"Nothing better than a burger for that."

"Would've been better with a few slices of beetroot." Back home, a burger isn't a burger unless it leaves purple stains on your fingers. He swallowed the last mouthful. "Look, I'm really sorry."

"Mate, you don't have to—"

He held up his hand. "I screwed up big time. I know it. For fuck's sake, you hardly know me. You could have ignored that phone call and no one would have blamed you. Certainly not me."

"Come off it, mate. You would have done the same."

"Would I?" He shook his head as if to answer his own question. "And then you took it upon yourself to bail me out."

"No worries." I followed my old man's credo — by all means do good, but not because you want the credit. Every Christmas when I was a kid, Dad would donate anonymously to the Salvation Army, even though they published all the donors' names in the newspaper. I never understood why he didn't give them his name but now I do.

"What I can't figure out," I said, "is why you hit Gina? She was only trying to help."

"I don't know, mate. I don't even remember doing it. Everything must have boiled up inside me. The fucked-up gig at the Living Room. All the booze. Plus I haven't been able to write a song to save my life since I got here, and that was the whole fucking point of coming."

"Gina said you kept yelling out the name Sharon."

He raised his eyebrows. "I did? Sharon was my manager in Australia when I went solo. We had what you'd call a love-hate relationship. Mainly hate. She persuaded me to sell the publishing rights to my songs, then helped me put the proceeds up my nose. And hers."

"Nice." I buttered a slice of rye and then spread some strawberry Smucker's on it. "One other thing I'm confused about. Why did you plead not guilty?"

"Partly because it's hard to plead guilty to something you can't remember doing. And partly because that's what the public defender recommended. He reckoned they would have probably thrown me out of the country right then and there if I'd admitted it."

"So this way you get another month or so?"

"Maybe more, depending on the next judge I get. My bloke reckons I could ask for a stay in proceedings, to prolong the whole thing. Plus you never know – if I have a word with Gina, maybe she'll drop the charges and then the whole thing will go away."

Not much chance there, I thought, but kept it to myself. Why dash whatever dollop of hope he had left?

"Anyway," he said, "no matter what happens, I owe you big time. And I won't forget."

"I just thought you needed some help. That's all."

"I still do." He sucked the dregs of his thick shake through a straw, generating a nasty guttural sound. A blue-rinse sheila at the next booth opened her mouth to protest but took one look at his disheveled state and closed it.

"You probably do need to get your shit together," I said, "but I certainly wouldn't lay any claim to being a life coach. It's all I can do to keep my own shit together."

"I need something more basic than motivational talks."

"Like what?"

"Somewhere to crash."

"I get it — you can't go back to the Blue Skies. But there are plenty of other hotels in this here town." About fourteen thousand, I reckoned, with varying levels of bedbugs.

"I know. But I've done my dough."

"You've what?"

"Done my dough. I've got no money left."

"Nothing?"

"Pretty much. Certainly not enough to stay in a hotel for weeks. Otherwise I would have paid my own bail," he said pointedly.

"Hold on a sec." I finally realized what he was driving at. "I live in a studio apartment. That means I don't even have a bedroom. Isn't there somewhere else you can go?"

He took one last pass at the thick shake, mostly sucking down air. "I only know one other bloke in town, this muso called Damian who lives at the Hotel Chelsea. But since it's a hotel, he doesn't even have a kitchen, let alone room for me. Plus he's a little suspect. I'm not sure I want to spend too much time with him." He took a sip of water. "It would only be for a week or so. Till I can get someone back in Oz to wire me some money."

"There's someone who can do that for you?"

"Sure. I still make royalties on the old Swallows hits."

The Swallows was the band he hit it big with in the Eighties. He'd had it all. Fame, fortune, and then more than enough drink and drugs to fuck it all up. But for a while there, he was a legend. Me and my mates, and about half the teenagers in Australia, were obsessed with The Swallows. Everyone knew their story. How they met at high school, playing at birthday parties and school dances. Then when they got old enough, they hit the Sydney pub scene. We were too young to go to go into pubs legally, but we'd still travel into the city by train from Liverpool every weekend to sneak into their gigs. If a publican wouldn't let us in we'd hang around outside, listening until the bouncers chased us away, saying we were lowering the tone of the neighborhood. Ah, those were the days, I thought, feeling like an old bloke at a country pub reminiscing.

"I thought you said you sold the rights to the songs?" I said.

"I did. But those were for publishing. This is for airplay. They're called performing rights royalties. You'd be surprised how much our old stuff still gets played on FM radio."

"Not really." FM radio has always liked old stuff more than new stuff. It's all about demographics and who's got the most money to spend on the products that the radio ads are selling. Which is usually older people, hence stations prioritizing older music.

"The music business is complicated," he said. "Anyway…my previous cock-ups have led to those royalties being held under lock and key, out of reach where I can't piss them up against the wall. My lawyer has to approve any requests but I can usually talk him around. Particularly if I tell him it's to get myself straightened out." He smiled and shook his head. "I've told him that God knows how many times, but it always works. I guess it's true what they say. Hope springs eternal."

"But you're serious this time?"

"Too right. Last night made me realize that I'm at the end of the line." His jaw stiffened. "That's it for me. No more fucking around. I'm getting back to work."

"Back to work? Doing what?"

"The only thing I know how to do, mate."

"What's that?"

"Writing songs."

I studied his face. He looked like he meant it. And there was an old adage in Australia. Never let down a mate who's in strife. Plus I'd already forked over five grand for his bail. In for a penny, in for a pound.

"Righto," I said. "If you get off the grog and knuckle down with your song writing, you can stay at my joint."

"Deal." He held out a hand heavy with rings. I shook it and, just like that, Ajax Farmer, rock legend and living Australian icon, was sleeping on my couch by day and writing songs in my living room by night.

5

"You what?" Anchor shouted over the jukebox.

"I told Ajax he could sleep on my couch for a while," I shouted back, feigning fascination with serving a punter so I could avoid the look that I knew was in his eyes.

Mondays at The Billabong were usually as slow as a wet week but for some reason that night the joint was going off. The place was chocka-block, crowded with hipsters, bridge-and-tunnel and regulars barking out orders for Melbourne Bitter, Fourex or whatever Aussie drops took their fancy. With the flag of the Eureka Stockade as our backdrop, Anchor and I did our best to keep pace behind the bar, doling out tinnies and stubbies, while Joe the Bouncer kept the front of house in order. The Sunnyboys, a trio of Sydney power pop practitioners from the early Eighties, sang on the jukebox about being alone with you tonight, quarters lined the edge of the pool table as punters waited their turn to play and, in a booth near a retro Toohey's beer poster of bronzed Aussie surfers, a bunch of sheilas were carrying on like headless chickens.

Anchor leaned closer, momentarily ignoring the outstretched arms holding cash and clamoring for a drink.

"Jesus, dude. How long's a while?" he said.

"I dunno." I stuffed a few bucks into Fort Knox, our tip jar. "A while."

"I hope you know what you're doing." Anchor had found Ajax and his drunken rock star persona a little smelly from the start. Past experience told me that Anchor possessed finely honed character judgement skills, something he'd developed while living on the streets, where gauging if a person is friend or foe in seconds can be a matter of life and death. He was rarely wrong but this time I wasn't so sure.

I glared at him. "Listen, I'm just putting a roof over his head so he can get back on his feet."

"So he can stagger to the next bar?"

AC/DC's "It's a Long Way to the Top If You Want to Rock'n'Roll" was on the jukebox and nearly everyone in the bar stopped to yell, "It's a long way to the shop if you wanna sausage roll!" when the chorus kicked in. It's an oft-replaced lyric Down Under and one that always warms my heart when I hear it.

"I won't deny that's a possibility," I said after the chorus ended. I poured myself a glass of water and one for Anchor, too. "But let's at least try and give the bloke some benefit of the doubt. I thought you of all people might have a little more sympathy for someone who needs a helping hand."

"I never went around looking for hand-outs if that's what you mean."

"Of course that's not what I'm saying." Anchor had wandered into my bar looking for a job, not spare change. A vagrant in San Francisco, Anchor had grown weary of living on the streets, rolled the dice and headed for New York. He had stumbled into The Billabong to ask for work just as I was getting ready to open the joint. I must have seen something in him because I had decided to give the underdog a chance and despite the lack of a roof over his head he'd never let me down. He was as dependable as a cold beer on a hot day and now things were starting to really work out for him. About a year ago he put down some long overdue roots by renting a studio apartment in Alphabet City, on Seventh Street near Avenue D. Lately he'd even been exhibiting definite signs of domestication. His trusty navy-blue woolen beanie, 501's and white Hanes t-shirts were a lot cleaner these days.

"God helps those who help themselves," I said, and pointed at him. "Case in point."

"Seems like all this Ajax dude wants to do is help himself to what's yours. He's sketchy, that what he is."

"Look, let's just give him a fair go, O.K?" I ripped the tops off two

Cooper's Pale Ale stubbies and slid them across the bar to a buxom lass wearing a "Total Eclipse of the Heart" t-shirt — ironically, of course.

"Thanks, Mel," she said, and I smiled back. I'd heard the Mel Gibson comparison before and, while I couldn't see it myself, I reckon it was understandable: same broad Aussie accent, same baby blues, same stocky build, same no-nonsense crew cut. I'm definitely not as bonkers as him, though, or at least I like to think so. I'm for damn sure not as anti-Semitic.

I decided to change the conversation with Anchor before he talked me out of anything.

"Listen, have you given any thought to what we talked about last week?"

I'd been encouraging him to do a night course, in the hope that he might be able to step up and manage The Billabong when I found a second bar location. Truth be known, Anchor was more suited to the bar business than me. He never tired of the endless circus of punters coming through the door, and because he didn't drink he wasn't prone to the major occupational health and safety hazard facing bar workers: alcoholism and its many related conditions. His dad had shot through when Anchor was an ankle biter, more interested in playing chasey with the bottle than with his young son, while his mum had struggled on through a succession of menial jobs only to die from cirrhosis of the liver when Anchor was a teenager — the chief reason why Anchor had dropped out of high school and ended up living on the streets.

"As a matter of a fact," he said, "I have. I've even looked into a few courses."

"Well, well. Do tell."

Bruce, one of our regulars, rapped his knuckles on the bar. A thirty-something bloke from Adelaide, Bruce was quite the pants man although he could never seem to hang onto a sheila once he'd nabbed them. He'd recently split up with his third of the year and it was only May. His wandering eye was to blame, always on the lookout for the next big thing.

Bruce was drinking against type, consuming glasses of Lazarus, our beer cocktail that was mostly popular with the sheilas. I took a fresh glass from the shelf behind me and a can of Victoria Bitter from the fridge, then threw three ice cubes into the glass and took a can of tomato juice from the fridge. I poured in a few inches, then cracked open the tinnie and topped it up with VB. I plonked it down in front of Bruce and he slid seven bucks toward me. I shoved six in the till and added the single to Fort Knox.

"The bartending courses seem like a bit of a joke," Anchor said. "I don't think they're going to teach me anything I haven't already worked out for myself."

"That's fair enough. You have been doing this for a while."

"But there are a few small business courses that I think could be better. A lot of them are one or two nights a week. Could be a little tricky for me to fit in around working here."

I thought about that for a moment. "If that's what you need to do to feel more comfortable about running this joint, I'm sure we can work something out." I served a plaid-drenched Wall Streeter three bottles of Cascade.

"Let me do a little more research," he said.

Ajax really did knuckle down after moving into my apartment. He was constantly bashing out chord progressions on his Maton, scribbling lyrics in a notebook, or pushing the buttons on a four-track recorder with headphones jammed on tight. In the confines of the small apartment it was impossible not to hear snatches of his new songs. They featured sharp lyrics, catchy choruses, killer hooks. In short, all the hallmarks of the earlier Swallows hits. Eventually he commandeered my Martin, claiming it tonally complemented his Maton, then borrowed a drum machine off a mate. When he brought home a cheap Ibanez bass, he had really put the studio in studio apartment.

Over the next week or so, the two of us settled into a strange pattern of domesticity. We both slept late — although Ajax, caught in the creative moment, would sometimes still be up working when I woke. I would tootle down the street to breakfast at Cosmo's while he continued to work or caught some shut-eye. Then most days after Cosmo's, I went on a long bike ride into Brooklyn, scoping out new bar locations. I had found an old butcher's shop in Red Hook that seemed full of potential but had trouble connecting with the landlord. For some reason, he was a hard man to catch. But I was pretty keen on the joint, so I vowed to keep trying his number several times a day while I explored other neighborhoods.

After the bar recce, I would return late in the afternoon to shower, throw on some fresh clobber and open up the bar. While I went about my business downstairs, Ajax would rise and go about his upstairs, and he'd still be fiddling with the four-track when I got home in the wee hours of the morning. We'd shoot the shit for a few minutes and then I'd hit the sack, so knackered that not even the twangs of his Telecaster could keep me from drifting off.

But before sleep beckoned, I sometimes had enough energy to realize that another day had passed and I hadn't called Hannah. In fact, I hadn't called Hannah since the night I'd met Gina.

And Hannah hadn't called me.

This domestic bliss persisted for about a week and a half — not long, but long enough to indicate that co-habitation was sustainable should anything delay the arrival of either Ajax's funds from Australia or his impending court case. With hindsight, however, we were in the eye of a Category Five cyclone that had begun forming the day Ajax first entered The Billabong.

The cyclone ramped up in intensity the following Wednesday when Detectives Malone and Lirianos wandered into the bar shortly after opening time. "Come Out and Play", a little-known gem by Sydney band Samurai Trash, was playing on the jukebox, its intricate guitar work trying in vain to sprinkle some pixie dust over an afternoon distinctly lacking in magic. Anchor sat perched at the end of the bar, wolfing down a tuna melt half the size of his head while chin-wagging with Bruce about his sheila troubles — although exactly what wisdom Anchor could impart in that department was unclear to me. When it came to women, Anchor had more in common with Robinson Crusoe than Errol Flynn.

"Detectives," I said, dropping the volume on the Trash. "Nice to see you again."

The three of us went back a ways. Malone and Lirianos had headed up the investigation when the sheila had disappeared from the bar. They made for a strange pairing — Malone, the voluble Irishman, and Lirianos, the quietly seething Latino — but they were a highly effective duo. Good copper, bad copper, with a little multiculturalism thrown in for good measure.

Malone tilted his head toward the far end of the bar, away from Anchor and Bruce. We walked down there and he pulled up a stool. Lirianos stood behind him, face impassive, his legs spread and arms crossed.

"It was nice to see you at the precinct the other day," I said.

"We're here in an official capacity," Malone said, in case their body language wasn't clear enough. "Not to shoot the shit about some drunk buddy of yours."

"What seems to be the trouble?"

"Murder seems to be the trouble, that's what."

"Oh. Crikey. Whereabouts?"

Malone cast his eyes around The Billabong. As usual, he looked disappointed with what he saw. I reckon his taste in bars ran to more than a few wobbly tables, torn beer posters and fridges full of tinnies. Walls of flat screen TVs and mounds of Buffalo wings were more his style.

His eyes stopped on Anchor, no doubt recalling the suspicion that Anchor had come under when the girl disappeared.

"Next door," he said.

"Next door? Jesus, that's a little close for comfort."

"Anonymous caller phoned it in." He was still looking at Anchor. Anchor held his gaze until Malone flicked his eyes back at me. "Did you hear anything around eleven o'clock this morning?"

I shook my head. "I was having breakfast."

"What? You can't chew and hear at the same time?" He sniffed, his signature sign of disapproval. I reminded myself to invite him to a poker game sometime.

"I was eating down at Cosmo's."

Malone sniffed again at my choice of dining establishment. "There was a fair bit of gunfire."

"At least three shots," Lirianos said.

"Three?"

"Appears as though one man was targeted and two others got caught up in the incident," Malone said.

"Oh." A four-alarm alert started ringing in my noggin.

"The two others were what you might call collateral damage."

"Hold on a sec. Which building are we talking about here?"

Malone tilted his head toward the uptown side of the bar.

"Shit," I said. "There wasn't loud music playing in the apartment, was there?"

Malone and Lirianos looked at each other.

"How did you know?" Malone said.

"Oh my God," I said, "they've killed Doof-doof."

6

"Doof-doof?" Malone said.

"The bloke next door." My mind was racing faster than a thoroughbred down home straight. I'd noticed two cop cars parked out the front of Doof-doof's building when I'd returned earlier but thought little of it.

"That much I figured," Malone said. "But why Doof-doof?"

"Because of the music he plays…played," I said, correcting myself. Malone still looked confused. "Dance music. In Australia, we call it doof-doof because of the relentless drumbeat." I made a sound like a bass drum to illustrate my point. "He played the stuff morning, noon and night."

And then some. Doof-doof had purchased the apartment about two years ago and undertaken an intense six-month renovation before moving in and partying often and partying hard. At first I'd tried yelling at him across the light shaft that our buildings shared but he either chose to ignore me or couldn't hear me over all the racket. So I resolved to confront him mano-el-mano, but that also proved fruitless. He rarely left his apartment, and when he did two bad asses shadowed him like some kind of fucked-up secret service detail. One had three teardrops tattooed on his left cheek, as sure a sign of a multiple murderer as you'll ever see; the other was the size of an MTA bus and looked about as welcoming. Trying to penetrate those two boofheads to lodge a formal noise complaint seemed bonkers, even to me. I didn't know what business Doof-doof was in, but I was pretty sure it wasn't legal and he wouldn't want me poking my nose into it. Plus I really was in no position to complain. The Billabong inflicted excessive noise levels on the neighborhood most nights of the week. We were, after all, living in the city that never sleeps. Live and let live — and buy some decent earplugs.

"Noise must've driven you crazy," Malone said.

"Not crazy enough to kill three people, if that's what you mean." I watched Anchor slide a can of VB over to a punter, take his cash and then return to his chinwag with Bruce.

"I'm not thinking anything." He did his sniff again. If I hadn't known better, I would have suspected him of cocaine use. "So let's get this straight — you weren't here, you didn't hear a thing, and you have no idea what happened?"

"Why should I? I've never even met the bloke. The only thing we have in common is the wall between our apartments."

"Is there anyone else who might know something?" His eyes scanned the bar and again settled on Anchor. With his street background, Anchor would always be suspect in the eyes of the law. Once a Bowery bloke, always a Bowery bloke.

"We don't open up till five in the afternoon."

"No one was here earlier?"

I shook my head. "We arrive at about four to prep, so no one was here at eleven." Except for Ajax, I thought, who would have been asleep upstairs at that time. I wondered if he heard anything. Probably not. And I didn't see much point in raising the possibility with these blokes. Ajax had enough on his plate without me dragging him back toward the coppers, and Malone and Lirianos weren't likely to go lightly on him either. Not after what he'd done to Gina.

"Well, we thought you might have heard something." He stood up and straightened his cheap suit as best he could. "Sometimes publicans hear things that never reach our ears. Something to do with a little truth serum called alcohol."

"That's true," I said, "but not in this particular case."

"Obviously."

"But I'll let you know if I do hear anything."

"You be sure and do that," Lirianos mumbled as they both pulled on their shades and headed for the door like half of the world's oldest, most badly dressed boy band.

I barely had time to collect my thoughts when another visitor came visiting. Bertha Oldfield, a reporter for the *New York Post* who I'd met a few years back, ambled in no more than a minute after Malone and Lirianos strutted out, sidling up to the bar like it was a daily occurrence rather than the blatant act of story chasing that it was. Only one thing drove Bertha: getting the next headline. She sniffed out stories like a great white shark sniffs out surfers.

"What kept you?" I said.

"Relax. At least I waited until they were gone." She hitched up the skirt of her shiny grey business suit and hooked her right leg over a bar stool, dropping her leather satchel on the floor beside her with a soft plop. "Worked up a fucking thirst, too, waiting across the street in the sun. Thought they'd never leave." She peered behind the bar. "You still got that beer cocktail thing? What do you call it? The Wanderlust?"

I pointed to the chalkboard behind me. "It went through a change of name and ingredients. It's called the Lazarus now."

"How come?"

"It's a long story. Wanna try one?"

She shrugged her shoulders. "Why not? As my father used to say, bless his heart, there's no such thing as a bad beer. Some are just better than others." She checked herself in the mirror of the back bar. Her hair was overdue for a trim, its salt and pepper dull like the fur of a koala bear flattened on the side of the road. Beneath a thin layer of foundation, the lines in her wizened face kept a pretty accurate tally of all the drinks, fags and late nights she'd notched up. Bertha was an old school journo, all right, from the top of her unpolished pumps to the bottom of her unchecked vices.

"So what did the Dynamic Duo have to say?" she asked as I went about fixing the Lazarus. I noticed that Anchor had stayed put down the other end of the bar, still talking to Bruce.

I slid the Lazarus in front of her. "Cut the crap, Bertha. You know why they were here or you wouldn't be here either."

"Did they tell you anything?"

"What do you think?"

She looked at the beer. "Tomato juice and beer. What will they think of next?" She took a sip and nodded with approval. "Well, I suppose they kept things to themselves as usual."

"Give the girl a kewpie doll."

"So they didn't mention that the murders were drug-related?"

"That much I worked out for myself." What else could it be? Three bad asses nailed in an area that was experiencing a...shall we say, realignment of its major industry.

"Oh, so Malone didn't tell you anything?"

"Didn't have to," I said. "I always knew what was going on in that apartment, what with all the loud music and yahooing. But I let it pass. It's New York City, not the Vatican. Besides, Doof-doof was my neighbor. I didn't want to make an enemy of him."

"Doof-doof?"

I made my drum and bass sound. "Morning, noon and night."

"From what I can tell, he didn't need any more enemies. Made plenty of those on his own. Comes with the job, when you're shifting as much product as he was."

"He was big?"

"Not top level. But according to my sources, he was a foot soldier in one of the biggest operations on the East Coast."

"Crikey."

She took another healthy gulp of Lazarus. "Part of a Mexican cartel."

"Really?"

"La Familia."

"Sorry?"

"La Familia. That's the name of the cartel. It means 'the family' in Spanish."

Even a language Luddite like me could figure that one out. But it raised another question. "What was his real name?"

"Sanchez. Jesus Roberto Sanchez. He moved up here about three years ago from Juarez. He was the head honcho's nephew. A bit of a loose cannon from what I've heard, but no one could do much about it because of who he was related to."

"Hence all the partying," I said. "But why wasn't he arrested when he entered the country?"

"No concrete proof," she said. "These guys are experts at covering their own tracks. Plus the coppers usually have the head of the cartel in their sights. They don't like to take any steps that might get in the way of taking out the top guy."

"Couldn't they have arrested him and put pressure on him to talk?"

She almost snorted some Lazarus back through her nose. "Those guys never talk."

"So who is the top guy?"

"An animal called Alejandro Navas. He's not gonna be too happy about his nephew getting whacked, either. Up until now, the drug killings around here have been pretty low level. Mules and a bunch of other losers who were more addicts that dealers. But this guy, he was connected." She sighed. "We could have a real bloodbath on our hands. These cartels are bad bastards, and La Familia is the worst."

Bertha was right. Cartel exploits from south of the Rio Grande had been all over the news of late. The cartels were killing small-town mayors who stood in their way, stringing their bodies up in town squares as a warning to all that no one can stop them. They had also murdered civilians, strapped their bodies with explosives and then them dressed in police uniform, human booby-traps detonated once the coppers arrived on the scene. All this was done without impunity. The cartels would stop at nothing to protect their illegal trade, which totaled in the billions of dollars. But now someone for some reason had decided to take out one of their connected operatives right next door to me. That took real balls. Or stupidity.

"So no one has any idea who did it?" I said.

"Not that I know of. You sure Malone and Lirianos didn't tell you anything else?" she tried again.

"You know those blokes. They play it so close to the chest you can't see it for all the hair."

"First thing they learn at the academy. Trust no one outside the department."
She sighed and gulped down the rest of the Lazarus, then rapped her knuckles on
the bar. "Hit me with one of more those. Just for the road, you understand."

I closed The Billabong around eleven thirty that night, the small matter of
three murders happening right next door spreading a slight pall over
proceedings. Anchor took the opportunity of an early night to hit Arlene's
Grocery for some homegrown rock'n'roll while I trundled upstairs to find
Ajax where I'd left him earlier — leaning over a four-track recorder with his
Telecaster copy slung around his neck, headphones jammed on tight, tapping
his foot to a drum and bass track that he'd laid down earlier as he waited for
the right spot to slot in a simple but effective piece of lead guitar. He
hammered out the riff and then hit the stop button.

"Nice work, Mister Clapton," I said.

He looked up, startled, then removed his headphones. "Gidday, mate.
Didn't see you there."

"I didn't want to interrupt you. You were deep into it."

"Yeah, that's just what happens. You start work and the next thing you
know the sun's coming up."

"Nice." It must be amazing to get that lost in something that you love.
The closest I had was the bar, but I reckon doling out tinnies doesn't really
compare to crafting your own music. Believe me, I'd tried the music caper
and soon learned that you either had it or you didn't. I most definitely did
not.

Ajax brushed his fringe of black hair out of his face, his expression much
brighter than the night we'd tossed him out of the bar. A steady diet of
takeaway Chinese, soft drink and hard work was actually doing him wonders.

"When he was working, Keith Richards would stay up for days at a time,"
he said with a grin. "Mick, Bill, Ronnie and Charlie would go home to get
some sleep and when they came back the next morning, the song would be
finished. Or completely different."

"There's only one Keef."

"Too right. I think his record was nine days without sleep."

"Jesus. Some days I can barely last nine hours."

"The bloke's a force of nature."

"A chemically-assisted force of nature." I pushed an old Lombardi's pizza box out of the way to take a seat on the couch. "Listen, you didn't happen to notice anything weird around here today, did you?"

"I don't think so."

"I don't want to freak you out, but some bad shit went down next door."

"Like what?"

"Three blokes were killed."

"What?" He removed the Telecaster copy from around his neck and put it in a guitar stand. Then he sat down beside me, his face whitening under the mop of black hair.

"Coppers came by the bar this afternoon, asking questions."

He winced at the mention of coppers, the wounds still fresh from his court appearance. "What did you tell them?"

"Not much. I had nothing to tell, except that I knew one of the blokes."

"You knew him?"

"Well, kinda. Doof-doof."

"Doof-doof?"

"Yeah, the bloke —"

"The bloke who plays techno all the time," he said, finishing my sentence. "I wondered who that was."

"I thought you hadn't noticed. You never said anything about the racket."

"Bit hard not to notice. But that's where these come in handy." He held up the headphones.

"Looks like you won't need them as much anymore."

"Maybe not."

"I don't think there's much to worry about. Looks like it's some kind of drug war thing."

Ajax looked at the common wall we shared with Doof-doof, presumably contemplating the fact that somewhere on the other side of that wall some bastard had laid three blokes to waste.

"Live by the syringe, die by the syringe," he said quietly.

7

Call me bonkers, but there's something about a mass murder taking place on the other side of your bedroom wall that just inspires insomnia. After a night of tossing and turning like the pre-iceberg Titanic, I rose early, deciding to ride out to Hannah's. The radio silence between us was taking its toll and I wanted to clear the air, for my own sanity as much as anything else. I needed to know what was going on between us. Plus the less I saw of Hannah the more I thought of Gina. Seeing Hannah, I reasoned, could put a lid on that.

I left Ajax working at his four-track and fifteen minutes later was coasting down Water Street's footpath to avoid DUMBO's bike-unfriendly cobblestones. If there is ever an Olympic Games for bad acronyms, DUMBO is a shoo-in for gold. DUMBO stands for Down Under the Manhattan Bridge Overpass. The area sits at the nexus of the Brooklyn and Manhattan bridges on the Brooklyn side of the East River. Closer to Manhattan than the rest of Brooklyn, DUMBO's warehouses were already well on their way to gentrification, although developers were schizophrenically converting them into both studio space for the artsy and expensive lofts for the rich. No doubt they'll all end up as the latter one day. Web start-ups and non-Madison Avenue marketing firms had also started infiltrating the area, taking the edge off a once-bohemian stronghold and pushing artists further north into Vinegar Hill, the Brooklyn Naval Yard and parts beyond.

Hannah's building, a cube of grey brick, stood at 135 Plymouth Street. It was spitting distance from the Manhattan Bridge. Across the road towered a pair of bridge pylons and the building's upper windows were adjacent to both the bridge's bike path and the train tracks that carried the B, D, N, R and Q lines. Shuttered loading bays stood to the left of the building's non-descript steel front door; arched windows framed with red brick sat over the loading bays, making a design feature of the delivery area rather than trying to disguise it the way most modern buildings do.

Overhead, a train grumbled across the bridge into Manhattan. I grabbed my bike by the handlebars and flipped it up onto its rear wheel to maneuver it into the building's goods elevator. Then I pulled shut the safety door and guided the lift to the third floor.

I leaned my bike against the hallway wall and tapped on Hannah's door.

"Han?" I whispered. "You awake?"

I heard stirring inside the loft, then the peephole darkened before the door creaked open.

"Gidday, stranger," I said.

"Luke? What are you doing here?"

"I was just in the neighborhood."

She blinked her eyes at the early morning light. "At this hour?"

"Yeah. Out for a ride. Can I come in?" It felt weird having to ask.

"Oh. Sure." She stepped aside, brushing her fingers through her hair. "What time is it, anyway?"

"About seven thirty."

"Really? Shit." She bolted the deadlock. "I slept in again."

"It's not that late."

She pushed her hair back, flustered. "There's stuff I need to get done. I'm trying to finish some prints for a showing next week."

"Don't be so hard on yourself. You must have needed the sleep." I hugged her and she hugged me back. Was it my imagination or was there a hint of resistance? "Sorry I haven't called for ages. I've had a lot going on."

"No worries. Me too." She broke our clinch. "Tea?"

"Abso-bloody-lutely." Hannah made one of the best cuppas this side of the subcontinent. Tea making is a pretty basic enterprise — boil some water, chuck in a few tea leaves — but for some reason I could never replicate the flavor that she achieved. My Mum had been the same. A cuppa always tasted better when she brewed it.

"Nice T," I said, nodding at three wolves howling at the moon on her T-shirt. The stretch cotton hugged her boobs, leaving little to the imagination. Hannah's beauty had seared itself into my retinas from the very first day we'd met. She was to die for — elegant neck, eyes like saucers of dark chocolate, narrow waist, enough in the hooter department to keep most blokes happy. But most blokes are also never happy with what they have, and since meeting Gina I was no exception, even though I should have been like those three wolves and howling at the moon with delight. Hannah wasn't just, as my Dad would say, a bit of all right. She was also a talented street artist in the vein of Banksy, mining a distinctive oeuvre that promoted animal rights. Kangaroos bearing rifles, koalas toting machine guns, and emus clenching daggers in their beaks to combat environmental injustice. She'd recently sold a piece for five grands. Not too shabby.

Hannah was also uncommonly healthy, a successful high school sprinter who still took excellent care of herself. And on top of all that, she was the original down-to-earth Down Under sheila who was up for anything. Not many women scale buildings in the dark of night to pursue their art or fancy a quick leg-over no matter where they happen to be. Hannah and I had done the dirty deed in many an unexpected location, including a janitor's closet at the Museum of Natural History and the top deck of the Staten Island ferry. I should have been thanking my lucky constellations that I'd met someone like her rather than counting off the minutes that we spent together, but somehow we'd fallen into a rut that Gina only served to accentuate. I had a feeling that Hannah felt the same way, too, but I didn't have the guts to ask her. I mightn't have been completely happy with what I had but I was definitely unsure of the alternative.

"Thanks," Hannah said, pulling the T-shirt tight across her chest to better display the wolves. Her nipples raised tiny bumps beneath the cotton. "A little irony goes a long way."

"Indeed." I tore my eyes away from her chest to focus on her face. She flicked on a paint-spattered radio; NPR filled the room. A sheila was lamenting the power of the gun lobby following another recent mass shooting. Americans talked incessantly about the gun problem without doing anything about it, then when the next inevitable massacre happened they talked more shrilly for a couple of days before returning to the normal level of talk. It was a war of words without end.

"So," Hannah said, going about her tea making, "what's happening?"

I pulled up a seat at a Fifties diner table that Hannah had scored on eBay for sixty bucks. That low price had also included four matching chairs. She'd furnished her entire loft scooping up bargains online, at stoop sales and wherever else she could find them. Her interior design approach didn't spring from miserliness, though. She was just a perfectionist looking for an eclectic vibe. A Danish coffee table, an Edwardian oak bureau and a Parisian four-poster bed somehow all worked together, with a drop cloth marking her studio in one corner of the loft. A half-finished canvas showed a platypus brandishing nuclear warheads.

"Well," I said, "three blokes were just murdered in the apartment next door to mine."

"Jesus. Really?"

"Yeah. It's pretty full-on."

"I'll say." She filled the kettle, put it on the stove and fired up the gas. She had her back turned to me, and as she rinsed the teapot her bum jiggled beneath her over-sized t-shirt. It might have been my imagination but she looked a little bigger than I remembered. Like she'd put on a few pounds. She had a tendency to do that if she was working on a new piece and didn't make time for exercise.

"You been working out?" I said.

"Not as much as I should. I want to get ready for the marathon. Thought I'd give it a crack this year."

"Right," I said, thinking of Officer Klein and his Timex.

"So what happened next door?"

"The coppers didn't say. But it was a drug hit, I reckon."

"Shit. That sounds serious."

"Yeah. I've heard talk in the bar that there've been a few hits in the neighborhood over the last couple of months. And a journo I know thinks the same thing."

"Nasty. Count your lucky stars it doesn't have anything to do with you."

"Yeah. It's funny, though. It was the bloke who was always playing that loud music."

"Doof-doof?"

"Yep. Doof-doof."

"At least you'll get some peace and quiet now."

The kettle whistled and she poured boiling water into the pot, spun the pot a half dozen times to mix the leaves with the water and then put a tea cozy over the pot to let it steep.

"I have some other news to report." I noticed a papier machete model sitting on her windowsill. It was a model of a Tiffany's jewelry box run over by a car, squashed flat with tire marks across its surface. Hannah's neighbor Patrick had probably given it to her. He specialized in sculpting faux fucked-up luxury goods. His art was cool, but I felt a twinge of jealousy that one of his pieces was taking pride of place in Hannah's apartment.

"What news?" She plonked herself down at the kitchen table opposite me.

"Remember Ajax?"

"The rock star from the Living Room who could barely play his own guitar?" She formed air quotes around the words rock star with her fingers.

"He was just having a bad night. He's been staying with me for a while. He had a fight at the hotel where he was staying and had to move out." A visual of Gina's battered face flashed through my mind and I decided to leave out those particular details.

"He's got nowhere else to stay?"

"No. So I'm letting him crash with me for a few weeks till he gets his act together."

"Good luck with that."

"Actually, he seems to be doing pretty well. He's off the grog and writing new songs. Working eighteen hours a day, some days."

She smiled at me. "My little Good Samaritan."

"I'm just trying to do the right thing, Han. What have you been up to?"

"This and that. Mainly working." She stood up and walked back into the kitchen to pour the tea. "Trying to keep up with the demand while it lasts.

I've had a lot of interest since that last gallery opening."

"That's a nice position to be in." I nodded at her latest creation. "I like the platypus."

"Thanks. It's getting there."

She slid a mug of tea across the table to me. I blew on it and took a sip, then winked at her. "Just like mother used to make."

Something passed across her eyes. She opened her mouth to speak but then changed her mind and closed it.

After two cups of tea and a bit more natter, we adjourned to the sack. It was a while between drinks in that department so we should have been hungry for each other, but I found myself distracted more than anything else.

Particularly by a papier-mache model that I spotted on her dressing table: a Mercedes Benz covered in bird droppings.

We both fell into a post-coital coma and dozed until lunch. Then Hannah rose to fix sandwiches of ciabatta, fresh mozzarella and basil. We ate through long periods of silence until I mumbled something about having to open up the bar. I'm not sure which one of us was more relieved when I slipped out the door.

I cycled home and then ducked up to the apartment to shower before prepping the bar. Ajax was still happily ensconced in his music. He must have been up for twenty-four hours straight, but there was no sign of what was to follow. Perhaps if I'd stayed around, not gone down to work the bar, what happened that night might not have happened. But hindsight, twenty-twenty, etc. I was never going to not open the bar and so any feelings of guilt stopped right there.

The Billabong was as quiet as the grave that night save for the sheila who overdid it with the booze and spewed an ocean of peanuts right outside the front door. Anchor and I hosed the putrid mess straight into the gutter, lest its sight scare away the punters, but a trace of its sickly-sweet odor still lingered at three a.m. when Anchor scooted off to Rosario's for a slice and I headed upstairs to find my apartment smelling like fireworks and bits of Ajax's brain decorating my living room wall.

8

Malone tapped a plastic sleeve on his desk that held a single sheet of paper. "But what about this?"

"I don't buy it." I took another sip of precinct coffee. The stuff tasted like axle grease but it wasn't flavor I was seeking. It was caffeine. I hadn't had a jot of sleep since I'd found Ajax's body and it was now six o'clock in the morning.

"Come on, Bales. Farmer felt guilty about beating on the girl, didn't see the point in going on." Malone tapped the plastic sleeve again. "Says so right here in the note."

"That's bonzer, if he wrote it," I said, tired of having a conversation I'd had three times. First with the coppers who arrived at the scene, then with Forensics and now Malone. These circular debates were making the situation even more surreal. A few weeks ago I'd been trying to work out how to get Ajax released on bail. Now he was lying in a refrigerator drawer at the morgue with a nametag hanging from his toe. He would have been better off if I'd left him to rot in the slammer, as he suggested, a notion that certainly didn't make me any more ebullient.

"We found some poems in Farmer's guitar case," Malone mumbled, still annoyed about his early morning wake-up call. The ends of his hair were wet from a recent shower.

"They're not poems. They're lyrics."

"Poems. Lyrics. Whatever. He was a regular Bob Dylan."

"He was a songwriter."

"All I know is that the handwriting on this note looks like a hell of a lot like the handwriting on those lyrics, and it won't take a Forensic Document Examiner long to confirm it." He adjusted the tie he'd thrown on as he left the house, succeeding only in making the pattern of orange and blue Knicks logos more crooked than when he started. "It's lucky for you we found it."

"I guess so." Even a law-and-order layman like me knows that whoever finds a body instantly becomes a prime suspect. Although how I could have killed Ajax was beyond me. I don't know one end of a gun from the other. Put me in charge of a weapon and I'd be more likely to blow my own noggin off than anyone else's.

"Look," Malone said, "we know that just last week Farmer smacked a woman around." He gestured across the room to Officer Klein's desk. "Marathon Man says he was a real mess."

I couldn't help but smirk at Klein's nickname despite the situation.

"I still don't buy it. Ajax was getting better, not worse."

"Because he gave up the giggle juice? That doesn't make him Mother Theresa."

"It doesn't make him suicidal, either."

"You don't have a clue what was going on inside his head. You said yourself that he was having a rough time of it since arriving in New York."

"The operative word being 'was'." I thought back to Ajax bent over his four-track, caught in the creative moment, excitement written all over his face. I just couldn't see how someone so invigorated with life, so in the moment, could do something so destructive to themselves.

Malone shifted in his chair. "We've known each other for a while now, Bales. And you seem like a good guy for the most part." Coming from Malone, that was a glowing reference. I wondered what this was leading to. "So I'll level with you. Forensics says that the angle of entry and gunpowder tests all confirm suicide."

"They must work fast to get those results so soon."

"Well, the preliminary trajectory from the crime scene will need to be confirmed with 3D modeling. But gunpowder tests can be confirmed in about half an hour if you have a good sample. Which we do. Your buddy's right hand tested positive." He tried a smile on for size that didn't quite fit. "You'll be pleased to know that both your hands tested negative."

So that's why they'd swabbed my hands back at the apartment. "That's very reassuring."

"Don't take it personally. You had to be classified as a suspect until proven otherwise."

"So I'm proven otherwise?"

"The absence of gunpowder doesn't completely rule you out. You could have been wearing gloves."

"I'm more of a mittens man myself," I said. "Look, everything adding up neatly just means that whoever did this knew exactly what they were doing. They did everything they needed to do to make it look like suicide."

Malone shifted his weight in his chair. "And why would someone do that? What's the motive? There were no signs of a robbery."

"True." If there had been a killer or killers, and robbery was on their mind, why did they leave Ajax's guitars behind? Musical instruments are usually a prime target for theft because of their portability – after all, guitars even come with their own cases — and easy hock-ability at pawn shops. "Well, what about the murders next door?"

"What about them?"

"Could the two be connected?" I took another sip of axle grease.

"Why would they be?"

"A little bird told me the murders next door were drug-related. Maybe Ajax got mixed up in it somehow."

Malone stared at me. "I have a fair idea who the little bird is. Fucking Bertha. She's been sniffing around here for days looking for a story. I wouldn't be surprised if she turned up outside my house one night." He leaned back in his chair and studied a brown water stain on the ceiling tile above his head. "Anyway, that possible connection had already occurred to me. Let's say just for a moment that the triple murder is drug related. A drug dealer gets bumped off next door and then a day later your buddy commits suicide in your apartment." He looked back at me. "Maybe. But an Australian, new to the country and with no priors, getting mixed up with a drug dealer so quickly? As much as I'd like to see a connection, it feels coincidental to me."

"Maybe Ajax heard or saw something that he shouldn't have?"

Malone leaned forward. "What do you mean?"

"Maybe Ajax somehow knew something about what went down in Doof-doof's apartment."

"How could he?"

"Maybe he was staying at my place at the time."

Malone's face reddened like he'd just bitten into a jalapeno hero. "Jesus, Bales. You mean to tell me that you had a potential witness to those three murders and you didn't tell us?"

I studied the plasmatic skin coating my coffee. "I didn't want to drop the bloke in any more shit."

"Very thoughtful of you. I'm sure he'll thank you the next time he sees you."

"So you think the two could be related?"

"I wouldn't go that far. Did Farmer mention anything to you?"

I thought back to when I'd told Ajax about the murders. His pale face. His look of genuine shock. "No. Quite the opposite. I specifically asked him and he said he hadn't noticed a thing."

Malone cogitated on that for a moment. "We'll look into it." He glared at me. "Thanks for mentioning now that he was at your place at the time of the murders, though, instead of when it really could have helped. In fact, thanks for not even letting us know that Farmer was staying with you."

"So, no progress on the Doof-doof murder?" I said guiltily.

In response, Malone sniffed.

I prodded at the skin on my axle grease and took a sip.

Around nine a.m., Malone told me that I was free to leave the precinct but not to wander too far. He also told me that my apartment would be off limits for another twenty-four hours while Forensics scoured the place for clues. In the absence of anywhere better to go, I decided to hit Cosmo's. It was fast becoming my second home.

No sooner had I slid into a booth than Maria scampered over.

"Crocodile Dundee, you look a little worse for wear."

"Rough night."

"I'll say." She dropped an early edition of the *New York Post* on the table. Its headline read, "Aussie Rock Star Appearing Dead Near You". Bertha's byline sat beneath the headline; underneath that was an old black and white publicity shot of Ajax.

"Damn, that was fast."

"Let's make this one my treat," Maria said softly. "The usual?"

"Thanks, but I think I need something a little simpler." All that cheap cop-shop coffee had my stomach doing backflips.

"Ah, you want your plan B. Grilled swiss and tomato on rye, mustard on the side?"

"Sounds bonzer. Just hold the mustard."

"Got it. Coffee?"

My stomach quivered at the thought. "No, thanks. Water will be fine."

She opened her mouth to say something else and then changed her mind, heading off to place my order. I turned on my cell phone, which I'd powered down at the precinct at Malone's request. Twelve voicemails chimed in, one after another, but I ignored them as I searched for Anchor's number.

"Dude," he answered, "I was beginning to wonder if I was ever going to see you again."

"What's that supposed to mean?"

"Have you clocked the papers?"

"Just saw one."

"I can't believe he did that to himself. I mean, I didn't think much of the guy but no one wants to see that happen to anyone. Not unless they're a complete douche."

"Quite."

"According to the article, you were right — Ajax really was the dude back in the day."

"Oh, so now he believes me," I sneered, but I wasn't angry with Anchor. It was the article that pissed me off. Ajax's life had always been a boon for the Australian media, whether he was a rising star or a crashing meteor, and now his bloody demise was flogging more newspapers. The thought that what I had found on my living room floor was now lining Rupert Murdoch's coffers made me want to puke.

"I haven't read the article yet," I said. "Is there any mention of me?"

"Not by name. Just that a Lower East Side bar owner called it in."

"Won't take people long to figure out who that is."

"What makes you say that?"

"Ajax was Australian. I'm Australian. The Billabong's Australian. It's not rocket science."

We paused as a fire truck sped past Anchor's apartment, siren blaring.

"Dude, maybe I should open up solo tonight," he said after the truck passed.

"No way."

"Why not?"

"Because we're not opening up, full stop."

"What do you mean?"

Maria slid the grilled sandwich in front of me and I gave her a thumbs up. I tested out one of the mandatory fries accompanying it and my stomach didn't object too strenuously.

"I mean we're not opening up," I said. "It just doesn't feel right."

"Dude, you're turning your back on a sick amount of cash."

"I know." There really is no such thing as bad publicity. After that sheila disappeared from The Billabong, a certain notoriety that hung over the joint had been unmistakably good for business. This latest drama would probably prompt a further spike in numbers. But if I exploited that, I was no better than Rupert Murdoch.

"You didn't see him, Anchor. I did. I found the poor bastard, and having a bunch of drunks cavorting around right below where it happened just doesn't seem right to me. Not yet." The whole thing was bonkers. I'd always known that opening a bar would come with its fair share of trouble, but I'd anticipated the sort of minor brouhahas that bouncers sort out, not life and death situations.

"So what went down?"

The sixty-four-thousand-dollar question. "Not sure. The coppers think it was suicide but I'm not convinced."

"I still think we should open up tonight."

"I already—"

"Hear me out, dude. If we don't open up, then the media will realize even quicker that you're the barman in question."

"True." But if I knew Bertha, she'd already figured that out.

"And if I open up by myself, I can handle any media heat that comes our way. Then you come back to work when things have chillaxed a bit."

What he said made sense. Opening up tonight would also look like we had less to hide. Not that we had anything to hide, but you know what they say: perception is everything.

"OK. But I should probably get shot of the Lower East Side for a while," I said.

"Where will you go?"

"I'll figure something out."

"Cool."

"Thanks, Anchor. I really appreciate it. Call me on my mobile if anything comes up."

"No worries, mate," he said in a terrible fake Australian drawl.

"See you tomorrow. Same Bat-time, same Bat-channel."

I rang off and went through my voicemail. The inbox held multiple messages from the same three people: Bertha, keen to learn if I knew anything about the death of a certain Australian rock star, no doubt placing the calls last night as she typed the story that lay on the table before me; Hannah, who'd seen *The Post*, put two and four together and figured out that I was the Aussie publican in question; and Gina, her words almost indecipherable, so distraught was she over Ajax's death.

I deleted all the messages and returned one call.

9

When I called Gina, she suggested that we meet. I figured that she'd want to rendezvous in a café or park. Who was I to argue when she suggested the privacy of her apartment?

Her reception was a little warmer than my first visit. A plate of biscuits sat on the coffee table and the smell of brewing coffee filled the air. I sat down on her sofa as she busied herself pouring the coffee. She carried two colorful hand-painted mugs into the living room and placed them on the coffee table then sat down beside me. The swelling around her eye had subsided since we'd last met, a few fading purple bruises all to show for her trouble with Ajax — on the outside, at least.

"You look better," I said, making small talk as much as anything else. Anything to avoid the topic of Ajax Farmer.

"Thank you. And thank you for coming over."

"No worries." I didn't want to get into how my apartment was still an active crime scene and how it was convenient for me to be elsewhere. It was either her place or Hannah's, and I had chosen hers. Exactly what that meant I pushed to the back of my mind.

She sniffed and blew her nose, then dabbed the handkerchief at her red eyes. "I've been going crazy," she said. "I do not know anyone else who knew Ajax well so I have no one to talk to about this." A white leather miniskirt and striped tank top struggled to constrain her contours almost as much as I struggled not to look at them.

"Not even the people at the hotel?"

She shook her head. "Most of the employees were wary of him. Perhaps with good reason."

"I didn't know him that well, either, to be completely honest. I only met him a few weeks ago."

"I shouldn't have been so harsh on him." Then she started sobbing and I realized why she had wanted to meet in private.

"Gina, what happened between you and Ajax had absolutely nothing to do with his death."

"How can you be so sure?" She looked at me with those eyes of hers. Even bloodshot from crying, it was one hell of a set of peepers. Round dark saucers that seemed to burrow into my soul. It was disconcerting, as if she could look right through me, but also comforting. I wanted to let myself fall into them, tumble to the bottom of that deep, dark wishing well.

"Because I was the one who found him."

"I thought that was you who the newspapers were talking about. It must have been horrible."

"It was no picnic, I'll say that much for it." The biscuits sat untouched on the plate and I took one out of courtesy.

"Elephant Ear," she said.

"I'm sorry?"

"It's called an Elephant Ear. My mother used to make them. Flour tortilla deep-fried and sprinkled with sugar. Very easy to make."

"Nice." It was, too. Simple and sugary. The flakes of pastry melted in my mouth.

"The newspaper said someone was taken in for questioning. That was you also?"

"Just a formality. I had to be ruled out as a suspect, since I found him."

"Obviously you have been cleared?"

"Pretty much. Ajax died from a single gunshot wound to the head. The police are working under the assumption that it was suicide."

Her hand flew to her mouth. "But why?"

"Well, he had gunpowder on one hand and—"

"No, I mean why would anyone think that Ajax killed himself? Was there a note?"

I nodded. I didn't see the point in complicating matters by telling her my half-assed conspiracy theory. "It said he couldn't go on."

"I hope it had nothing to do with the bad blood between us."

"Nothing whatsoever," I assured her, neglecting to mention the salient fact that the suicide note specifically called out his remorse over assaulting her. "Ajax had much bigger problems than that." Like someone blowing half his head off.

Outside the front window, a delivery truck beeped as it reversed into a parking spot. "Anyway," I said, "what's done is done. At least he's at peace now."

"It was very kind of you." She blew her nose with a geese-like honk that somehow made her more attractive. "No matter how it turned out."

"What was?"

"Allowing Ajax to stay at your apartment."

"It was no biggie. He was an Aussie in need. Any bloke from where I'm from would have done the same thing."

"No, not most. Just you."

She was wrong about that. Any Aussie would help a mate in need. That's just the way we're raised. But I didn't have time to tell her that because she had leaned over and taken my hand, just like she had when we last met. Only this time, I didn't stand up and walk away. I probably should have, but I didn't, and I still don't know why. Sure, she was most blokes' dream, but it was more than that. Perhaps it was the waste of life I'd just witnessed. Or perhaps it was because I was feeling on the outs with Hannah. But mostly, it was that when our hands touched something shifted in that room.

I'm not sure which one of us made the first move but suddenly her lips were crushing mine, tasting of coffee. She climbed onto my lap and I tugged her tank top over her shoulders as she struggled with my belt and the top button of my jeans before pulling them down. I hiked up her skirt, pulled aside her underwear. She maneuvered into position and lowered herself onto me, moaning as we went about our business. I finished in moments, feeling like a semi-trailer had flattened me, but somehow conjured a repeat performance that lasted long enough to satisfy the two of us.

I stood up and carried her down the hall to the bedroom. We lay listening to the slowing of our heartbeats as the room grew darker, night falling on the other side of the window. From my vantage point I could see a nylon string guitar leaning in one corner and a framed photo sitting on a desk: a handsome, swarthy bloke about her age, drinking a cocktail on a patio overlooking a river. Perhaps this was the love interest, I thought. The way she looked, there had to be one tucked away somewhere.

"Are you working tonight?" I said, my voice loud in the quiet that had formed around us.

"No. I worked earlier. Although I was in such a state after I heard about Ajax that I was not much help to anyone."

"I don't blame you. The whole thing's pretty bonkers."

"I feel so terrible." She took a deep breath. "But what he did. Suicide. It is never the answer."

"Too right."

"Maybe he just felt overwhelmed."

"Maybe."

"He was a long way from home. That can be difficult."

"Indeed." There were many times after my ex Suzie took our daughter Phoebe back to Sydney that I wasn't sure if I could make it on my own. I'd never considered topping myself, though. But I reckon once you start that downward spiral you never know where you're going to bottom out. Sometimes at the very, very bottom.

"I have spent many years alone," she murmured.

"I find that hard to believe." I ran my hand over her bum.

"I…" She stopped for a moment. "I moved to New York by myself."

"Shush. You don't have to—"

"My twin brother, he died," she continued quickly, like she needed to tell someone. "A car accident near our home in Spain. We were so close, it was too much to take. I came here to start over, away from the memories. My parents, they didn't understand, but I had to leave. He was everywhere, everywhere I looked. It was hard at first and it took me many years to feel comfortable. But I concentrated on my English classes, then getting a job and saving money…" Her eyes flicked toward the photo on the desk as her voice ebbed away. That's her brother, I thought with relief, not a competitor for her affection.

"You're Spanish," I said.

"I'm sorry?"

"I thought you were from somewhere over there. Your olive skin." I ran my hand over her bum again.

"Yes. Spanish." She drifted into a reverie, presumably thinking about her homeland. In the silence, a soft mew came from under the bed and then a cat jumped up. A mostly white tabby with two dabs of black fur on its face like a moustache.

Gina giggled. "This is Alberto."

"Gidday, Alberto."

Alberto meowed again and then rubbed his cheek against Gina's shoulder, igniting his purring. Then he smooched up against my face.

"That is a compliment," she said. "He is normally afraid of strangers."

I ran my hand over him and he arched his back.

"Luke…" Gina said after Alberto had curled up at our feet.

"Yeah?"

"I can't understand why Ajax would do such a thing."

I was suddenly tired of pretending that I agreed with the coppers' theory. Besides, after what we'd just done, surely it was time for a bit of honesty. "I'm not totally convinced that he did."

She raised herself up on one elbow. "What do you mean?"

"I'm just not sure that he killed himself, that's all. I mean, it doesn't really make any sense." Then again, suicide rarely does.

"What about the note?"

I shrugged my shoulders. "Maybe it was fake." It sounded far-fetched, even to me.

"Is that what the police think, too?"

I thought back to my conversation with Malone. "No, they bought it hook, line and signature."

She rested her head back on my chest and fell silent again. Eyelashes brushed against my skin when she blinked.

"About this afternoon," she said after a few minutes. "What just happened."

"Uh huh."

"I hope you do not think that I do this often."

"Gina—"

"Because I do not. But there is something between us. I noticed it the first time we met."

"Believe me, I noticed it, too."

"But Hannah? She is your girlfriend?"

"Yes, she's my girlfriend. But I'm not sure for how much longer. Things have been weird between us lately."

"Weird how?"

"That's a very good question. I'm not sure. Just different."

She sighed, as if she'd just made up her mind about something. "Do you...do you think it will happen again?"

"Well, I hadn't given it much thought," I said, then groaned as she slipped her hand underneath the sheets and began certain ministrations.

Around nine p.m., Gina reheated the coffee and brought in the leftover Elephant Ears. She nibbled at a cookie slowly, as though food was the last thing on her mind. It was completely at odds with Hannah's approach to eating – every meal with her was like competing in the Coney Island hotdog eating contest — and I felt more than a touch of guilt at the thought.

After finishing three cookies, I let Alberto lick the sugar off my fingers with his sandpaper tongue and then hit the bathroom to wash my hands. When I returned, Gina was strumming the guitar that had been leaning in the corner. I lay down on the bed and listened to her lilting voice as she sang:

A la puerta del cielo
Venden zapatos
Para los angelitos

Que andan descalzos
Duérmete niño
Duérmete niño
Duérmete niño
Arrú arrú
A los niños que duermen
Dios los bendice
A las madres que velan
Dios las asiste
Duérmete niño
Duérmete niño
Duérmete niño
Arrú arrú.

She played four more bars and then finished with a soft flamenco flourish.

"Beautiful," I said, clapping softly.

"It is nothing." She picked absently at the strings. "Just a children's song."

"What's it about?"

"That there are shoes waiting for the poor children in Heaven." She strummed a few chords. "I taught at a local school back home. There were many poor children."

"You were a schoolteacher?"

"That's right."

"So why are you working as a cleaner in a hotel?"

"I cannot teach in the United States."

"Why not?"

"My qualifications are not recognized in New York. I thought that once I found regular employment I would be able to attend college part-time and do a bridging course to teach here. But so far that has not been possible. My job is too demanding and I am very tired at the end of the day. Occasionally I volunteer at an elementary school on Fourth Avenue to keep myself familiar with the feeling of being around the children. The school is grateful for the extra help. It is very underfunded and overcrowded…although not as badly as the ones at home."

"Who are you? Mother Theresa?"

She blushed and shook her head, nodding at the tangled bed sheets as proof of her unsuitability for sainthood. "And you?"

"Me? I'm just a humble publican from Australia."

"No, I mean do you play?"

"A little."

She held out the guitar to me. But I shook my head.

"Not in your league, I'm afraid." Sure, I could have busted out a Paul Kelly tune, but it would have had none of the charm of her performance. First rule of performing — never follow a better act.

She leaned the guitar in the corner and then lay down on the bed beside me.

"But that," I said, rolling over to face her, "I reckon I can take a crack at."

10

A car door slamming out in the street woke me around eleven the next morning. I rolled over to find the bed empty; a note on the kitchen counter told me that Gina had left for a morning shift and opted not to wake me. I scribbled out a response — procrastinating for a long time about drawing a heart on the bottom before doing just that — then tracked down some cat biscuits to satisfy a complaining Alberto.

I let myself out, floating down Fourth Avenue beneath grey skies while contemplating whether it was lust or something more serious I felt for Gina. And where my indiscretions left Hannah. I felt like an explorer navigating the Land of Lotharios without a map or compass. Contrary to what the previous night's exploits suggested, I was definitely no philanderer. I had never cheated on Hannah — or Suzie, for that matter. In fact, I was a damn sight more monogamous than most blokes if I was to believe the tales I heard nightly behind the bar.

I rode the D express to West Fourth and then changed to an uptown F, surviving an acapella combo covering the Pet Shop Boys in the cramped carriage before alighting at Twenty-Third and Sixth. All that horizontal cha-cha with Gina and no breakfast had left me ravenous so I ducked into Mai Fun, a cheap and cheerful Chinese joint across Twenty-Third Street from the Hotel Chelsea. I inhaled a lunch of spicy prawns, steamed broccoli and brown rice doused with sriracha while perched at a window seat, contemplating the hotel's red awning across the street. Dylan Thomas, Oscar Wilde, Bob Dylan, Iggy Pop, Sid Vicious and many more icons had graced that entrance, making the hotel itself a prominent player in counter-culture history. It was also where Ajax's only other New York mate lived, according to the dead man himself, and that was the reason for my uptown excursion. I reckoned it was high time I had a chat with the only other bloke in New York who had gotten close to Ajax – that I knew of, at least — to see if he could shed some light on why Ajax might have topped himself. Or not topped himself, as the case may be. Just because Malone and his ilk were comfortable with the unofficial verdict of suicide, that didn't mean that I had to lie down and accept it. I owed it to Ajax to try and figure out what really happened. I was damn sure that if someone offed me I wouldn't want everyone thinking that I took the easy way out – not that there's anything easy about firing a bullet into your own noggin.

My stomach full of shrimp, I waddled over to Chelsea Guitars, the shop next door to the hotel. I perused their vintage axes while I gathered my thoughts then ventured into the hotel lobby. The joint's lighting was so low I half-expected to trip over a stalagmite. A grungy bloke and a mangy tomcat sat at the front desk. The bloke had a few days' growth and the pasty look of a man marking time until his next drink. The cat had the look of every cat. Undisguised insouciance.

"Gidday," I said, resting my elbows on the front desk, "I'm looking for someone called Damian."

"Is that so?" the bloke replied with a Southern drawl.

I should have asked the cat, I thought. It might have been more helpful.

"I owe him some money."

"Is that so?" he said again. "What do you make of that, Moonshine?"

The cat rolled over and licked its bum.

"I have a little extra, if that helps," I said. The bloke raised his eyebrows. "Money," I clarified.

He held out his hand and I slapped a twenty into his palm.

"Room 412," he said. "But it won't do you much good. He sleeps all day, that boy."

"No worries. I'll just slip the dough under the door if I can't wake him."

"Is that so?" he said, but my back was already turned as I headed toward the stairs.

The stairwell featured local artwork executed to varying degrees of success, each with a price tag underneath boasting an excessive figure. Good luck with that commercial enterprise, I thought, as I took the steps two at a time, panting like a greyhound by the time I reached the fourth floor.

Damian's room was one in from the corner of the building, tucked away from the din of Twenty-Third Street. The hallway was deathly quiet. The tenants had either left for the day or were still in bed.

I pressed my ear to the room's lime green door and heard nothing.

"Room service!" I shouted, pounding on the door.

Some sheets rustled inside the room, then silence.

"Room service!" I yelled again.

"Fuck off!" said a bloke's voice.

"Room service! I have your breakfast order."

"I didn't order any fuckin' breakfast so fuck off!" the voice yelled. If it was Damian, he sure liked his F-bombs, like many an English compatriot before him. Perhaps that's where we Aussies got our penchant for cursing.

"Compliments of your mate," I said.

"What fuckin' mate?"

"Ajax Farmer."

That prompted some silence, followed by more rustling of the sheets before the door's tumblers clicked over. It squeaked opened on its chain to reveal a sliver of a face. One bloodshot eye and a few inches of dry, flaky lips.

"You knew Ajax?" Damian said.

"Knew him?" I fought the urge to recoil from the sour smell of beer and fags. "I found him."

The inflamed eye studied me until the information sunk in. "Jesus. You're the fuckin' Aussie bloke who was puttin' him up?"

"Yep."

He stared at me, waiting for me to talk. "Well?" he said eventually.

"Well what?"

"What do you want from me?"

"Seems that you're pretty much the only bloke in town that knew him. Apart from me. So I wanted to talk to you about...well, you know."

"No, I don't know."

"His final days."

"I didn't know him that well, I'm afraid."

"You spent some time with him. You must know a bit about what he was up to. I won't stay long. Unless you have something to hide…"

"I've got nothing to hide," he said a little too quickly.

I stared at him, not saying anything but also not going anywhere. He thought about that for a moment and then flicked the security chain off its latch and opened the door.

I stepped into a bohemian room with yellow walls, banks of built-in bookcases and a Persian rug at its center. The room was a bloody shambles, with the sort of after-party look I'd always imagined Doof-doof's apartment to have. Pizza cartons and Chinese takeaway boxes littered the floor, empty beer and liquor bottles crammed every available surface and half a line of coke lay unsnorted beside a copy of yesterday's *Post*. The photo of Ajax from his heyday stared at me from the front page.

The two of us stood on the Persian rug like boxers sizing each other up in center ring. Damian was a few inches shorter than me, probably around five seven, with the pointy snout and alert eyes of a weasel. He looked like he'd be a nasty bugger in a fight. Squirrely and hard to pin down. His haircut was a shaggy mullet and he wore a short-sleeved Manchester United jersey over navy blue track pants that rode low on his waist and had two white racing stripes running down each polyester leg. A tattoo of a Chinese Dragon graced his left inner forearm, the sharp blue line work telling me it was a recent affectation. An older tattoo, a sword with wings, graced his right inner forearm, with the words *Who Dares Win* written in a flowery olde English font across a scroll beneath the sword. *Who Dares Wins* sounded like the name of a hit game show to me, but I reckon there's no accounting for what people will permanently grace their bodies with.

"Luke," I said, and stuck out my hand.

He took it in a strong grip. Again the word squirrely came to mind. He looked somehow familiar, but then again a lot of blokes do after you've been serving drinks on the Lower East Side for a while. I'd opened The Billabong shortly after 9/11 so I'd been doing just that for more nights than I cared to — or even could — remember.

"Love what you've done with the place," I said.

"Me and the mates got a little carried away last night. Thinkin' about Ajax and all." His accent was from the north of England. Manchester, I reckoned, judging by the choice of football jersey. He was from The North, as the Poms call it, managing to be both functional and derogatory in the same breath.

"How well did you know Ajax?" I said.

We were still standing awkwardly in the middle of the room because he hadn't invited me to sit down. Perhaps because there weren't any available surfaces to sit on. Party detritus covered everything, and a shiny cream Musicmaster bass occupied most of the couch.

"Not very. I knew him more as a muso than anything else."

"I see."

"He tried out with us when we was lookin' for a new front man."

"Really? How was he?"

"He had the right moves and the right voice, but he was just too old. Anyway, we liked him enough and shared some...ah, common interests." He couldn't stop himself from glancing at the line of blow on the table. "Anyway...yeah, we hung out a bit. He had some amazin' stories from back in the day. Back when rock stars were rock stars."

"I'll bet. He was huge in Australia. What kind of band are you in?"

"Retro glam. Think Gary Glitter meets The Killers. Without the pedophilia."

"Glam. That would have been right up Ajax's alley."

"Like I said, he would have been fuckin' perfect if he was twenty years younger. Fellas these days don't move like those old geezers do. Today's kids just stare at their sneakers and mumble into the mic. Ajax had all the moves, but like I said, he was just too old."

"So you knocked him back."

"'Fraid so. We didn't have a choice, really. It just wouldn't have worked out."

"How'd he take it?"

"Well, knock-backs are never fuckin' easy. But, you know, you been doing this for as long as he has I'm sure you get used to the ups and downs."

"You don't go and top yourself, is that what you're saying?"

"Wouldn't know about that. Who knows what goes through a fella's head. Shame, though. He played me some of the new tunes he was writin'. They were fuckin' good."

"When did he do that?"

He thought for a moment. "A few nights back. I guess a night or two before he died."

"Where was this?"

He stood there awkwardly, scratching his noggin.

"My place?" I ventured.

"Yeah." He ran his hand through his mullet. He looked uncomfortable and why not? He'd been inside my apartment without my knowledge. It made me wonder who else Ajax had invited over while I was working my bum off downstairs.

Then he smiled unexpectedly, displaying sharp carnivorous teeth and oversized gums. "He was fuckin' amped. Lovin' what he'd written. It was good stuff, too. We agreed to be his backin' band when it came to layin' the stuff down."

"Looks like that'll never happen."

"Yeah, like I said, a real shame that. He had the time booked and everythin'. He was fuckin' itchin' to get things moving."

"He had studio time booked? Jeez, he was keen." It also meant a few other things. One, Ajax would have been much less likely to top himself if he had this recording session lined up, and two, he was much more financially liquid than I had assumed. Ajax had supposedly been staying with me because he didn't have enough money to stay somewhere else, and now this bloke was telling me that Ajax had enough money up his denim sleeve to pay for a recording session.

"Which studio?" I said.

"I pointed him in the direction of Blue Million Miles. A coupla blocks uptown from here. Twenty-fifth and Sixth. Run by a top fella called Eric. He was a foundin' member of The Chairs. Great guitarist."

"The Chairs? They were big."

"Too right. But Eric and Ross Olshansky didn't see eye to eye so he quit The Chairs just before they made it."

That sounds about right. Nearly every unsuccessful artist in New York City has a coulda-woulda-shoulda story. The Chairs were massive in the nineties, a polished pop metal band that weren't to everyone's liking, including mine.

"How could Ajax afford that?" I said.

"What?"

"The session."

"Search me." He scratched his nuts through his track pants and changed the subject. "So you said you found him?"

"Yeah. It wasn't pretty."

"I'll fuckin' bet."

I nodded at the unfinished line of coke on the table. "You wanna be careful with that stuff. Addiction is only one of its many dangers."

"Ah, that's nothin'," he said. "Me and the mates call that an alarm clock."

"Why's that?"

"It's just enough to get you out of bed. Anyway...we was just partying."

"No need to get all defensive. Just making an observation. Listen, can I hit your dunny? Too much Diet Coke."

"Knock yourself out." He bent down to grab a packet of Silk Cut from the coffee table.

Silk Cut. How terribly British, I thought, as I closed the bathroom door.

When I returned, Damian had moved the Fender bass and was lying on the couch blowing smoke rings at the ceiling. I watched as one formed a heart shape and then turned in on itself and fragmented.

"You gonna be in town for a while?" I said.

"What's it to you?"

"You know — in case something comes up."

"What do you mean, in case something comes up?"

"I dunno. Loose ends."

He sat up and turned to face me. "Loose ends to what?"

"I'm not sure. I just feel like there's more to this whole Ajax thing than meets the eye."

"Looks pretty simple to me. The fella topped himself. He was a strugglin' muso, it happens all the time. It's sad, but I don't see what all the hoo-haa is about."

"Yeah, I reckon you might be right. But I think I'll dig around a little more and see what I can find out."

He lay back down and blasted two more smoke rings at the ceiling. "Knock yourself out, fella."

I considered trudging the few blocks uptown to Blue Million Miles but soft rain was falling so I let my fingers do the walking. I slipped into a nearby café, ordered a skinny latte, and then called 411 on my mobile. I asked the operator to connect me to the studio.

"Blue Million Miles," answered a chirpy sheila. "You rock and together we'll roll."

"Cute," I said.

"Thanks."

"Is Eric there?"

"Sorry, Eric's in an all-day session." She sounded like she said it fifty times a day.

"I'm not sure if you can help me but I'm from out of town and—"

"Let me guess — South Africa."

"No, I'm—"

"Don't tell me, don't tell me — New Zealand."

"Getting warmer."

"England!"

"Australia," I sighed. "But you were close. I was —"

"Australia! Is it true that there are kangaroos hopping down the streets there?"

"No, love. Not unless you live in Goondoowindi."

"Goonga-da-windi. You guys have such funny names."

"That's us. The funny names blokes. I was wondering how much you charge for time in a recording studio."

"That depends," she said, followed by the snap of gum hitting her front teeth.

"On what?"

"On how much you want to record. An album's cheaper than one track, pro rata, because of the economies of scale." She sounded a lot smarter when she was on her own turf. I reckoned she should stick to that.

"We're talking an album here."

"Then the rough figure would be ten grand."

"Crikey."

"Plus you have the recording engineer's fee on top of that, and another five hundred or a grand to get the album mastered."

"So I wouldn't get much change out of fifteen thousand?"

"That sounds about right."

"O.K." I said. "Lemme think about it."

"What's the name of your band, just in case I'm out and about and come across it?"

"We're called The Didgeridoos."

"Really?"

"Fair dinkum. From Goondoowindi."

"I'll keep my eye out for you," she said, sounding confused.

But not as confused as me. How in the hell had Ajax come up with fifteen thousand dollars?

11

As I ambled back to the Lower East Side that afternoon, lost in a swirl of thoughts, a sight-seeing boat ploughed into Pier Eighty-Three at West Forty-Second Street killing three Belgian tourists and trapping another seven passengers below deck. The accident, while unspeakably bad luck for the tourists — the trip of their lives had, after all, cost them their lives — was good luck for me. Because that error in seamanship shifted the New York media's attention away from Ajax's death and onto the round-the-clock effort to save the trapped passengers.

With all media hands on deck down at Pier Eighty-Three, I could return to work at The Billabong that night without fear of journalists accosting me. If the blanket TV coverage was anything to go by, every single one of them — even Bertha, who had probably never left dry land in her life — was riverside, jostling for pole position in the race to win front page of the day.

Then events took another turn for the better when, just before nine o'clock, my landlord rang to give me the all clear to move back into my apartment. As the owner of the building, it was his responsibility to arrange for trauma scene cleanup after Forensics had released the crime scene. He outsourced the job to a private company that specialized in such matters, the aptly named Aftermath Services. They did a stand-up job, stacking Ajax's music gear neatly to one side before removing all traces of his brain matter and body fluid. Yet despite their sterling efforts, I couldn't sleep that night until I had carted a mop and bucket up from the bar and given the joint a once-over myself.

Over the following days I continued to run the puzzle of Ajax Farmer around in my head as I went about running my business, but if I was fair dinkum about it I'd have to admit that I was fast losing steam. Maybe Ajax did top himself, I decided, because I couldn't see any other answer. I certainly couldn't work out where the fifteen thousand dollars for the recording session had come from — perhaps song royalties from Australia, although I had no way of proving that because when I tried poking around into his financial affairs I came up against a brick wall. Neither his Australian bank nor the bloke who held the power of attorney over his remaining assets would give me the time of day. And who could blame them? Some bloke they didn't know calling from the other side of the world to ask personal questions about Ajax and his finances? I would have blown me off, too.

Perhaps the fifteen grand came from drugs. Ajax could have been in cahoots with Damian, dealing coke and Lord knows what else, although in the time that Ajax had lived with me I'd glimpsed no evidence to support such a hypothesis. And Ajax had been in the country for such a short amount of time that it would have been almost impossible for him to build up any kind of profitable network. Buying and selling drugs operates on trust and it's hard to establish that in just a few weeks.

As for Ajax's mental state…well, I'm no head doctor so I can't say for sure that he wasn't depressed. Many people close to committing suicide appear at peace, possessed by an inner calm after wrestling with the biggest question anyone can ever ask of themselves. Ajax was definitely more chilled out in his last weeks than when we first met, but I wasn't sure that meant much one way or the other. Perhaps the serenity was the result of making up his mind to act with such terrible finality, or perhaps it was the result of successfully channeling his efforts into song writing. Eventually I realized that I might never know for sure.

And ultimately, Ajax's death was a mystery that no one else — certainly not the coppers — considered a mystery at all. Plus I didn't have oodles of spare time to put into it. I had a going concern to run and was trying to get another one off the ground. Then when Anchor started attending night school, undertaking a course in small business administration at The New

School, I had to run solo on Wednesday nights. I was busier than a one-armed juggler with an itchy bum. I considered hiring a freelancer, but then decided to persevere and save the dough for the new bar. Renovations were hopefully just around the corner, which of course would mean even less time to delve into the Ajax conundrum.

For the next few weeks, I also gave Hannah and Gina a wide berth but for different reasons. Hannah because I wasn't sure I could look her in the face after what had happened with Gina, and Gina because I was scared of what might happen again if I could look her in the face. I was no doubt postponing the inevitable, but whenever Gina rang I fought against infatuation and let the call go to voicemail. I'd seen too many blokes fall into a new relationship just to get out of an old one and I didn't want to make the same mistake. Plus I wasn't completely convinced that I wanted out of the old one. So whenever Hannah called, I engaged her in brief conversation but avoided making any concrete plans. Funny thing is, it didn't click with me that she was employing exactly the same strategy.

All that's a long way of saying that I made little headway trying to figure out how Ajax might have come across that fifteen grand and its possible link to his demise. Perhaps there was no connection, I concluded, and had almost abandoned the entire sad experience to history when on a sunny Friday afternoon another bike-powered reconnaissance mission to Brooklyn was interrupted by a phone call. A blocked number appeared in the caller ID of my mobile and then Malone announced himself.

"Detective Malone," I said, "lovely to hear from you. I've missed your dulcet tones."

"Cut the crap, Bales."

"My, aren't we the testy one today?"

He sniffed. "You better get your ass down here."

"I'm kinda in the middle of something."

"You're in the middle of something, alright."

"I'm out riding the streets of Brooklyn." I was scoping Park Slope, South Slope and Windsor Terrace for more bar locations. The old butcher's shop in Red Hook still held appeal, but until the landlord got back to me I needed to gauge the potential of other Brooklyn 'burbs.

"How lovely for you."

"It would take me a good thirty minutes or so to ride back to the precinct."

"Wrong."

"OK, maybe a tad longer. But no more than thirty-five."

"I mean wrong, we're not at the precinct."

"Oh."

"We'll meet outside your apartment."

"My apartment?"

"You've got thirty minutes," he said.

Then the line went dead.

"So what's this all about?" I said, wiping off the sweat running down the back of my neck. I had hightailed it back to the Lower East Side and found Malone and Lirianos waiting for me outside the bar on Essex Street. I threw my bike in the basement and then Malone indicated we should go upstairs. He and I took a seat on the couch while Lirianos, as usual, remained standing, blocking the door like he was expecting someone to attempt a hasty exit. Me, presumably, although I had no idea why.

Malone sniffed. "So this is where it happened." He looked at my tatty Ikea couch, my two milk crate side tables and my chipped particleboard desk with my computer sitting on it. After years of piecemeal existence, I should have upgraded my furniture but I had never gotten around to it. The bar always seemed to take priority.

His eyes stopped on Ajax's music gear piled in the corner.

"If you're talking about Ajax," I said, "then yes, this is where it happened."

"Where Farmer offed himself." He accentuated the verb. A trace of white bread sandwich was stuck between his front teeth; it stood out against the coffee-stained enamel.

"Uh huh. Although you know I have my doubts about that."

Lirianos stifled a chuckle but when I looked over he wasn't grinning.

"Come on, Detectives," I said, tiring of their games. "Piss or get off the pot."

Malone reached into his jacket pocket and pulled out a zip-lock baggie. It contained a gun. A gun that looked suspiciously like the one I'd seen lying next to Ajax's dead, outstretched hand. It was gunmetal grey, of course, boxy and functional in appearance. The Bauhaus of weapons.

"That's the gun?" I said.

Malone turned the bag over in his hand. "Glock 19. Third generation. Nine-millimeter. Four-inch barrel. Plenty of fans on both sides of the thin blue line. It's a bit smaller than most handguns so it's easier to carry." He rubbed the rectangular barrel of the gun through the plastic in a fruitless attempt to polish it, probably more out of habit than anything else. "Registration marks have been filed off."

"How would Ajax get hold of something like that? He only just moved here."

"You might be surprised how easy it can be to get a gun in this country, especially if you want it bad enough." He held it out to me but I didn't move. I didn't want to touch it. "Forensics finished their ballistics testing yesterday."

"That took a while." I'd assumed that everything was hunky dory when I hadn't heard anything further following Ajax's death.

"They ran the tests multiple times, just to be sure."

"Sure of what?"

"The tests confirmed that the bullet that killed Farmer was fired from the gun found with his body."

"Hold on a sec. They found the bullet?" Last I'd heard, it had passed clean through Ajax's head and out the other side.

Malone turned and pointed upwards towards the cornice. A chunk of wood was missing where the wall met the ceiling. I hadn't noticed the hole before, but then again after finding Ajax's body I hadn't exactly craved closer inspection of the area.

"They removed part of the wall around the bullet, too. The angle of the indentation can help confirm the bullet's trajectory."

"I reckon that makes sense."

"The trajectory matches with the theory of a self-inflicted wound."

"How neat and tidy."

"Except for one thing," Lirianos said.

"What's that?"

"Forensics ran a couple more tests," Malone said.

"They did?"

Malone nodded. "On the bullets and casings from next door."

"Doof-doof's?"

Malone rolled his eyes at the nickname. "Yes, Doof-doof's."

"Why would they do that?"

"Standard operating procedure when two crimes happen so close together. You'd be surprised at what can turn up." He pulled out another plastic bag from his other jacket pocket. It held three bullets and three casings, each bullet mashed and bent out of shape, their ends exploded outward rather than dented inward. I hated to think what had caused that.

"Case in point," he said.

"Pun intended?"

He ignored my joke. "These are from the crime scene next door. You want to hear something really amusing, Mister Funny Guy?"

I nodded, although I had a feeling that I wasn't going to like the punch line.

Malone held up the bag of casings. "These here bullets match this here gun."

12

"Those bullets match this gun?" I said. "Are you sure?"

"I could bore you to death with the ballistics," Malone said, "but it's probably easier if you just take my word for it."

"O...K..." My mind tried connecting the dots but ended up with an inkblot test. "So what does that mean, exactly? That Ajax's death is connected to the drug hits? How is that even possible?"

"We thought you might be able to tell us," Lirianos said.

The bloke might be short on words but he had timing, I'll say that much for him. "Me? I know fuck all about guns."

"They're not that complicated," Malone said. "You hold the end without the hole in it, point the end with the hole in it at someone else, then pull the trigger."

I looked at him, then Lirianos. I'd known these blokes for a few years now. I wouldn't say we were mates, exactly, but I thought that we had built up some kind of rapport. "You blokes don't seriously think that I had anything to do with this, do you?"

Malone ignored my question. Not a good sign. "When Forensics matched this weapon to the crime scene next door, they also ran tests against any bullets found at the scenes of the other drug hits that have taken place over the last few months."

"And it matched those as well?" My stomach was sinking faster than an eight ball into the side pocket.

Malone shook his head.

"No?" I said. "It didn't? So that means…?"

"We don't know yet." His hand made a sandpaper sound as it kneaded his five o'clock shadow. "It could mean that the other killings are unconnected to your buddy Farmer and Juan Travolta next door. Or it could mean that the killer or killers decided to change weapons. You know, throw a spanner into the ballistics works."

"If they're smart enough to think that far ahead," Lirianos said, staring at me.

"What's that supposed to mean?" I said.

Lirianos suppressed another chuckle. He loved watching me squirm.

Malone put the gun and the bullets back in his pockets. "The bad news for you is that in the eyes of many, you're the logical prime suspect in both these deaths."

I'd be lying if I said my heart rate hadn't accelerated markedly at this point. "Just because I phoned in Ajax's death? Seems like a bit of a stretch."

"Statistics would suggest otherwise," Malone said. "As you know, those who are first on the scene turn out to be the guilty party in a surprising number of cases. And you're conveniently forgetting that you've already lied to us once."

"When?"

"When you neglected to mention that Farmer was in your apartment at the time that this Doof-doof was killed."

"I was just looking out for Ajax."

"Not gonna help your cause any, holding back the truth." Malone sniffed and looked hard at me. "Then there's the fact that you've managed to keep your bar open for four years and yet whenever we swing by there's barely a soul in there."

"Come on, detective. Now you're drawing a long bow. Try visiting on a Friday or Saturday night. You won't be able to get in the joint."

"Maybe he has a silent partner," Lirianos said, ignoring me. "Someone who likes to peddle more than booze."

"Now hold on a sec." I raised my hands. "Leave my bar out of this." I did indeed have a silent partner: Charlie Bertolucci, a retired NYPD top cop with political aspirations. And if he heard that kind of talk he'd have a fit. Charlie could be a tad sensitive about PR matters.

"No, you hold on a sec," snarled Malone, exposing a Rottweiler side of him that I had never seen before. "We've got a stiff in your apartment that you discovered alone, three more stiffs next door, and a bar that somehow stays afloat despite the absence of customers for large portions of time."

Even I had to admit that the optics weren't stellar.

"And who knows what else we'll find when we start digging deeper," he said.

I knew what they'd find. Charles Bertolucci, mayoral aspirant, linked to at least three drug-related murders. Wouldn't his political adversaries just love to get their hands on that juicy little tidbit? They — and the press — could run with that for months. And while Charlie's power and reach could sort out most problems, not even he could control the New York press. Not to mention that that really could be the end of The Billabong. I could be out of a partner and possibly lose my bar, as well as any chance of opening a second one. My dream of world pub domination would be so much Pavlova in the sky.

"So what are you saying? Are you arresting me?"

"No. Not yet. What I'm saying is that it would...what's the word...?"

"Behoove," suggested Lirianos.

Malone nodded. "Thank you. *Behoove* you to tell us anything you know."

"But I know jack—"

Malone held up a hand. "Yeah, I know, I know. You know jack shit. But maybe you know something that you don't know, you know?"

Malone was beginning to sound positively Rumsfeldian with his known unknowns and unknown unknowns. But what did I know? That Ajax was a failed rock star who had fled Australia for New York to take a crack at getting his act together. That Ajax didn't have enough money to keep a roof over his head yet somehow he found fifteen grand to cut a new album. That he had one mate in New York, a dodgy muso who appeared to be somehow involved in drugs, at the very least as a casual user but possibly on a more serious level. Perhaps there was something there, I thought, but Damian seemed pretty rough around the edges. He didn't seem like kingpin material, the kind of bloke who went around whacking other blokes.

"I've got nothing," I said, keeping my powder as dry as the outback dust. The less I said, the better.

"That's what you said when we asked you if anyone was around when Sanchez was killed," Malone said. "Why should we believe you this time?"

"Because I'm not a complete fucking idiot. I know I'm in the shit, so why wouldn't I speak up if I knew something that might help clear the air?"

"The criminal mind works in mysterious ways," Lirianos said, running a finger over the Twizzler-shaped scar on his cheek.

"Indeed it does," sighed Malone, and stood up. "We'll be in touch."

"I'm sure you will," I said.

It was the only fucking thing I was sure about.

I worked in a daze that Friday night, my mind in a swirl. I might have served one beer, I might have served a thousand. Around two a.m., when Anchor and I kicked the last punters out the door — a bunch of Price Waterhouse accountants who to everyone's dismay had monopolized the pool table for almost the entire evening — I was no closer to a plan of action than when Malone and Lirianos had left my apartment. But I knew that I needed to do something, anything, to try and work out what the hell was going on. And for several reasons, the best place to start would be Charlie Bertolucci. While the last thing I wanted was for him to learn about this sad and sorry mess, I needed to come clean with him. Better that he heard about it from me than one of his many sources about town, which wouldn't take long given the extensive network of NYPD contacts he'd garnered over the years. And I also reckoned that network might be able to help me. So first thing the next morning, I bit the bullet and called him.

"Ah, Luke. To what do I owe the pleasure?"

His voice echoed on speakerphone and a shaver hummed in the background. I pictured him in his marble-tiled bathroom on the Upper East Side, reducing his five o'clock shadow to four-thirty before spending another day in the spotlight. Charlie was quite the local boy made good. He had clawed his way up from the slums of Hell's Kitchen to the second most senior position in the NYPD. Popular with his men and the public alike, he had surprised no one by retiring a few years ago to seek a career in politics, only to lose the mayoral election against the bloated media spend of Michael Bloomberg. Last I heard, he was planning to run when Bloomberg's eight years were up, and in the meantime he was concentrating on his various business interests. Hot dog carts. Security consultancies. The Billabong and I were but a minor player on the fiscal stage of Charlie Bertolucci.

"I have some news to report," I said.

"About the new bar?" We had spoken about opening a new bar a few weeks ago and he had thought it was a splendid idea. And why not? For minimal investment, he would do virtually no work and receive half the profit.

"Kinda," I said, hoping to ease myself into the conversation.

"You found a location yet?" The last few words came out garbled as he ran the shaver round his chin.

"I think so. Red Hook."

"Bit of a commute, isn't it?"

"Not Hudson River Red Hook. Brooklyn Red Hook. There's an old butcher's shop down on Van Brunt that could be perfect. I'm waiting to hear back from the landlord about getting in to view the property."

"Isn't it a little sketchy down there?"

"Used to be," I said. "But that's quickly changing." I gave him a quick précis of what I observed to be Red Hook's shifting landscape: a new Ikea was going in, hipster waterside condos were under construction, and there was even a plan to run water taxis to Lower Manhattan. Plenty of disposable income would soon be in the offing, I suggested — some of which should be disposed of in our general direction.

"Sounds good," he said. "I say pull the trigger if you like the place when you see it."

"I will," I said, taken aback — not for the first time — about just how much faith Charlie placed in me. Blokes like Charlie and me ordinarily wouldn't share the same postcode, let alone the same profit and loss statement. But when our paths crossed a while back he must have seen something he liked, because he offered to become my silent partner just when I needed one most. Who was I to argue?

"So what else is going on?" he said.

"Well…I was paid a visit by Malone and Lirianos yesterday."

The shaver switched off abruptly.

"Seventh Precinct?" Charlie never forgot a name or face. His men – or ex-men, since he was technically retired – were like family to him.

"Yep."

"Tall Irish fella and Latino with a scar?"

"Yep again."

"What did they want?"

"You heard about that Aussie rock star who died on the Lower East Side?"

"I did. I thought you might be the bar owner in question."

"I am."

"So what? You can't help it if a friend commits suicide."

"True. But a few…how shall we say, complications, have arisen."

I heard a short sharp beep as he took his phone off speaker and picked it up. "Complications?"

I told him about Malone's visit, about the ballistics tests and the matching bullets. He listened, then said quietly, "Jesus, Luke. That doesn't sound good."

"I know. I'm sorry."

"It's not your fault. I know you don't have anything to do with drugs."

"Believe me, I don't."

"I dealt with those low-life scumbags for over thirty years. I know what kind of character disorder it takes to profit from misery. Believe me, you ain't got it."

"Nice to know."

"But this is a very tricky situation," he said. "It needs to be handled carefully. What are you planning to do?"

"Well, first of all I thought I'd try and get a little more intel on the situation."

"How so?"

"I was hoping you might be able to use your connections."

"Really? And what would I be looking for, exactly?"

"I dunno. But Malone must have held something back. You of all people know how detectives operate."

"That I do. Rule number one: know more than you let on in case you can use it later." He mused for a moment. "You're right. It might be useful for you to know what else they know."

He thought some more. I let him think. It wouldn't take him long to figure out that he would be covering his own ass as much as mine.

"Give me a day or so," he finally said.

"Thanks, Charlie," I said, but he had already hung up.

13

There really wasn't much I could do about Malone's visit until Charlie came back with more information. But there was some other unfinished business I needed to take care of. Half an hour later, I was coasting down Van Brunt Street into Red Hook, past car repair shops and lots crammed with school buses. I slammed on the brakes outside the old butcher's shop then dialed the landlord's number from a rental sign in the window. I was sick of waiting for him to call me back and thought that perhaps putting in a personal appearance might help move things along a little.

Lo and behold, someone answered after the third ring. "This is Antony."

"I'm standing outside the property you have for rent on Van Brunt."

"That would be Rizzo's. Great space. Great location. Wanna take a look-see?"

"Sure. How soon can you get here?"

"About two seconds."

"Two seconds?"

"Look left."

I swiveled and saw a fat Italian bloke leaning out the front door of the weatherboard house two doors down, holding a cordless phone the size of a brick.

"Just let me put my shoes on," he said, then hung up and disappeared inside the house.

He reappeared a moment later, locking his front door behind him. He was a short, fat piece of work, a few parallel lines of black hair greased flat across his clammy pate. He looked like a piece of gnocchi with spectacles. He tottered over, the heel of his left shoe two inches higher than the right, compensating for some kind of injury or congenital defect.

He put his hand out when he reached me. "Antony."

"Gidday," I said, taking it. "Luke." His shave was patchy, like he'd done it without his glasses on and missed a few spots. "You're a hard man to get hold of."

He looked sideways at me. "You that Aussie that's been leaving me voicemails?"

"Well spotted." Most Yanks thought my accent was from either New Zealand or South Africa, and both interpretations can be somewhat insulting to an Aussie. Australia has a good-natured rivalry with New Zealand, much like the rivalry between the U.S. and Canada, while South Africa…well, let's just say that their history of apartheid means it's a country most Aussies don't want to be associated with.

"I'm sorry I haven't returned your calls," he said. "I've been down in Baltimore for the past few weeks. Sick sister. She's not long for this world."

"I'm sorry to hear that."

"Ah, it's all right. That's just the cycle of life." He looked sideways at me again. "I fought with a few of you fellas in Korea. They were good men."

"We do our best."

He pulled a jumble of keys from the pocket of his shapeless pants, worn low to accommodate an ample gut. Deodorant stains marred the armpits of his short-sleeved business shirt and a pair of scuffed loafers finished off the whole package. "So you're interested in Rizzo's, eh?"

"That's right."

"You don't look like a meat man."

"I'm a publican. I run a bar in the city and thought Red Hook might be a good place for another one."

"You thought right, my boy. The skies the limit out here." He looked down a main drag devoid of traffic, a stray dog ambling along its centerline. "Might look quiet now, but it's a whole different box of dice on the weekends." He nodded at my bike leaning against the front window. "You might wanna bring that inside. They'll lift anything around here that isn't bolted down."

He unlocked the door without explaining who 'they' were. He flicked on the fluorescent lights while I carefully rested my bike against what had once been the shop's glass counter and display case. Behind it, running along one wall, was a thick butcher's block, sunken and worn in the middle by years of cleaver and knife action.

"You own the place?" I said, scratching my nose. A layer of dust covered everything and I detected a faint smell. Was it pork chops or just my imagination?

"Uh-huh. My great-grandfather was the first real estate agent down here. Bought the place next door, where we still live. Then when shipping containers came in, these narrow streets couldn't handle the semis. Everything moved to Jersey, the dock work dried up. People started defaulting on their mortgages and he started buying up the foreclosures. Don't get me wrong. He wasn't no slumlord. His plan was to hold onto them until they got back on their feet. Trouble is, they never did. The properties have been in the family ever since."

"What happened to the butchers? The Rizzo's?" I said, reading their name from where it was spelled out in blue and white tiles on the back wall.

"That was a shame," he said, shaking his head. "A real shame. Three generations spent building up the business and then poof."

"What happened?"

"The third generation was just one son and he wasn't interested in the meat business. He moved to San Diego and became an architect." He shook his head again, like he couldn't understand how anyone in their right mind would pass up the opportunity to be elbow-deep in lamb cutlets all day. "So what do you think?"

"Let me take a sniff around."

"Be my guest."

The space was about thirteen hundred square feet, a good size for a bar. Big enough to hold a decent crowd, small enough to keep an eye on what was going on. Nice wide timber floorboards, original pressed tin ceiling. I liked the idea of keeping the glass counter as the bar and working around that. Its three glass cases that once displayed T-bones, sausages and the like would be an excellent showcase for Aussie memorabilia. Behind the counter, beside the long butcher's block, two farmhouse sinks gave the place a rustic feel. There was plenty of room for extra shelving and lighting on the walls. The joint's dunny was its weak point, a single crapper built for the occasional needs of one or two butchers. It would need serious expansion to cope with the bladders of steady drinkers. The joint would take some work, all right, but the bare bones were there.

"What are you asking?" I asked casually.

Antony looked me up and down. "Three and a half grand a month, first and last month up front, one month security."

Crikey. The Billabong was costing me almost twice that much. Plus I reckoned I could shave off a few hundred when we got down to negotiating.

It was my turn to look him up and down. "Kinda steep for something all the way out here," I said. "Is there a cellar? A bar's pretty useless without one. Need somewhere to keep all that booze."

He nodded through the front window at a pair of padlocked steel grates built into the footpath. "Delivered clean and vacant." He turned to face me. The look in his eye said he was about to play his trump card. "Of course, the price also includes the apartment."

"Apartment?"

"Upstairs. Railroad. Two bedrooms, living room, separate kitchen, good size bathroom. Nothing fancy, but you can see the water from the front bedroom without putting a crick in your neck. Wanna take a look-see?"

"I guess so," I sighed, although in truth I'd already made up my mind. Two bedrooms and water views. In New York City, that was bloody luxury.

I intimated to Antony that there was another property I was interested in and that I'd call him in a few days, just to let him sweat a little before we started talking about the terms of the lease. Then I rode back to the Lower East Side, plans for the new bar whizzing around my brain and competing for attention with my Ajax-related problems to the point that my thought processes were in danger of short-circuiting.

I reached my apartment around lunchtime. Exhausted, I stripped down to my undies and lay on the bed, the significance of the surrounding silence not lost on me. For once I longed to hear that familiar bass and drum thudding through the wall. Then everything would be as it should be: Doof-doof shifting truckloads of blow next door, Ajax crafting songs in my living room, and me focusing on my new bar rather than the NYPD focusing on me.

Two hours later, I woke to the ringing of my mobile phone. I ignored it and the subsequent voicemail chime. But when two texts messages arrived in rapid succession, I picked it up.

Hannah. She was waiting outside.

I didn't have a clue what she wanted but after our recent radio silence something told me that it wasn't good. I texted her back and then buzzed her in, flinging on some jeans and putting on the kettle as she came upstairs. I also dropped the metaphorical needle on a CD: "Gossip", the classic Paul Kelly double album from the early Eighties. "Leaps and Bounds", an ode to watching Aussie Rules at the Melbourne Cricket Ground, its guitar work sparkling and its bass line walking, filled the apartment.

A moment later, Hannah knocked on the door.

"Jesus, you look like shit," she said when I opened it.

"Nice to see you, too." I closed the door behind her. "I just woke up from a disco nap."

"You OK? Not crook, are you?"

"Nothing that a few weeks in the Bahamas wouldn't fix." We hadn't hugged when she walked in and now it felt like it was too late to try. We stood awkwardly facing each other. "How are you?"

"Pretty good." She nodded at the sofa. "Mind if I sit down?"

"Of course not." I cleared off several sections of *The New York Times* to make way for her. "I've got the kettle on."

"Awesome."

"Sorry I didn't answer your call. I was totally knackered."

"Really? What's been happening?"

I sat down beside her. "I've been busy...you know, trying to figure out what happened with Ajax."

"But I thought the verdict was suicide?"

"I'm not so sure. And now neither are the coppers."

"Why not?"

I didn't feel like going into all the gory details about the link to the murders next door so I glossed over them. "He just didn't seem like the type to top himself and there's also some other stuff that makes it seem unlikely." The kettle whistled and I moved into the kitchen to make the tea. "Why all the drama?" I said over my shoulder.

"What do you mean?"

"Turning up here unannounced." For some reason, I found myself getting annoyed. "How come you didn't call me before you came over?"

She looked at her hands. "I wanted to talk to you face to face. I knew that if I called to tell you that I was coming over that it might end up being a phone conversation and I didn't want it to happen that way."

"Fair enough." I wondered what on Earth 'it' was. "Cuppa?" I asked, confirming before I added an extra teaspoon of Bushels tea leaves to the pot.

"Sure."

"I haven't had time to shop lately so the fridge is a little bare. You'll need to take it black...like your men." It was a bad joke and it hung in the air like a bad smell.

After I stirred the teapot and left it to steep, I decided to try again. "So what's with all the mystery, Han?"

"Mystery?"

I reclaimed my seat beside her on the sofa. "I've barely seen you for the last few weeks and then you turn up out of the blue on my doorstep."

"Sorry about that. I've had a lot on my mind lately and it didn't feel right seeing you until I'd worked it all out. Or tried to, at least."

"That's fair enough. I've had a lot on my mind, too."

"Really?"

"I reckon you're right. We do need to talk. Things have been weird between us for a while now." Ever since the night I met Gina at the Living

Room, I thought, although our relationship had been way too comfortable for a long time before that. Maybe Hannah had met someone else, too. Maybe that Patrick bloke from her building, the one who made the papier-mache models. I felt a niggle of jealousy and then reminded myself of my own infidelity.

"O.K." she said. "So where do we start?"

I made a grand sweeping gesture with my hands. "Ladies first." Here it comes, I thought. She's met someone else. Or fallen out of love. Or just wants to see other people. I'd be lying if I said that my heart didn't sink a little.

"Here goes," she said.

"Come on, Han. Spit it out."

She inhaled deeply, then exhaled.

"I'm pregnant."

14

"Pregnant?"

"Six weeks, give or take a couple of days."

"Six weeks," I repeated. Pregnant. Jesus. I wasn't ready for that. "Are you sure?"

"Sure I'm sure. Do you think I'd be telling you otherwise?"

"I'm sorry. It's just that…" I thought about what she had told me the last time we met. "So I guess you haven't really been so busy that you couldn't find time to work out."

She blushed. "I had to tell you something."

"I don't know what to say."

"I know. It's a head fuck. It took me a while to get mine around it."

"How did it happen? Well, not how, but why? I thought you were on the pill." Hannah had always taken responsibility for birth control, just like everything else in her life. When we first met, we used condoms until HIV testing confirmed that we were both clean. Then Hannah had gone on the pill. But she hadn't minded. She reckoned it helped regulate her cycle.

"I was. But I stopped after I found out. Not much point taking it now."

"I guess not."

"Plus my doctor says it could be bad for the baby."

"No point taking chances." The baby. It was weird hearing that word. It sounded like she'd already made up her mind to keep it.

"But that still doesn't explain why it happened," I said.

She pushed her hair back, suddenly annoyed. "Why does anything happen?"

"True."

"Unbeknownst to anyone who doesn't read the fine print, there's a one in ten thousand chance of falling pregnant while you're on the pill."

"Fair dinkum? I thought it was fool-proof."

"Apparently not. To wit, one fool."

"Come on, Han. It could happen to anyone. Anyway, I always thought you were more like one in a million."

"Luke, this is serious."

"I know." I reached out and took her hand. "So what do you want to do?"

"I don't know. I've been trying to decide. That's why I've been avoiding you. I wanted it straight in my own mind before we sat down to talk."

"And?" I said, not sure I was ready to hear the answer.

"I still don't know. I know on a practical level that having the baby would be crazy. I'm too young."

"Han, you're nearly twenty-seven. There are plenty of younger mothers in the world than you."

"I know. But I have so much more I want to do with my art and who knows where that might lead. I'm not sure how a baby fits into all of that."

"If you really wanted to, I'm sure you could figure out a way."

"Easier said than done but, yes, there's always a way." She let go of my hand. "To be honest, the thought of getting rid of it disgusts me. Like the poor thing is an inconvenience that can be removed with a surgical procedure, like a wart or a carbuncle."

"Nobody's saying that, Han."

"I know." She wiped her nose with the back of her hand as tears welled in her eyes. "What do you think?"

"Well, I haven't had much time to think about it. You caught me with my pants down. Literally." I pointed to the disheveled bed.

"Come on, Luke."

"It's different for me, Han."

"How? Because you're not carrying it?"

"Yeah, that. But also because I already have a kid." I didn't need to say that I didn't want another one, or the financial burden that goes with it. She already knew that from previous conversations we'd had about Suzie and Phoebe back in Sydney.

"I see."

"But it doesn't really matter what I think, does it? I reckon it's your body and your choice." I squeezed her leg, the thought of not seeing Gina again crowding my mind at the most inopportune moment. "Look, Han. I love you and I'll support you in whatever decision you make, in whatever way I can."

"That's nice to know. But the thing is…"

"Yeah?"

"I said I wanted to make my mind up before we talked about it?"

"Sure."

"I kind of did."

"Yeah?"

"Of sorts. I reached the decision that it's my decision."

"That's fair enough. That's what I've been trying to say."

"But I need to know that if I have the baby, you'll support it. Us. Financially and…well, like any other father. Not married, but…you know…" She looked at the floor. "I realize that it's a big decision, with a lot of moving parts, so I'll give you as much time to think about it as I can." Then her voice trailed off.

I sat there speechless, holding her hand, listening to Paul Kelly sing about going about his father's business.

We reached no conclusion that afternoon. Around five o'clock I headed down to prep the bar for another Saturday night while Hannah stayed upstairs. She was still there when I knocked off ten hours later. We ordered in a late-night Sicilian pizza from Rosario's and talked some more before hitting the sack. But there was no love making that night. An unexpected pregnancy can crush even the strongest libido, and Han seemed more than happy for me to hold her in my arms until she fell asleep.

It was several long hours before I followed suit. I loved Hannah and would do everything I could for her, but that night I spent with Gina had left a lasting impression. I wondered if it was possible to love two people at once and decided it probably was. Hell, ask some Mormons and they'll tell you that a man can love a dozen women simultaneously. Two would seem like child's play to them.

I lay staring at the ceiling, listening to Hannah's steady breathing as I shifted mental gears. I began contemplating the options available to me while I waited for Charlie to unearth more information. Eventually a plan formed in my mind and I decided to get cracking first thing in the morning.

Fortunately, the first port of call was close to home.

A thick brick wall separated my living room from Doof-doof's apartment. But a narrow light shaft was all that separated our kitchen windows. Designed to let sunlight and fresh air permeate the tenements' lower floors, the shaft was three feet wide, presumably the minimum distance allowed by law. Prior to the murders I had occasionally seen shapes moving around behind Doof-doof's frosted windows. He always kept the windows closed, though, even on warm summer days when I would raise mine to grab whatever breeze I could.

Hannah left early the next morning to finish working on some prints and that's when I went to work. Crossing the three-foot gap between the buildings held some risk, to be sure, given that my prior history of feline burglary was non-existent and a twenty-foot drop onto concrete awaited any slip. But I steeled myself and pushed headfirst through my kitchen window, then leaned out and grabbed the top of Doof-doof's window frame while I kept my knees on my windowsill. Then I inched into a standing position and shifted my left foot across the void, straddling the gap between the two buildings with one foot on each windowsill. I bent to slide up Doof-doof's window but it wouldn't budge. When I pushed harder, the pressure forced my left foot to slip from the windowsill. I grabbed at the window frame for dear life, snagging hold just before losing my balance. A shower of brick dust rained down, crashing onto cement twenty feet below.

I pulled my dangling foot back up onto the windowsill, my heart beating ten to the dozen, took a few deep breaths then examined the window latch. Someone had locked it tight from the inside: either Doof-doof or one of his muscle before the hit went down or a diligent copper charged with protecting the crime scene. I paused for another moment to slow my heart rate, then returned to fetch a knife from my kitchen drawer and repeated my journey back across the abyss. I slid the blade of the knife between the window's upper and lower panes, pushing up until it reached the latch. Some older scratches scarred the bottom of the window frame. On the third attempt I managed to flick the latch to the right. I tucked the knife into my back pocket, heaved up Doof-doof's window and clambered inside.

I stood still, listening for signs of life where death had been a recent visitor. There were none, save the soft hum of a refrigerator.

I knew from personal experience that Doof-doof had undertaken major renovations when he moved in because his builders had created an unholy racket from daylight till dusk. But despite aurally witnessing the renovations, I was unprepared for the scale of the apartment's makeover. Craftsmen had finished the kitchen counters with expensive white marble and paved the floor with slate. Mahogany cabinets, stainless steel sinks and high-end Bosch appliances — a dishwasher, a convection microwave, a two-door fridge and a half-sized bar fridge — were all accented with shiny fixtures that, judging by Doof-doof's obvious penchant for ostentation, weren't made of fool's gold. He might not have been perched at the top of the cartel's totem pole but clearly he liked to give that impression.

The pantry held pretty much what one would expect to find in a Mexican drug dealer's pantry by way of groceries. Cero, except for bags of corn chips and jars of salsa. He and his cronies probably ordered in their meals three times a day. The two fridges also contained no foodstuffs or provisions. They were reserved exclusively for alcohol. Cases of Carta Blanca — a beer I'd not heard of but presumed to be a Mexican drop — filled the bodies of the two fridges, while bottles of Grey Goose were stacked in the freezers. I also found a cupboard full of Riazul, a high-end Mexican tequila, ready to be consumed at room temperature. I was not much of a tequila man myself, having had an adverse experience with the stuff when I was barely of drinking age, but every self-respecting publican knows that experts once rated Riazul the world's best tequila. Doof-doof certainly had good taste in liquor, if not interior design or music.

The slate flooring flowed into an open plan living room where glass and leather became the order of the day. A glass coffee table, its legs metallic vines of golden intertwined ivy, separated a black leather couch and two matching easy chairs. An eighty-inch Aquos flatscreen filled one wall, probably worth a lazy ten grand, its hi-tech screen ideal for watching the soccer matches that I sometimes heard Doof-doof and his mates cheering on. On an adjacent wall hung welcome signs for the border towns of El Paso and Cuidad Juarez, presumably purloined from the highways of Doof-doof's hometown. Rusty bullet holes pocked the latter but the U.S. sign was pristine. Side by side, they offered an instant snapshot of the uneasy co-existence of two border towns operating under completely different national jurisdictions.

My daily nemesis dominated the rest of the living room: a six-speaker Bose sound system, four speakers mounted just below ceiling height in each corner of the room and two freestanding subwoofers in dark timber cases directed at the sofa and easy chairs. It wasn't difficult to envisage Doof-doof and his mates seated around the low coffee table, grooving to the music as they snorted lines of coke and went about their business.

I put off inspecting the scene of their demise by scanning the rest of the room. Serious fortification faced Essex Street. Double-glazed windows and iron bars kept out both street noise and intruders, while a state-of-the-art video surveillance system augmented a steel-plated front door. I flicked the two deadlocks, pulled the door open and inspected its edges. Smooth as a baby's bum. The door had never seen a jimmy in its life. I relocked it, then scrolled through the surveillance system's different camera angles: the building entrance, lobby and hallway outside the apartment. Its coverage was thorough. Arriving at the apartment unheralded would have been virtually impossible.

I returned to the couch. White crime scene tape still outlined where the three felled bodies had slumped together on the sofa. Blood and other indistinguishable body fluids marred the upholstery. Clearly Aftermath Services had not yet been engaged. On the wall behind the sofa, three chalk circles highlighted the final resting places of the bullets that Malone had had in his pocket when he visited me. Playing cards littered the floor and three half-finished bottles of Carta Blanca sat on the coffee table. The gunman had caught Doof-doof and his henchmen deep into a game of Texas Hold'em, completely unawares, and not given them the time to so much as move a muscle before nailing each with a single shot to the head. Whoever the assailant was, he was quite the sharpshooter. He also must have held the element of surprise, almost certainly not coming through the front door because Doof-doof and his mates would have easily spotted him. Unless Doof-doof knew and trusted the killer, which granted was a possibility, then the assassin's probable point of entry was through the kitchen window. It would have been relatively easy to open it unnoticed because, as Malone had confirmed when he told me about the murders, Doof-doof was playing deafening music at the time of the attack. And if I could gain entry through the kitchen window in a matter of minutes, then someone with experience could do it in a flash.

Of course, if the kitchen was the killer's point of entry then they probably came through my apartment — a suspicion I'd harbored since I first saw the scratches on the window frame. I had no idea how that was possible, or what it meant for Ajax. But it did seem unlikely that the killer had come from an apartment above mine. That would have required abseiling down the interior of the light shaft, an activity that surely someone would have noticed at eleven o'clock in the morning.

My stomach turned as fruit flies buzzed around the sofa. What a terrible way to die, I thought. But as Ajax himself had said, live by the syringe, die by the syringe. These blokes would have known what they were signing up for the day they decided to embrace the lucrative but volatile world of drugs, checking into a self-imposed prison of steel bars and security cameras that held all the riches in the world but left no way of spending it outside those four walls. It didn't seem like much of a life to me. Better to be poor and free, I reckoned, although that's easy to say if you've never truly been poor.

I wiped clammy sweat from my forehead and ventured down the hallway, its walls decorated with wooden carvings of animal heads painted in bright colors. The first two bedrooms I encountered were tightly configured affairs and, in marked contrast to the rest of the joint, furnished like university dorm rooms. Open suitcases holding clothes and personal effects sat on the floor beside baseless Futon mattresses. However, further down the hallway a third bedroom, the master, exhibited a gaudiness similar to the kitchen and living room: thick shag-pile carpet and a king-size waterbed covered by a velvet comforter embroidered with a tiger's head. Above the headboard hung more hometown memorabilia: a framed antique map of Juarez and its sister city, El Paso, divided by the Rio Grande and the United States border.

Inside Doof-doof's wardrobe I found a three-foot square safe, its heavy door ajar, its shelves empty. The assailant had presumably cleaned out its contents. And why not? Any cash or drugs stored therein were illegal and therefore untraceable. No one could ever report them missing.

Above the safe hung a clutter of western shirts and beside it stood an impressive array of cowboy boots. The shirts looked about my size, but while I loved a good cowboy shirt as much as the next bloke I drew the line at wearing a murdered man's clobber. I left the shirts where they hung and returned to the kitchen.

I studied the scratches on the window frame again, convinced that I was following in the footsteps of someone else. But who? Ajax? Doubtful. When it came right down to it, he just didn't seem the type for cold-blooded killing. That required a level of ruthlessness that I was pretty sure he didn't possess. Damian? Perhaps. I knew for a fact that he had been in my apartment because he had told me so. But I also wasn't sure he could blow away three blokes while they sat around playing Texas Hold'em. Still, I decided that a harder look at Damian was probably warranted.

If that proved fruitless, then logically a third party was involved that I had yet to encounter. A third party that had somehow gained access to my apartment and then killed three hardened criminals with single gunshots to the head.

With that realization, I decided I'd done enough breaking-and-entering for one day and left through the front door. I saw no harm in that. After all, the building had other occupied apartments and would therefore be subject to other comings and goings. No one would notice little old me leaving.

Or so I thought.

15

I nipped upstairs to the apartment and called Charlie to see if he'd made any progress. He had, and suggested that we meet for a mid-morning coffee at Cora's, his regular diner in Hell's Kitchen. I rode an F train to West Fourth, swapped to an A, and one hour later was safely ensconced in a booth with a steaming cup of watered-down Joe in front of me. The air-conditioning was set to a pleasant seventy-two degrees, "Daydream Believer" was playing on AM radio, and I was the youngest bloke in the place by a good forty years. In short, Cora's was a pensioner's paradise.

I had arrived five minutes early because Charlie was always bang on time. Sure enough, he strutted through the door at exactly ten-thirty looking like a cross between John Cleese and a mortician. Dark pin stripe suit, dark brogues, pale skin. He shook my hand and slid into the booth, nodding and smiling at a few star-struck locals as he smoothed some stray hairs back into place. I felt rather than saw his two meathead bodyguards, Freddie and Phil, jam into the booth behind me, the sheer size of them causing the back of my seat to flex inwards and press me closer to the table.

"Ho, if it isn't Lance Armstrong," Freddie boomed, taking his usual dig at my cycling ways.

"Freddie," I said through tight lips, not bothering to turn around. He and Phil had roughed me up a bit when we first met, although Charlie claimed that it was all a misunderstanding. Easy for him to say when he wasn't the one left holding the rough end of the pineapple.

Charlie stared at me, then clicked his fingers at the waitress and made a pouring motion. She winked and rushed off to fetch his coffee.

"So how'd you get on?" I said.

He tugged on both shirt cuffs and straightened them so that they were just so. Then his eyes darted around the diner as he spoke in a low voice.

"Not so loud." He paused as the waitress, who was just a little too perky for her middle age, delivered his coffee with a shimmy in her shoulders and a bobble in her breasts. "I've known most of the people in here since I was a kid and they're all half deaf. But you can never be too careful." He heaped two teaspoons of sugar into his coffee, added some Half and Half, and then stirred it thoughtfully. "I'll say this for you — you've got a knack for getting yourself mixed up in some serious fucking shit."

"Happens all the time to Jerry Orbach."

"First of all, this is not *Law and Order*. Second, you don't have his talent for wisecracks. And third, no pantomime DA is going to swoop in with five minutes to go and stick it to the bad guys."

I didn't have an answer for that so I took a sip of coffee. I'm not a huge fan of the jittery caffeine buzz but I do enjoy a cup of cheap diner coffee. I reckon it's because the brew is so weak I can enjoy its flavor without getting too amped.

Charlie put his spoon down. "Let's get one thing straight before we start. I'm only telling you any of this because we're partners. This stays between you and me. This is privileged information that no one outside the force is party to."

"OK, OK. Relax."

"Ordinarily I wouldn't tell you a word of it. But too much is at stake." Meaning his reputation.

"Sure. So, about Doof-doof—"

"Doof-doof?"

"Sorry. The drug dealer next door. It's a bad joke about his musical choices." Bad now that he was dead. While he was alive, it had just been the truth. I explained to Charlie where the name came from.

"His family calls him Jesus Sanchez," he said, pronouncing the Christian name fluently in Spanish: Hey-soos.

"I know."

"You know? How do you know?"

"Let's just say a little bird told me." It was probably a long time since someone had called Bertha a little bird. "It's funny…I hadn't even thought about his family till now."

"With these kinds of crimes you tend to forget that everyone has one. Even the worst criminal in the world leaves a mother behind. We were all somebody's baby once." He blew on his coffee and took a sip. "Although I hate to speak ill of the dead, Sanchez was a real bad bastard." He shook his head. "La Familia. They get up to some nasty business. Bloodthirsty doesn't begin to describe it."

I took a belt of coffee too, but the way this conversation had turned I felt more like a beer. "Is the other side the same?"

"Other side?"

"The other side of the turf war. I assume there are two sides. La Familia is one. Have you learned anything about the other?"

"What do I look like? An idiot? It's a gang based in Harlem. Run by a nightclub owner called 2Pay."

"Toupee? As in wig?"

"Yes and no." He spelled out the name. "Rumor has it that 2Pay is bald, but no one has been game to ask him."

"I see." I subconsciously ran my hand over my Number Two.

"But it's also 2Pay, as in, 'You are going to pay.'"

"Economical. Catchy moniker and veiled threat all in one."

"My friends at Narcotics tell me that 2Pay may be attempting to expand into La Familia's traditional downtown stronghold. Four of his dealers have been murdered in the last two weeks. Same number as La Familia."

"That's one lethal game of tit for tat." "Under My Thumb" by the Stones had hit the speakers and an old bloke two booths away was nodding along to the bassline. Either that or he had early onset Parkinson's.

Charlie took another sip of coffee. "How well did you know this buddy of yours? This Farmer guy?"

I shrugged. "Not very. I only met him a few weeks before he died. I was just doing the bloke a favor, giving him somewhere to crash."

"Did you know that he was a heroin addict?"

"A what?" I said, figuring I must have misheard him.

"A junkie."

"I...ah, no, I did not know that." Ajax a junkie? Jesus. I hadn't noticed him nodding off or needle marks. How could I have missed that? "Are you sure?"

"Positive. I spoke to Forensics. They found high levels of opiate in his blood and hair samples that point to long-term, sustained drug abuse."

"Fucking hell."

Charlie nodded, ignoring my profanity. "Apparently he used within an hour of his death."

"Jesus."

"They also found needle marks on what was left of his forehead."

"His forehead?"

"Just above the hairline." He carefully pushed back his coiffed fringe until I could see the roots of his hair. "Virtually undetectable, if you do it correctly. Or so they tell me. It's the best place to hide track marks, unless you hit a major artery, in which case you'll end up looking like you just went ten rounds with Muhammad Ali." He patted his hair back into place.

I thought of Ajax's jet-black hair. Maybe the dye-job wasn't just a fashion statement after all. "But he seemed fine. Wouldn't I have noticed something?"

"Not necessarily. Any heroin addict with a regular supply of high-quality product can function quite normally. To all outwards appearance, they look just like you or me. There are even a few on the force, unbeknownst to most of their fellow workers. Desk jockeys mainly." He took a sip of coffee. "Forensics also found Farmer's kit at the crime scene. Stashed in a secret compartment of a guitar case. He had half a gram of Grade Four heroin in his possession."

I recalled my conversation with Ajax about Keith Richards and his drug-fuelled creativity. Looks like Ajax had been employing the same strategy. But how could he afford that much heroin? And where would he get it?

"Jesus. I feel like such a bloody idiot."

"You weren't to know."

"It definitely puts a new spin on things."

"It does indeed. Do you have any idea where he might have been able to get his hands on high-grade heroin?"

"None at all."

"Well, if you can find out, you might be halfway home to figuring out what's behind all this."

"How so?"

Charlie clicked his fingers at the waitress, then made a circle with the thumb and forefinger of one hand and held up two fingers with the other. I didn't understand the sign language but she seemed to get the drift, scurrying off towards the kitchen.

"I hate to say it, but the way I see things your little friend was no innocent bystander in all this. I had a discussion with the commander of the Seventh Precinct. Strictly on the QT. The two detectives investigating the case, Malone and Lirianos, are following two lines of enquiry. One, as we know, is you. The other is that Farmer may have seen something to do with the Sanchez shooting and then been silenced."

"What do you think?"

"Hard to say for sure, but to me his drug use suggests that your friend was somehow involved."

"OK," I said, even though it was very fucking far from OK.

He drummed his fingernails on his coffee cup, thinking. "Did Malone mention anything to you about the bullets?"

"He showed them to me, if that's what you mean."

"Showed them to you?" he said, grimacing.

"Uh huh."

"That's strictly against departmental policy."

"Why?"

"It breaches chain of custody procedures. Taints the evidence. Wouldn't have happened on my watch."

"He kept them in a zip-lock bag. I didn't touch them."

"Doesn't matter. But it's probably OK if no one else knows, although if there's ever a trial and that comes out, the whole thing could blow up in his face. He could be in some seriously deep shit."

"I reckon he was just trying to shock me."

"Did you notice anything strange about the bullets when you saw them?"

"They looked kind of fucked up to me, but I'm no ballistics expert."

"According to my buddy at Forensics, they were seriously misshapen. They expanded on impact, which is highly unusual for a weapon of that caliber."

"What are you saying exactly?"

"I'm not saying anything. Forensics is saying that someone, presumably the killer, crosshatched the bullet tips so that they would burst on impact. It causes a larger exit wound by creating a larger surface area that does more damage. Only someone who is very familiar with weapons would know how to do that."

I pictured Ajax's head, blown asunder like an overripe watermelon, and took a swallow of coffee.

"Anyway," he said, "it seems unlikely to me that Farmer had that kind of weapons expertise."

"True."

"So putting that aside for a moment, the way I see it there are three options." He held up a finger. "One, Farmer was the triggerman for all the drug killings, using different weapons. Then someone decided to silence him."

"Impossible. He hadn't been in the country long enough, and then there's the bullet thing you just mentioned."

"Could be," he conceded.

"What's the second option?"

"That his was one in a series of killings meant to establish some kind of new order."

"Even more impossible. That presupposes that he was part of some order in the first place. I just can't see Ajax being involved in something like that. Plus, again, he'd only been in the country for a month."

"It does seem unlikely. Although you said yourself that you didn't know him very well."

"What's the third option?"

"That he saw something when the Sanchez killings occurred and was silenced before he could talk."

The same thought had crossed my mind. "There is a fourth option."

Charlie raised his eyebrows.

"That he killed himself, just like the note said." I realized for the first time that suicide might be the best outcome. When that's the case, you know you're in real trouble. It reminded me of Michael Hutchence, the front man for INXS. A housemaid found him hanging behind a hotel room door in the Sydney Ritz Carlton and word on the street was that he accidentally strangled himself during a bout of autoerotic asphyxiation. But such is the shame associated with that act that to this day his family prefers the official coroner's verdict of suicide.

"I highly doubt that it was suicide," Charlie said.

"Why?"

"It's too simple. Too pat. There's more to this than meets the eye, you mark my words."

I decided to play devil's advocate. "What about the note?"

"Easy to fake. Or coerce."

The waitress slid a plate holding two chocolate-coated donuts onto the table, explaining Charlie's earlier finger semaphoring.

"Thanks, Marcie." Charlie tapped the plate. "Help yourself."

I did as he instructed, too busy thinking about how someone could convince Ajax to sign his own death warrant to worry about the caloric hit to my waistline.

"What can you tell me about this bloke 2Pay?" I said.

"I can tell you that he's someone you should stay well clear of."

"Come on, he can't be that bad."

"Oh, really?" He took a bite out of a donut and put it down, then leaned back in his chair and formed a steeple with his long-fingered hands. "Let me tell you a story."

"Should I sit on your knee, Grandpa?"

He ignored my jibe. "For about ten years, 2Pay has run drugs out of a jazz club in Harlem."

"What club?"

"The Calloway."

"As in Cab Calloway? 'Mini the Moocher'?" My old man is a jazz fiend. When I was a kid, he used to drag out his old seventy-eights when he had a few beers under his belt. Which was more often than not. Every suburban butcher needs an outlet.

"2Pay has a Cab Calloway fixation, right down to his moustache and slicked back hair. Wears Thirties clothing, too."

"Makes a change from the usual rapper-slash-drug-dealer with his pants on backwards or down around his knees."

"Sometimes he even carries a conducting stick, like he's some kind of bandleader."

"I guess in some ways he is."

"He sees himself as a cut above the other New York dealers."

"A drug dealer with a superiority complex. Go figure."

"Indeed." Charlie pushed his cowlick back into place. "2Pay also has a very nasty streak."

"Don't they all?"

"Not like this guy. 2Pay doesn't just like to hurt people. He likes to hurt people in ways that will hurt them most."

"I don't follow."

"That's where the story comes in. There was once a bandleader at the Calloway, a trumpeter by the name of Fitzie Fitzgerald. One night, he was found dumped outside Harlem Hospital Center, literally drowning in his own blood."

"What? Choking on it? Was he stabbed?" Charlie shook his head. "Shot?" Charlie shook his head again. "So what was it?"

"Think about it. What's the best way to hurt a trumpeter?"

"Search me." I was beginning to regret even starting this conversation.

"Take a wild guess."

"I dunno…break his fingers?"

Charlie shook his head. "Not permanent enough. Bones heal." He drummed on the table's edge with his fingers as he spoke. "If you want to make sure a trumpeter never plays again, never makes money again, never has a reputation again, you know what you do?"

I shrugged my shoulders. "Search me."

"Cut out his tongue."

16

"Cut out his tongue?"

"And gouge a couple of holes in his cheeks for good measure."

"Crikey."

"2Pay did not get to where he is on wardrobe choices alone."

"But why didn't he just kill this bloke, this…"

"Fitzie. Because that would have been too easy on him. Word is that he dumped him at the hospital after mutilating him so that Fitzie would survive. That way, he'd have to live the rest of his life with the knowledge that he'd never play the trumpet again. The one and only thing that he was ever good at, apparently, apart from sleeping with women that he shouldn't."

"That's why 2Pay did it?"

"Word on the street, although no one knows for sure."

"Well, whatever the reason, I have to admit that's kind of amazing, in a fucked-up, evil genius kind of way."

"Maybe. But the thing is, it didn't work."

"What do you mean?"

"Fitzie didn't have to live with his shattered dream for very long."

"He died of his wounds?"

Charlie shook his head. "He survived those, only to hang himself two months later with a length of Time Warner cable left at his apartment."

"Cable?" I pondered that for a moment. "I hate to be morbid, but wouldn't that stretch?"

"You'd think so, but no. The outside of the cable might be plastic, but the inside wiring finishes the job. It gets used in suicides more often than you'd think, probably because there's so much of it left lying around the city."

"So 2Pay in effect killed this bloke. But he was never charged over any of it?"

"Nope. No one would talk. Especially not Fitzie, even while he was alive."

"Bit hard to without a tongue."

"Quite. Then there was the small matter of what else 2Pay might remove if Fitzie did talk. So, do you still want to go around poking your nose in where it might not be wanted?"

I realized that I was subconsciously running my tongue around inside my gob and stopped. "You've definitely given me food for thought."

"I thought that might be the case. Although with you, it probably wouldn't be the tongue that 2Pay would go after." He thought about that for a moment, sizing me up, and then asked, "Tell me, do you think it's possible to ride a bicycle without feet?"

Charlie and I chewed the fat for a while longer, trying to work out exactly what we should do with the information he'd learned. He reckoned that with two drug syndicates involved, the situation was far too dangerous to play around with and that we should wait and see where the police investigation led. With a little luck, Malone and Lirianos would clear me of suspicion and we wouldn't have to act, or that was Charlie's theory, at any rate. He warned me in no uncertain terms not to get involved and with hindsight he was probably right. But with so much at risk — my freedom, the bar, Charlie's and Ajax's reputations — it was going to take more than a campfire horror story to stop me from doing some digging around of my own.

Who knew where 2Pay was at that particular moment — removing a crucial body part of a competitor, perhaps — but thanks to Charlie I knew where he would be that evening. I scooted back to my apartment and searched the Village Voice music listings online. The Calloway Club's first act was scheduled for seven p.m. An early start, to be sure, but it was Sunday night.

I'd not visited Harlem in quite some time. Like most Manhattanites, I succumbed to the truism that everything within a twenty-block radius of my apartment held what I needed and, except for my Brooklyn forays to visit Hannah or scout potential bar locations, I seldom ventured further afield. So I decided to make something of my uptown expedition. I called Anchor to let him know that he would be flying solo at the bar that night and then walked over to catch the B train at Broadway-Lafayette. It was a further walk than Grand Street but the weather was conducive to a bit of toddling, about eighty degrees with low humidity, and the route decidedly less malodorous than the streets of Chinatown.

Forty minutes later, the B train dumped me at One Hundred and Twenty-Fifth Street and Dr Martin Luther King Junior Boulevard. I climbed out of the subway fifteen blocks north of Central Park into the fading light of Harlem. At the top of the stairs, my mobile chimed: a voicemail from Antony, the owner of the butcher's shop, claiming that another party was chomping at the bit to lease the property but he was giving me first option on signing. According to him, if I was still planning to lease the shop I should do so toot sweet. He was probably bluffing, trying to force my hand, but even if he wasn't he was right. I needed to make a decision.

But first things first. I hoofed it two blocks east along footpaths dotted with black circles of long-ago discarded gum until I reached Sylvia's, the most famous southern restaurant in Harlem. Sylvia's is a tourist trap, to be sure, but it's a tourist trap with damn fine tucker and I had worked up the appetite of a sumo wrestler. I opted for chicken livers with brown gravy for starters followed by a main course of blackened catfish with sides of collard greens and black-eyed peas, all washed down with an Abita pale ale.

Not for the first time, however, did I underestimate the size of American portions. I left the restaurant holding a foam takeout container crammed with leftovers, resolving to lay it at the feet of the first homeless person I saw. It didn't take long. An old bloke was sleeping on the footpath three doors down from the restaurant, the passers-by paying him no more mind than those old pieces of chewing gum. I placed the tray next to him, ready for when he awoke, hoping like hell that he liked catfish.

The Calloway Club was a short stroll from Sylvia's, situated on One-hundred-and-nineteenth Street between Fifth Avenue and Malcolm X Boulevard. The sun had set so I skirted the perimeter of Marcus Garvey Park, Harlem's bad press causing me to obey my baser instincts even though I frequently traversed more dangerous areas downtown. The far east section of Alphabet City, for example, was no urban picnic. Anchor lived there, purchasing his milk and provisions at a corner store where bulletproof glass protected its owner twenty-four hours a day, seven days a week.

Halfway down One-hundred-and-nineteenth Street, the flamingo pink door of The Calloway Club stood out like tits on a bull. The steel bars lining its windows were also painted the same garish color. A neon sign announced the club's name in a pre-war font that was all curlicues and scrolls.

Accustomed as I was to running a bar on the hyper-vigilant Lower East Side, where the liquor authority was constantly fighting an endless tide of underage Bridge-and-Tunnel drinkers and so bars carded everyone without exception, I expected someone to challenge me at the club's door as to my age and/or attire. But I leaned on the unattended front door and it swung right open. I walked right in. My eyes took a moment to adjust to the room's low lighting but eventually I made out a rectangular room that gave every table a clear line of sight to a stage at the rear. A bar ran down the left-hand side, where a black barman wearing a well-pressed tuxedo and pink bow tie chatted to a waitress while mixing drinks. She wore a pink frock that clenched tight at her waist and billowed out around her knees. On stage a solo clarinetist in a green zoot suit played to the sparsely populated room, just a few tables occupied by nattily dressed couples trying to enjoy the ephemeral sensation of the weekend never ending when in reality the work week was just a few songs away.

I pulled up a stool at the bar and eventually the gangly barman ambled over. He had the walk of a basketball player, rhythmic without trying. He looked at my black t-shirt and white skin but didn't comment. Not with his mouth, anyway.

"What's your poison?" he muttered.

I nodded at a fridge full of Red Stripes.

"Kinda quiet, isn't it?" I said, as he ripped the top off the bottle and placed it on a coaster in front of me.

"Early yet. We's only just opened." I noticed he had a lazy left eye. Maybe he wasn't a hot shot at the hoops, after all.

The clarinetist finished his song with a flourish and polite applause twittered from the crowd, such as it was. Then the musician said he'd be right back and disappeared offstage.

I turned to study the back bar, where the personality of an establishment almost always presents itself. At the Billabong I had sundry memorabilia on display. Mostly Australian, of course, but amongst its number was an ivory elephant gifted to me by my first partner, a memento of a hunting trip that now held greater meaning. This bar's Jamaican theme intrigued me: antique postcards advertising 'rhum', a sweatband in the country's national colors of black, green and gold, and an autographed miniature cricket bat signed by the West Indian cricket team, once the rock stars of the cricketing world who had now fallen on hard times.

"Who's the Jamaican?" I said to the barman, nodding at the objets d'art.

"The owner."

"He's not a local?"

"He is. His parents come to Harlem from Kingston when he was a boy."

"Interesting." An idea emerged from the depths of my brain. It happens sometimes. "Is he around?"

He tilted his head almost imperceptibly toward a door at the end of the bar and beside the stage. Black, no-nonsense lettering spelled out the word *Office*. "He is. But he don't like to be disturbed."

"That's fair enough. Got a pen?"

He found one under the bar, the club's name inscribed down its side in the same pink script as the neon sign out front. I scribbled four words on a coaster and handed it to him. "Can you give this to him, please?"

He stared at the message, looked at me for slightly longer than was necessary and then disappeared through the office door. He reappeared a moment later but stayed at the other end of the bar, mixing drinks and chatting with the waitress, not bothering to signal one way or the other whether my note had reached the hands of its intended recipient.

I sat at the bar nursing my beer, unsure of my next step. The barman would give no answer when I probed him about the message, only to say that the owner was currently busy. So I sipped my Red Stripe, not wanting to get legless in case I needed to front the big man but also needing to do something to kill time and not appear any more conspicuous than a white bloke drinking alone in a Harlem nightclub already was.

Fifteen minutes later, the clarinetist gave way to a three-piece ensemble that eked out a living covering Cab Calloway hits. It was like time-traveling back to pre-Second World War Harlem, and I realized that the world had changed some for African Americans since then. They had made real progress, like voter rights and the great hope of the Civil Rights movement and Martin Luther King. But still, the lot of the average African American seemed grim to me. They might not be in chains anymore but they sure as hell weren't running Wall Street or Silicon Valley, either. There were exceptions to the rule, of course, but if I were a working-class black man in the United States with children I would be more than concerned about the hurdles they face. There were still vast sections of New York, and the country, where black people seemed to live without much hope on the horizon and the eye of the law always upon them.

I was in the middle of this depressing reverie when someone tapped my shoulder. I turned around to see a goon. He might have been clean-shaven and wearing a tuxedo, but he was a goon, all right, right down to the dim-witted look on his face and his confrontational manner despite there being nothing to be confrontational about. He stood like aggression had been his default setting from the moment he came out of his mother's womb, and almost nothing could change that. I wondered what would. A free Big Mac? Copping a blowjob? Winning the lottery?

He held up the coaster I'd scribbled on. It looked small in his Hulk-like hand. "You send this?"

"I reckon I did."

"Whatchoo playin' at?"

"No playing. I just noticed the Jamaican stuff behind the bar and thought that Mister Pay and I might have something in common."

"Mister Pay?"

I corrected myself. "2Pay." I must admit that I had trouble coming to terms with his name. Give me a good old-fashioned moniker like Tom or Jack or Bill any day. Although I reckon one day even the president could have a name like 2Pay. Maybe 2Pres. Or would it be 1Pres, like Air Force One? Only time would tell.

He looked me up and down and then spat out, "Shee-it. O.K., come with me."

I stood up and surveyed the room. No one was paying us the slightest bit of attention. I half-hoped that someone would be, just in case I wound up abandoned outside Harlem Hospital with my unmentionables missing. But everyone was too busy zoot-suitin' along with the trio onstage to care about some honky who had somehow tricked his way into an entrée with the club's owner.

I took a last swig of Red Stripe for Dutch — or perhaps that should be Jamaican — courage. The barman watched, his lazy eye impassive, as The Hulk led me to the door marked *Office*.

When he opened it, what lay beyond was like no office I'd ever seen.

17

By the laws of physics, the room behind that door should have been about as spacious as a broom closet: the width of the club's bar and the depth of the stage to the right. But 2Pay, presumably empowered by drug dollars, had pushed through to the adjoining building on the left and occupied its first floor, creating, by New York standards, a large rectangle of open plan space that was roughly the size of a basketball court.

Space, however, was not the room's sole distinguishing feature. In marked contrast to the Thirties-style Calloway Club, this joint oozed modernity. Sure, the man's desk was a mountain of mahogany that wouldn't have looked out of place in the Eisenhower Oval Office, but beyond that was an eighty-four inch home theater with surround sound, a liberally stocked bar, a full-size billiard table, three pinball machines (including Playboy, a particular favorite of mine) and a vintage glass-topped coffee table whose inbuilt screen and buttons enabled the playing of Space Invaders. In an open-plan work area furnished with wooden workbenches, blokes nattered away on mobile phones: presumably disposable, so that the calls couldn't be traced. A laptop was open in front of each of them. Clearly the business of getting people high was now hi-tech.

A spiral staircase in the back corner of the room pushed through the ceiling to the second floor. Presumably it led to 2Pay's living quarters.

I followed The Hulk across a lion skin rug to where the man in question waited behind the Eisenhower desk. He stayed seated, holding out a long-fingered hand to greet me.

"Mister Bradman, I presume." His voice was deep, cultured, with no discernable Jamaican lilt. But nor was his accent Harlem-based. He'd gone to quite some trouble to make his speech more refined, more befitting of a respectable nightclub proprietor.

I took his hand. His skin was soft, no doubt well acquainted with quality moisturizer. "Hardly. I barely know one end of a cricket bat from the other."

He gestured to a wooden chair upholstered with burgundy leather. I sat down and studied him. My mind's eye had painted a 2Pay of considerable size but now I could see that, while he was tall, his frame was slight. He wore a loose-fitting zoot suit cut from purple velvet cloth, a purple silk shirt and orange tie, and a single ring on the index finger of his right hand — a silver horseshoe studded with diamonds. His black hair was short at the sides and left long on the top, all the better to execute an elaborate slicked-back look that clearly was not a wig. The smell of Brylcreem wafted across the desk, the same citrus scent that my grandfather had exuded when I sat on his lap as a child. 2Pay trimmed his moustache Cab Calloway style, the thin black streaks of hair accenting smooth caramel Caribbean skin that showed no signs of equatorial sun damage — probably because he had moved to New York at an early age.

He clicked his fingers and The Hulk handed over the coaster I'd scribbled on. He read my words out loud.

"'Lara sucks. Bradman rules.' You say that you don't know how to bat and yet you know enough about cricket to claim that Bradman is better than Lara?"

He was trying to sound pissed off but I knew that he was feigning annoyance. His eyes had come alive, just as I thought they would at the mere mention of cricket. West Indians are mad about the game, as are most inhabitants of the former British Empire: Indians, Sri Lankans and the like. And, of course, Australians. Wild colonial boys, the lot of us.

"Statistics would seem to support my case," I said.

"A batting average of almost one hundred is impressive, I'll grant you that."

"Pretty hard to beat." Cricket aficionados widely recognize former

117

Australian captain Sir Donald Bradman as the greatest batsmen who ever lived. His average was just shy of a hundred runs per innings, more than half as much again as the next bloke. But the West Indians have known some swashbuckling batsman in their time, including Brain Lara, a cricketer from Trinidad who not only holds the record for the highest first-class innings of 501 not out but also the record for the highest Test score. Who the better batsman of the two was has long been the subject of much conjecture. Of course, most Aussies side with their countryman Bradman while West Indians side with Lara.

"As is the highest first-class score in history," he said, referring to the masterful innings by Lara. He touched up his hair to make sure everything was just so.

"I'll go for the bloke with longevity over the odd flash of brilliance," I said, deliberately downplaying Brian Lara's feats.

"This is an argument neither of us will win. But it is enjoyable none-the-less. I don't get the chance to talk cricket much these days."

"I know the feeling." I'd visited London after living in New York for three years and attended a Test match between England and South Africa at the Oval. I spent a delightful six hours discussing the game with the complete stranger beside me.

2Pay sneered at The Hulk. "These philistines and their baseball. If forced I can watch, but there are just too many damn games to care about. It all seems meaningless until the playoffs."

"Amen to that."

"Shee-it," the Hulk said from over my shoulder. "Isn't that game of yours the one that goes for somethin' like four days?"

"Sometimes five," I said. "And even then, there might not be a result."

"A draw can be the most exciting game of all," 2Pay said. "But a lot of people don't understand the notion of delayed gratification." The Hulk grunted and shook his head. "So, Bradman, what brings you to my club?"

"Oh, you know. A little music, a little drinking."

His eyes flicked over my black t-shirt. "If you'll pardon my saying so, the Calloway Club doesn't seem your style."

"Don't judge a book by its cover. But, yes, I reckon you're right. I do have an ulterior motive."

He smiled to himself. "Everyone does."

I sat there, staring at him as his smile faded, unsure of what to say next. Wheedling my way in to see 2Pay had turned out to be the easy part. Now, how to steer the conversation around to the indelicate topic of Doof-doof's murder? I realized that there was no easy way so I just came straight to the point.

"Seems like you've got a bit of a turf war going on."

I heard a whisper of sound behind me and then my arms were pinned to my sides. For a hulk, The Hulk sure could move. He held me tight to the chair in a bear hug.

"Easy, big guy," chuckled 2Pay.

"What's this honky playing at?" The Hulk grunted from somewhere behind my left ear.

"Now, now. Calm down. He's not a narc."

"How can you be sure?"

"Even Serpico was better dressed than that. Let him go."

"Aa-ight."

The Hulk released me as 2Pay picked up a very shiny, very sharp letter opener from the desk. The conductor's baton that Charlie had mentioned earlier lay nearby.

2Pay made a show of cleaning his fingernails with the letter opener even though they looked freshly manicured. "What do you know about turf wars, Bradman?"

"Not much." I readjusted my T-shirt and tried to look undaunted, like bodily attacks were an everyday occurrence for me. "Just that my apartment seems to be stuck in the middle of one."

"Sounds inconvenient. Tell me more."

"I run a bar on the Lower East Side."

"Ah, a love of cricket is not the only thing we share. You are a fellow publican."

"My joint is a little...how shall we say, down market from yours."

"Most are. What's yours called?"

"The Billabong."

"Billabong?"

"It's Aboriginal. It means watering hole. You know, where animals come to drink."

"Cute." He wiped the letter opener on the purple leg of his trousers to enhance its shine. "But what's all this got to do with a turf war?"

"My apartment is right above the bar. And next door to where Jesus Sanchez lived."

He continued his letter-opener routine but fixed his eyes on me. "You don't say?"

"I do say. I reckon you've heard about what happened to Sanchez."

"I don't know the man personally, but yes, when three people get shot and killed in this town I usually hear about it."

"Shortly after Sanchez was killed, a mate of mine staying at my apartment also died of a single gunshot wound to the head."

"How unfortunate." He almost sounded like he meant it. "And you think these two," he said, pausing to choose his next word carefully, "*events* might be related?"

"Forensic testing has established that the same weapon was used in both killings."

2Pay put down the letter opener and leaned back in his chair. "Mister Bradman, you have played a number of attacking shots here."

"Offense is the best form of defense."

"True. So let me respond with some offense of my own. This drug war that you speak of, what makes you think I'm involved?"

"I have my sources."

"Your sources are mistaken. I categorically deny any insinuation that I am."

"Denial noted." Of course he'd say that. But only an idiot would believe him. What else paid for all the pinball machines and gadgetry, not to mention the enormous office space? Surely not the turnover from his nightclub, no matter how successful it was. I was in the nightlife business myself so I knew roughly what kind of financial return was possible, and it wasn't anything like the amount of money needed to fund the ostentation on display around me.

He picked up the letter opener again. "Mister Bradman, against my better judgment, I like you. You have testicles of steel, coming in here to front me on behalf of your dead friend and accusing me of involvement in his death."

"I'm not accusing you per se. Just trying to clear up a few things."

"Be that as it may, let me give you a word of warning. Believe me, it's more than most people get."

"Don't do me any favors."

"This is the last one, I can assure you." He held the letter opener vertically on the desk and spun it on its point. "Stay the fuck away from me and my club," he hissed. The letter opener stopped spinning and fell flat. Reflected in its shiny blade I saw The Hulk, looming over my shoulder, smiling for the first time since we'd met. It was at that moment that I realized what could cheer a man with a predisposition to violence.

The thought of more violence.

2Pay looked at the Hulk and said, "Time for Bradman to retire hurt."

The Hulk tossed me out a side door into an alley. I landed with a thump beside a dumpster alive with rats; they scurried off into the darkness and I followed suit, lest the Hulk wanted to inflict more pain.

"Fuck off," he grunted succinctly, then slammed the door.

I dusted myself off and limped back to the B train, trying to work some circulation back into a slightly corked thigh. When I reached the top of the subway stairs, my mobile rang. I paused where I still had a signal, expecting to see the butcher shop landlord's number in the display but seeing Hannah's name instead. I debated whether to take the call but decided that, despite what had just occurred to me, dodging her was definitely not the right thing to do given her condition. A condition that I was at least half responsible for.

"Hello, stranger," she said when I answered.

"I know, I know," I said. "I should have called."

"No worries. I figured you needed some time to think things through." She hummed a few bars of the music from *Jeopardy*.

"You're in a good mood," I said.

"I think I'm finally over the morning sickness I've been having."

"That's good."

"Yeah, it just cleared up. Maybe that's a good sign." She cleared her throat. "So what have you been thinking?"

"To be honest, I've been kinda busy and haven't had much time to myself." Too busy sleeping with another sheila, facing off with a drug-dealer-cum-torturer. You know, just your usual shenanigans.

"The clock's ticking," she said.

"I know. What do you think?"

Impatience entered her voice. "Luke, I've already told you what I think. That if I have the baby, I — no, we — need your full support. It's a huge part of my decision. I'm not sure I want to bring a baby into a single mother family."

"Right."

"So will we have it?"

"I honestly don't know, Han." I could barely think straight after what had just happened with 2Pay. Things had not exactly gone the way I'd planned. But what had I expected? Charlie had warned me that 2Pay was a tough nut. I was lucky to be leaving with all my extremities intact.

And then there was Gina. I had either met her at the perfectly right or perfectly wrong time. But either way, she was complicating an already very complicated situation.

"The ball's in your court, Luke," Hannah said.

"I know." Although it sure as hell didn't feel like I was calling the shots. I felt more like a cork bobbing about in the Bondi surf, just waiting for the next wave to swamp me.

A wave that, unbeknownst to me, was just a subway ride away.

18

I heard a click then felt the cold touch of metal behind my right ear.

"Move one fucking inch and you're a dead man," someone said.

A dark shape in front of me kicked my legs apart and frisked me. Hard and fast. Left leg, right leg, groin, stomach, chest, underarms. Then back through them again in reverse order.

"*Limpiar*," the frisker grunted.

The other bloke took the gun from my head. He pushed me in the bum with his foot, propelling me into my apartment. Then he hit the lights.

I spun around to face them. Two short Mexicans, about five feet four with stomachs drooping over their belts. The gunman had two droplets tattooed on his left cheek. I was pretty sure they didn't symbolize his love of precipitation. He wore Wranglers — the loose-fitting Wranglers you buy in Texas, not the skinny Wranglers you buy in Williamsburg — a sweat-stained white T-shirt and scuffed, unlaced worker's boots. The frisker had more of a south of the border vibe. Snakeskin cowboy boots, checked shirt, string tie. But differences in attire aside, these blokes had one thing in common. They were the meanest-looking motherfuckers I'd ever seen. Their eyes were as dead as a red-belly black snake's.

"Sit," the gunman said, flicking the gun barrel at the sofa.

Seeing no reason to argue, I sat.

"What the fuck you playin' at?" he barked.

"What do you mean?"

He nodded at the wall I shared with Doof-doof's apartment. "Breaking into a dead man's home."

"I never—"

"Bullshit. We been watching his place since the hits. We saw you leave yesterday."

"I...well..."

"Well, what?"

"I thought I might —"

"Might what? See if you left anything behind? Some fingerprints? Coupla bullet casings?" His finger turned white as it tightened on the trigger.

"Can you put that thing down? I can't think straight with it shoved in my face."

"No can do. Not until we know what we're dealing with."

"'What we're dealing with?' What's that supposed to mean?"

"You went into a dead man's apartment," he repeated. "Returned to the scene of your crime."

"It's not like that."

"Then tell me, what is it like? Why else would you go in there? Like I said, you was worried you left something behind. Or maybe you just get your kicks out of seeing what's left of what you done."

"It's not like that," I said again. "I was just digging around. Trying to find out—"

"Find out what?" he said, growing impatient. He looked at the other bloke. He was raring to go, an overweight Doberman straining at its leash. "Three of our amigos got their heads blown off in there. Good men, with good families and good lives. Three men who right now my boss thinks you killed. So you better start telling me fast what the fuck you was doing in there or —"

I held up my hands. "OK, OK. Calm down." Jesus. He was like Samuel L. Jackson with that piece. Righteous fury and all that crap. "I went in there to see what I could learn. My friend, he died in this apartment the day after your mates were killed. I thought the deaths might be connected."

"Your amigo died here?"

I pointed to the floor. "Right there. Single gunshot wound to the head."

He looked at the spot like it was nothing special. "That so?"

"Yes, that is so." I was starting to get pissed off myself. How many times did I have to tell this story?

The other bloke muttered something in Spanish and the gunman grunted back.

"What did he say?" I said.

"He said a gringo like you wouldn't have the cajones to kill three men."

"I reckon he might be right."

He sneered. "It's not up to him to decide."

I didn't want to think about whose decision that was. I wiped my chin with my hand and decided it was time to take a chance. "Look, you can either shoot me now or just put down the gun. I'm not gonna try and pull anything."

To my surprise, he chuckled, and then the other bloke caught on and they were both giggling. They were like two school kids who'd stuck a post-it note to the teacher's bum.

"What's so fucking funny?"

"You. Mister Tough Guy. Like there's only two options."

"What do you mean?"

"Stand up."

I did as I was told. He gestured toward the front windows of the apartment. The other bloke coughed and lit a cigarillo.

"Look outside, gringo."

I walked over to the window and saw the usual view: Essex Street traffic crawling in both directions, downtown toward the Williamsburg Bridge, uptown toward Houston.

"I'm looking."

"See that van across the street?"

A non-descript work van sat outside Essex Street Markets. A cream Toyota Hi-Ace. "Uh huh."

"Right now, we're s'posed to be in it."

"Don't let me keep you."

"I said we. As in the three of us. We been waiting here all night for you, ever since your little buddy downstairs told us you wasn't working tonight."

I spun around. "You leave him out of this."

"Our boss wants you disappeared," he said, ignoring me. "Come on, let's take a ride. Go for a little swim."

"Swim?"

"My man here knows the Jersey swamps like the back of his hand."

"I'm not much for road trips," I said. "I get a little car sick."

"I got something that'll take care of that."

And then everything went black.

I came to in the back of the van. My head felt as though a mob of wild emus had trampled on it. My wrists, bound tight in front of me, ached like there was no tomorrow —which for me, I was beginning to realize, there might not be. Two plastic garbage-bag ties dug tight into my wrists, threatening to break the skin. I lifted my right hand to check the back of my head where the bloke had king hit me and, momentarily forgetting about my bound hands, got a rush of shoulder pain for my trouble.

I lay still, getting my bearings. The van had sliding doors on both sides and a small window in each of the two rear doors. The Mexicans had stripped the interior walls of paneling, presumably to better secrete illegal substances therein. No plumber, or any other kind of tradesman, had ever been near this van. Its sole purpose was transporting misery in either human or pharmaceutical form.

Up front, the two Mexicans talked low in Spanish. Yellow lights flashed at regular intervals through the windscreen. Overhead lights. We were driving through a tunnel. The Lincoln or Holland, I reckoned, headed west out of the city to dump my sorry ass in the swamps of New Jersey like many a hit before me. I could never have imagined that digging around would land me in such deep shit. I should have listened to Charlie, taken his advice and left it to the coppers.

But it was too late for coulda-woulda-shoulda's. I needed to act now and get out of this van. Whichever marshland had my moniker on it, I definitely did not want to be there for the naming ceremony.

I eased myself into an upright position and leaned against the side of the van. My head throbbed with the mother of all headaches. I stayed upright and peeked through the windscreen. The van had slowed to a crawl, its engine barely ticking over. The tunnel's two lanes were merging into one to make room for a road crew undertaking late-night maintenance. I could hear jackhammers pounding in the distance. The traffic was merging left to right, which meant that the road crew was working in the lane on the driver's side of the van. Keeping my eyes on the backs of the Mexicans' heads, I lay down and rolled sideways until I was facing the wall on the passenger's side of the van, figuring that the driver was less likely to turn around to check on me and that it would take considerable effort for the passenger to look behind his seat. I ran my fingers along the exposed substructure of the van until I found a rough metal edge. Pain flared in my head as I placed my bound hands against the metal. I drew my hands back, scoring a small mark into one of the plastic ties. As the jackhammers grew louder and covered any sound I made, I repeated the act, maintaining steady pace and downward pressure as I drew my hands back and forth over and over. It was slow going, and just as I was beginning to question whether I was making any progress the tie snapped in two and fell away from my right hand.

One down, one to go.

I took another quick peek out the front window. The road crew was closer now, the traffic almost at a standstill. The driver cursed the delay under his breath. I placed the second tie against the metal and went to work. With the removal of the first tie I had a bit more freedom to move. I could work harder and faster. In thirty seconds, it too broke free.

I unraveled the tie from my wrists, the left one bleeding where the plastic had dug into my arm and broken the skin. I rolled back over to the driver's side and put my hand to the door handle, silently sliding its latch to the unlocked position. Then I jiggled the handle until it clicked open less than a half inch.

I sat like that for an eternity, holding the door slightly ajar, my hand poised on the handle as the rat-a-tat-tat of jackhammers grew closer. One backward glance from either Mexican and it would have been all over, but they were looking straight ahead, the driver fuming at the traffic while the passenger hummed along to REO Speedwagon.

When the jackhammers sounded like they were right outside the van, I sat up and tugged at the door with all my might. I pulled so hard that the door slid open and then instantly rebounded to its closed position. The passenger cried, "*Joder!*" and scrambled between the front seats like a man half his size. I was fumbling with the latch to open the door again when he fell on me. I raised my feet, pushed him in the stomach and sent him sprawling sideways. He struggled to his feet to take a second go at me. But right then the driver stomped on the brakes, bringing the van to a screeching halt and upsetting the bloke's balance. It gave me the millisecond I needed to open the door and tumble out, landing at the feet of a stunned road worker.

Now it was the driver's turn to shout, "*Joder!*" while his sidekick rolled around in the back of the van. The driver screamed again in Spanish and then hit the accelerator; the other bloke slammed the rear door shut as they sped off. Horns blared as the van swerved onto the shoulder beside the one open lane, squeezing between slow-moving cars and the side of the tunnel. The front of the van ground against the tunnel wall, sending up a shower of sparks as they sped toward New Jersey.

The Mexicans had clearly decided that they were in no position to retrieve me, and they were right. How would it look, two blokes holding another bloke captive in the back of their van, brandishing weapons to thwart his escape? It was much smarter to flee the scene and avoid any potentially awkward questions from the bevy of authorities who patrolled the Holland Tunnel post-9/11. Particularly if you had links to La Familia.

The road worker, a young bloke with red hair and freckles, looked down at me lying on the ground.

"You OK?" he said, holding out a hand to help me to my feet. A few feet away, a jackhammer operator who must have stopped work when I made my escape was shaking his head as if to say, "Only in New York."

"I think so." My shoulder had taken the brunt of the impact. I flexed it but nothing felt broken.

He reached for his mobile phone.

"What're you doing?" I said.

"Sorry, but I gotta call this in. I have to report any irregularities in the tunnel. Terrorism and all that."

"Come on, mate. It was just a prank. I'm getting hitched next week and the lads had one too many and got carried away. That's all there is to it."

He looked doubtfully at the van disappearing into the distance and then back at me. Then he put his phone away.

"What's the best way out of here?" I asked before he could change his mind.

He pointed to a maintenance catwalk about four feet off the ground. "That runs the length of the tunnel. There'll probably be some cops at the other end who'll want a word with you, though."

I thanked him for his trouble and set off towards Manhattan, rubbing some circulation back into my wrists as I walked.

Coppers? Right now, they were the least of my problems.

19

As it turned out, I waltzed out of the Holland Tunnel like I was taking a Sunday evening stroll. I stepped straight off the maintenance catwalk and walked past three vacant cop cars that were parked askew at the head of the tunnel. Their lights were flashing but there was nary a uniform in sight. New York's Finest were no doubt off scoring a late-night Dunkin' Donuts fix.

I took cover in the shadow of a lone row of brownstones that had somehow escaped demolition during construction of the tunnel and then scurried down Broome Street, taking Varick south to Canal. My homing instincts drew me east, toward the Lower East Side and the bar, but my head told me otherwise. The Mexicans had probably chucked a U-turn as soon as they exited the tunnel in Jersey City and were now heading back to scour the streets of the Lower East Side. They would need to fix what they had fucked up before Alejandro Navas found out. I'm sure he was not a man to anger.

The streetlamps of Canal Street felt like prison lights bearing down on me. I was a fugitive with nowhere to go. I couldn't return to my apartment. I couldn't call Anchor to seek sanctuary at his place because the Mexicans could easily find out his address from one of the regulars at The Billabong, if they hadn't done so already. I thought about heading out to Hannah's in DUMBO but that would only put her and the baby at risk. That left springing for a hotel, but I didn't fancy being alone after what felt like a near-death experience.

I patted my pockets and realized that I still somehow had my phone and wallet. The Mexican who frisked me must have figured that I wouldn't be doing much talking or shopping from my watery grave.

Procrastinating, I slipped off Canal Street and found an all-night bodega tucked away on the corner of Wooster and Grand. I bought some extra strength Tylenol for my head and washed them down with a surprisingly good cup of black tea while sitting at a counter in back of the store. The Pakistani bloke behind the counter raised an eyebrow at my appearance but then quickly returned to reading a Stephen King paperback.

After twenty minutes I had reached a decision. The way I saw it, I really didn't have much choice. But once again an ulterior motive was baked in there somewhere.

As I sandwiched my empty styrofoam cup into an overflowing bin, I pushed that thought to the back of my mind.

"Hello?" came her voice through the intercom.

"Gina," I whispered, relieved to find her home. "Let me in."

She hit the buzzer and then met me at her front door. Her hand flew to her mouth.

"Luke! What happened?"

"It's a long story."

She ushered me onto the sofa. "Here. Sit. I will get some hot water and towels."

"Maybe I should just take a shower."

"No. Let me clean the wound first."

She disappeared into the bathroom. I stood up and checked myself in the reflection of the TV. I could feel dried blood caked to my hair and my clothes looked like…well, like I'd been rolling around unconscious in the back of a van. No wonder the road worker and Pakistani shopkeeper had looked at me askance. It was a miracle they hadn't called for the men in white coats.

Gina came out of the bathroom carrying a towel and an ice bucket filled with warm water. She ordered me to sit back down on the sofa and then dabbed at the wound at the back of my head, cleansing the towel in the warm water every few moments, gradually turning the bucket of water a deeper red. Then she put the towel down and started parting my hair to further investigate the cut.

"Ow," I said.

"Sorry."

"Does it look bad?"

"Not really. There is quite a lump but the skin is not too badly broken. No need for stitches, I think. Wait here. I have some antiseptic left over from…" Her voice trailed off. But we both knew what the end of that sentence was: the time that Ajax assaulted her.

She went to the bathroom to retrieve it. "So what happened?" she sang out.

I stayed silent, debating how much to tell her and also whether the story would sound like the ravings of a madman.

She walked back into the room and I was once again blind-sided by her beauty.

"Come on, Luke. You can not arrive on my doorstep at this hour in this condition and provide me with no explanation."

"Fair enough."

As she finished cleaning my wound, I spat out the full story. How I still wasn't convinced that Ajax had killed himself so I started looking into the murders next door, and how that had led me to 2Pay and La Familia to me. I omitted Charlie's role and the part about me being under suspicion and the impact all this might have on my bar and any future plans. Even so, it felt good to speak to someone about it, to share the insanity with someone who wasn't involved. As I spoke, I looked for signs that she thought I was crazy, a few sausages short of a barbecue, but she seemed to nod in all the right places. I finished with my escape in the Holland Tunnel and explained how coming to her place had felt like my only option.

"Well," she said when I finished, "I am glad that you felt that you could come here."

"Thanks, Gina. I really do appreciate it."

"That is quite a story."

"It's not a story. It's the truth."

"I know. It's just that it is all a little incredible. Drug wars, cartels. Shootings, kidnappings."

"I have more than a little trouble believing it myself."

"And you think Ajax was mixed up in all of this?"

"No, I'm beginning to think that he wasn't."

"Really?"

"Well, to be completely honest I'm not sure. Maybe 2Pay is responsible for the drug murders and killed Ajax because he saw something. Although inflicting a quick and painless death doesn't really seem his style." I winced as she applied antiseptic to the cut. "But if he didn't do it, then who did? Maybe be a third party I don't even know about."

"What about La Familia? Maybe they could have killed him?"

"I don't think so. They were certainly involved in some of the earlier drug murders, but not Doof-doof's."

"How can you be so sure?"

"I don't think they'd bump off their own bloke, for a start – especially if he was related to the head honcho. And if they didn't kill Doof-doof, that pretty much rules them out of any involvement as far as Ajax's death goes, too."

She thought about that. "What will you do about them?"

"What do you mean?"

"The cartel. They are looking for you, yes?"

"I reckon I'll just hope that if I can get to the bottom of everything then they'll be satisfied. I think they really just want to know who killed Doof-doof." And then exact their own unique brand of revenge, I thought, but kept that to myself.

Gina took my hand. "You need to be careful, Luke. This is serious business you are mixed up in."

"Believe me, if I didn't know that before tonight, I do now."

"After what happened to Ajax, I could not bear it if something also happened to you."

It was the first time she'd articulated her feelings for me and I knew I was beginning to feel the same way about her. This relationship was taking its natural progression and deepening without any conscious effort from either of us. It felt like a natural evolution. I still hadn't made up my mind about the baby and this sure as hell wasn't making that decision any easier. But as I looked into Gina's eyes, I had an inkling that perhaps she was too good to be true. Then I told myself not to be so stupid. That was the old Luke talking, the bloke with no confidence who had screwed up pretty much everything in his life. Of course a sheila this beautiful, this exotic, could be interested in me. I just needed to believe in myself to be able to believe in her love.

"I think you should go to the police," she said, snapping me out of my reverie. "They will protect you."

"Not much the coppers can do," I said. "These drug cartels are a law unto themselves." Plus I would need twenty-four-hour protection and there was no way Malone or Lirianos would give me that. Not without concrete proof that I was in danger and I didn't have a single witness to support my story. Well, except for the Irish road worker, and I didn't fancy my chances of tracking him down. Plus I'd lied to him, so why would he support me?

"Even in the United States?" Gina asked. "In Mexico I can understand, perhaps, but is it not different here?"

"Not as different as you'd think. Not when there's millions of dollars to be made."

"I see." She put the bowl and towels aside then led me to the bathroom. She turned on the shower and undressed me.

Then she undressed herself.

"How's work?" I murmured. We were lying in bed, my wet hair soaking into the pillow, her wet hair dampening my chest. Alberto was curled up on the end of the mattress, purring softly.

"Work?"

"Yeah, at the hotel."

"It is OK. Just a job."

"Do you like it?"

"Yes and no. I am grateful for the money but would rather be teaching. Doing something more meaningful."

"Are you making plans in that direction?"

"There is a bridging course I have found. After I save more, I will try and find a part-time job and complete it."

"Sounds like a plan, Stan." I tried to picture myself fitting into those plans. I wondered if there was room for me. Or if she even wanted me there.

"I owe it to my brother," she said.

"Owe what?"

"To make the most of my life. He never got to live his, so I need to do it for the both of us."

I kissed her forehead. "I'm sure you'll do just fine."

"And you? Do you have plans?"

I told her about the second bar, how I wanted to keep the business growing.

"I'm sure you can do it," she said, then smiled. "I have full faith in you."

Who is this woman, I thought. She had been through so much — the death of her brother, then leaving her parents and homeland to emigrate to another country — yet had so much to give to others. I searched her eyes and saw nothing but tenderness looking back at me.

"I love you," she said.

Without even thinking, I said the same words back.

When I woke the next morning, it hit me.

Damian.

In the violent swirl of 2Pay and La Familia, I had forgotten all about him. It seemed unlikely, but perhaps he was the as yet unidentified third party. To my knowledge, he was the only bloke in town who Ajax knew that was involved in drugs, even if he was just a user. And if he wasn't the third party, perhaps talking to him might lead me there.

I tucked a note under the pillow and left Gina sleeping. I hobbled to an early morning café on Fourth Avenue, aching in places that I hadn't known I could ache. My knees and elbows were also sore from crawling around the back of that van. I ordered a breakfast burrito of black beans, chorizo and egg, splashed it liberally with Cholula hot sauce, then ate as I rode the D train to Chelsea.

As I exited the subway at Twenty-third and Eighth, my phone chimed three times: text messages from Hannah, not so subtle reminders that her biological clock wasn't just ticking but fast forwarding. I needed no reminders. But my own clock was also ticking, the alarm set to go off as soon as those Mexicans caught up with me again.

I called Hannah back as I walked to the Hotel Chelsea but the call went straight to voicemail. I left a short message telling her I'd try again soon. Once I'd had my little chat with Damian.

Standing outside the hotel entrance, I decided to opt for the element of surprise. I ducked around the back and soon found an alley that ran behind the Hotel Chelsea. However, climbing its fire escape proved more elusive. It took five minutes to maneuver an overflowing dumpster into position beneath the ladder and balance myself on its lip to reach the bottom rung. I grabbed hold at full stretch, then hauled myself up hand over hand until my feet reached the lower rung. I then sweated and grunted my way to the top, my battered body straining as I climbed, watched all the while by a bemused homeless bloke huddled in a cardboard box in a corner of the alley.

Once I reached the bottom landing of the fire escape, however, it was a relatively easy climb up three flights of stairs. Most rooms had the blinds drawn against the morning sun, including Damian's, but his bathroom window was still ajar, just as I recalled from my first visit. I eased the window further open and climbed through, stepping onto the toilet to break my fall. My foot landed on the lid with a heavy thump. I held my breath, waiting to see if Damian had heard me.

After five seconds of silence, I stood up and eased the bathroom door open. A lump lay on the bed, covered in a tangle of bed linen. I crept over and grabbed the sheets with both hands.

"Rise and shine, mother fucker!" I shouted, and ripped them off.

But it was not Damian lying beneath.

A black sheila, naked as the day her mother had pushed her out into the world, rolled over to the far side of the bed, screaming like Jack the Ripper had woken her. She curled herself into the fetal position, trying to cover her nether regions. It was a losing battle, though, her big tits flopping about like over-filled water balloons.

"Oh, shit," I said. "I'm so sorry."

"What the fuck do you think you're doing?"

"I…I…"

"Get the fuck out of my room!"

"I thought you were my mate. It was…you know, a joke."

"A joke?"

"I'm so sorry." I realized that I was still holding the bed sheets. I tossed them to her and she quickly covered herself. "I'm really sorry. My mate, he was staying in this room."

"Well, he's not anymore."

"Clearly."

She tilted her head as she looked at me. "Is his name Damian?"

"Yeah."

"I thought as much. I've had people knocking on my damn door day and night looking for this Damian."

"What kind of people?"

"I don't know. Some fella who said he was in some kind of band with him. Then some girl who said she works with him. Damian," she said, spitting his name out like it was on the schedule of restricted poisons. "I've asked three times for another room but that fool downstairs keeps telling me the place is fully booked." She glared at me. "But this is the last damn straw. I ain't taking no for an answer now."

"I don't blame you. When did you check in?"

"Day before yesterday. Seems your friend Mister Damian gave this room number out to half the damn city. Lords knows what he was getting up to in here."

"I've got a fair idea," I said, thinking about that half a line of coke I'd seen on his coffee table. "I truly am sorry. I didn't mean any harm."

She looked at me uncertainly. "That's O.K…I guess."

I knew grudging acceptance was the best I could hope for. I blurted out goodbye, then let myself out before she had a change of heart and called the coppers.

I barreled down four flights of stairs into the lobby. The drink-ravaged Southerner and his feline companion were still manning the front desk.

"Didn't see you come in," the bloke said.

"You must have been too busy patting Puss in Boots. I'm looking for that Damian bloke again."

"Is that so?"

"Yes, it is so."

"Well, he's moved on. Checked out a few days ago. Most curious behavior."

"How so?"

"He was paid up till the end of next week. Isn't that so, Moonshine?"

Moonshine licked his chops in response.

"Any idea where I might find him?"

"You could try his place of employ."

"And where would that be?"

The bloke scratched his left ear, feigning memory loss.

I sighed and pulled out a twenty.

"Much obliged," he said, slipping it into the pocket of his greasy pants. "He works at a bar."

"Thanks, mate. That really narrows it down."

"The bar is in a hotel down on the Bowery. Very fancy pants. Maybe you've heard of it."

"Maybe. What's it called?"

"The Blue Skies."

20

I stumbled out of the hotel lobby and onto the footpath, nearly colliding with a bloke on a skateboard as I wrapped my head around the fact that Damian worked at the same hotel Ajax had been staying at. I had assumed that they met when Ajax auditioned as a singer with Damian's band. Obviously I assumed wrong.

I scooted around the corner from the hotel and whipped out my mobile. A quick call to the front desk at the Blue Skies confirmed that Damian did indeed work there. He had been out sick for two days, though — since the day he'd checked out of the Hotel Chelsea, I reckoned, according to what the black woman and the desk clerk told me.

I hung up and made another call, this time to the same place that I'd called after I first visited Damian.

"Blue Million Miles," the same sheila chirped, "you rock and together we'll roll."

"Gidday. Remember me?"

"Kinda." Her chewing gum snapped against her front teeth. "You're the guy from New Zealand, right?"

I fought back an urge to sigh. "Yeah, that's right. From somewhere down there, anyway. It's all the same."

"You called about making a demo?" she said, suggesting that perhaps she possessed some short-term memory after all.

"That's right."

"So do you want to?"

"Not right now. I was just wondering if you could help me out a little."

She giggled for no apparent reason. "I can try. What's it about?"

"Well, I saw this band last night and they were incredible."

"Really? Who were they?"

"That's the thing. I was kind of out of it by the end of the night. I can't even remember how I got home."

"Been there, done that." The gum hit her teeth again.

"Yeah. Feeling pretty crap today. Anyway, I can't remember their name but I really want to speak to their manager. I might have something they'd be interested in."

"That's cool, but I don't know how I can help you."

"Well, you must see a lot of bands, right?"

"Un-huhn. My mom says way too many."

"So maybe you know these guys. They were kinda glam rock. Gary Glitter meets The Killers. Scrawny little bass player."

"Sounds like The Knock."

"The Knock?"

"Yeah. You know, like The Knack." She mimicked the guitar sound of The Knack's most famous riff. "Da-na-na-na-na-na, na-na-na-na, da-na-na-na-na-na, my Sharona."

"Oh, right." I was more than familiar with that song. An ad bloke that hung out at the bar was always banging on about using it for a Toyota commercial. He wanted to change the chorus to, "My Toyota". Ad men. They'll beg, borrow and plagiarize anything to make a buck.

"That sounds like them," I said. "Definitely the right genre. Do you know anyone in the band?"

"Not really. But my friend Danielle once had a thing with the drummer."

"She did?"

"Yeah. He turned out to be a pig. Fuck 'em and forget 'em, that was his motto."

"Men. They're the worst. Any idea where I can find this little drummer boy?"

"Nope, but I can probably call her and find out."

"That would be cool. Very cool."

I gave her my number and she hung up, promising to call back as soon as she had the information. Twenty minutes later, just as I was finishing up a caffeine injection at one of several dozen nearby Starbucks, she did just that.

"He lives in the East Village," she said. "Avenue A between Seventh and Saint Marks." She gave me his name — Keith — plus the street and apartment number. "So what kind of offer do you have for The Knock? Are you an A&R man from a record company?"

"Something like that."

"But I thought you said you were in a band? The Dodgery-somethings?"

"What can I say? I'm a man of many talents."

"I hope it all works out," she said uncertainly.

"I think it will. I have a feeling this might be an offer he can't refuse."

On my walk over to the East Village I stopped at K-mart in Astor Place to buy some Tylenol for my throbbing head. Gina's healing powers had worked wonders last night but the afterglow was wearing off. I needed some pharmaceutical assistance.

Rolling around in the back of that van hadn't done my wardrobe any favors, either, but I didn't dare go home to change in case the Mexicans were watching the joint. So I bought a black T-shirt to replace the one that I was wearing. I slipped into the department store's surprisingly clean restrooms and chugged two Tylenol before changing T-shirts, dropping the dirty one into a bin beside the door.

It was around ten o'clock by the time I reached the East Village. Avenue A was Sunday-morning quiet despite it being Monday. All the gainfully employed locals had already headed off to work, leaving the rest of the population — students, artists, drug addicts and general no-hopers — still asleep in their beds. Which is where I expected to find Little Drummer Boy, given most musos' aversion to the pre-noon hours.

His apartment building was directly across from Tompkins Square Park, a mecca for Manhattan's drug worshippers. I hit the apartment's buzzer and then watched a woman wheel her life by in a shopping trolley while I waited for a response. None came. So I loitered outside the front door until a young sheila dressed in blue hospital fatigues and juggling an aluminium coffee thermos dashed from the building. I slipped through the door in her wake, mumbling something about forgetting my keys, but she was so preoccupied with getting to work on time that she couldn't have cared less if she had just allowed entry to the Boston Strangler or Jack the Ripper.

The building's lobby smelt of garbage, the culprits a half dozen wheelie bins lined up under the stairs. Takeout menus had spilled from the mailboxes and littered the floor. Little Drummer Boy's apartment was 3L, a third-floor walk-up. I didn't pass a soul on the way. I knocked on his door and yielded the same result as downstairs.

I didn't fancy jimmying the door but I had to talk to this bloke if I wanted to find Damian. I also didn't fancy wandering the streets, waiting for the Mexicans to spot me and resume our life-threatening relationship. I scooted around the corner to a thrift shop that was just opening for the day and bought the cheapest suitcase I could find. It was almost new, but pre-wheels, so I carried it back to Keith's apartment, scraping it against mailboxes and garbage bins along the way to give it that pre-loved look.

Once I reached his building, I rang the buzzer for the superintendent's basement apartment.

"Ola?" came the response. I could also hear a soccer match broadcasting in Spanish.

"Gidday, mate, I was wondering if you could help me."

"'fraid not."

"But you don't even know what I want," I said. No wonder the lobby was such a mess if this was the super's approach to his duties. In Australia we would call him a bludger. A shirker of his duties. He would be a hard one to budge.

"Whatever it is you want, I'm sure I can't help."

"Just hear me out."

"Make it pronto," he said, the sound of his voice changing as he turned away from the intercom to watch the game.

"I've just arrived from Australia after a twenty-four hour flight to visit my mate."

"So?"

"Well, he's not at home. I was wondering if you could let me into his apartment."

"Whassis name?"

"Keith. Keith McFarlane," I said, reading his last name off the intercom.

"You coulda just read his name off of the intercom."

"Come on, man. What do you take me for? Look, he's my mate. I know him. He's a drummer," I said. "Skinny bloke." I made up that last bit, based on the fact that nearly every drummer I've ever met is thin, a side benefit of all the exercise they get behind the kit.

At that point, I heard the commentator on the TV scream, "Goaaaaaaaaaal!"

"Yesssss!" hissed the bloke.

"Come on, mate," I pleaded, "Do you know how far away Australia is? Ten thousand fucking miles. I'm completely and utterly knackered."

"OK, OK," he said. "Jesus. I'll be witchoo in a minute."

He buzzed me into the building. I climbed the stairs to Keith's apartment with the empty suitcase. A few minutes later, rapid footsteps followed me up the stairwell. A wiry bloke in a wife-beater and denim shorts arrived out of breath. He quickly clocked me and the suitcase, then unlocked Keith's door and bolted back down the stairs.

"Thanks, mate," I said to his back, then stepped inside.

The joint was a three hundred square-foot studio apartment. Every inch was visible from the front door so it took just one look to confirm Little Drummer Boy wasn't home. The apartment was so small that in most other cities in the United States it would be considered a vestibule, a place to store coats and shoes before entering the house proper. A poor excuse for a kitchen lined the wall to the left: a half sink, a two-burner electric stovetop and a bar fridge. A bathroom — although 'shower-room' was technically more accurate since it only had a shower stall — stood to my right. The bathroom had no door and the showerhead was leaking at the base, a brown line of rusty water marring the tiles. Straight ahead was the everything-else-you-might-want-to-do-in-the-comfort-of-your-own-home room.

Little Drummer Boy, like many New Yorkers including yours truly, paid upwards of several thousand dollars a month for the privilege of living like a lab rat.

I crossed into the everything room. A Murphy bed was folded down from the wall. Its sheets soiled and creased, it took up half the space. Assorted drum kit paraphernalia took up almost all the rest of the room, a worn leather armchair the only other furnishing. It faced a TV balanced on a wooden crate, its wires trailing to a cable box on the floor. A portable stereo sat on the floor in one corner, hundreds of CD cases scattered around it like discarded playing cards.

I flopped down into the armchair. Perhaps Little Drummer Boy was at a diner eating breakfast, I surmised, or had crashed the night at some sheila's apartment. Either way, I didn't see much point in leaving only to return later. And keeping my face off the street seemed particularly prudent considering the rabid Mexicans that were giving chase. So I found a copy of the *New Yorker* dated from several years ago, pulled the lever to raise the armchair's footrest, and leaned back to read the profile of a young black senator from Chicago who was making waves in Washington.

And that's when the Tylenol kicked in.

I awoke as the door burst open.

"Who the fuck are you?" a bloke yelled from the doorway.

I rubbed my eyes. "Keith?"

"That's *my* fucking name. I asked yours."

I leaned forward to get out of the armchair but my legs became tangled in the footrest and I ended up bent forward and off balance. Keith walked over, pushed my shoulder, and I toppled back into the chair.

He looked at my filthy jeans. "You some kind of junkie, is that it? Crawled over here from the park to see what you could find? Come to rip off my gear but nodded off instead?" He glanced at the empty suitcase I'd used as part of my ruse. "Is that what that's for? To carry the loot to the nearest pawn shop?"

He pulled a mobile phone from his inside coat pocket. He was wearing a stylish single-breasted pinstriped suit, a grey button-down shirt and a narrow black tie. Polished black Doc Martins covered his feet. Decidedly dapper in contrast to the squalor of his apartment. His build was rangy and long-limbed, like a lot of good drummers; his brown mop of hair was cut Mod-style. He reminded me of a young Paul Weller when he was with The Jam, singing about going underground. Hardly the scruffy, Ramones-ish East Village rocker I'd been expecting.

"What are you doing?" I said. The clock on the cable box read five twenty-seven. Had I really been asleep for six hours? I had been running on adrenaline for a while — ever since Ajax died, if I was honest about it — and my body must have decided that it was time to stop.

"What's it look like I'm doing? I'm calling the cops."

"Don't do that. Please."

"Sorry, buddy, but I've had it up to here with you guys. Hanging around the park, looking for the next bastard to rob so you can score more shit to shoot into your arms or God knows where else. The genuinely homeless I have some sympathy for, but you guys – it's totally self-inflicted."

"It's not like that. I—"

"9-1-1? I'd like to report a break and enter in the East —"

"I'm looking for Damian," I said.

The phone chirped as he hung up. "That little prick. Always fucking trouble." He looked at me. "Okay. Talk."

My heart was racing but I was still half asleep. So instead of starting with the truth, I made an ill-advised decision to sling some bullshit. I told him that I had met Damian at the Blue Skies hotel bar and he'd lent me some money. Now I was in a position to pay him back so I was trying to find him.

His eyes flicked over my dirty jeans again. "Bullshit." Then his phone rang. "Hello?" he said. "Yes, I did." He studied me before his next response. "No, everything is OK. False alarm. Thank you." He hung up. "9-1-1, calling back to make sure everything is all right. Now, where were we? Oh, yes. I was calling bullshit on your pathetic explanation."

"I swear it's true. I have —"

"Have what? The money for Damian? OK. Show it to me. Right now."

I pulled out my wallet. It had twenty bucks in it.

"You're chasing Damian all over town to pay him back twenty bucks?"

I didn't know what to say as I put my wallet away. This was not going the way I had planned. It was supposed to be me pressuring Keith, not the other way around. So I took the only course of action left open to me. I threw myself on the mercy of the court. I looked him square in the eye and told him the truth: how I reckoned someone had murdered Ajax and that maybe Damian had something to do with it. I could feel his stance softening with each word. Perhaps he remembered Ajax from his audition with the band, or perhaps he was thinking that Damian was more than capable of murder. Either way, the truth had an impact. It often does.

"I wouldn't be surprised if Damian was mixed up in it all somehow," he said when I finished.

"Really?"

He sat down on the end of the unmade bed. "Damian is trouble. Always has been, as long as I've known him, and probably always will be."

"In what way?"

"I dunno…he's always looking for that easy score, that easy way to make it big. I mean, he was serious about the band and all, but I always had this feeling that he just wanted money and he would do almost anything to get it. I think he was always that way. A couple of the guys in the band said he had done some bad shit in the past."

"What kind of bad shit?"

"Search me. I didn't need to hear the details. I took them at their word. They said that Damian was not someone to fuck with."

"Jesus." I'd never given much thought as to what Damian might have done before he moved to New York. That's one of the benefits of coming here. You can start with a clean slate, at least in other people's eyes, and be almost anything you want to be. But I also knew that reinvention had its limits. You take your problems wherever you go. I found that out the hard way when my many shortcomings followed me from Sydney to New York. You can run away from a lot of things, but not yourself. Just ask Ajax.

"So maybe music isn't his life's calling," I said. "Whereas you…?"

"Playing music isn't about the money for me. It's about the music. Don't get me wrong — I want to be a filthy-rich rock star as much as the next guy. But if that doesn't happen, I have back-up plans."

"Hence the suit."

"Wall Street," he said, nodding. "They're a bunch of money-grabbing scumbags, but…well, you know, if you can't beat 'em, join 'em. I'm an office shit-kicker. Start low, end up high, that's my plan."

I gingerly touched the lump on the back of my noggin. "You said Damian was serious about the band? What do you mean, 'was'?"

"We fired him."

"Wow. When?"

"A couple of days ago."

Right around the time he'd checked out of the Chelsea and done a runner from his job. "How'd he take it?"

"It wasn't pretty. But it had to be done. Damian was average on bass. At best."

"Really? I thought he knew his stuff?"

"He's only been playing for a year or so. Since he came to New York. He was a quick learner, but not quick enough. So we found a new bass player with better chops. And a much better attitude."

So that's why that Musicmaster bass lying on Damian's sofa was so shiny. It was almost brand new.

"No time wasters," I said.

"Sorry?"

"Nothing. Just a cliché that used to be on every musician-wanted ad I ever saw in Australia."

He laughed. "As if most musicians aren't experts at wasting time. That's almost part of the job description."

"Do you know where Damian is now?"

"I assume you tried the Chelsea?"

"Yeah. He checked out a few days ago."

He winced, doing the same mental arithmetic I'd done and arriving at the conclusion that that was right around the time that they fired him. He thought for a moment. "You know what? He called me yesterday." He pulled out his mobile. "I let it go to voicemail because I knew it would just be another one of his rants. I haven't even listened to it." He found the voicemail, then hit the speaker button.

"Keef…it's me," a disembodied voice said. The reception wasn't great and there was a hell of a ruckus in the background, but it was Damian, all right, right down to his Northern England accent. "You know, the bloke you blokes knifed in the back. Well, I just wanted to let you know that I don't need you fuckers. You're a bunch of no talent bumbags and I'm better off without you. I've got big plans and something big has already happened for me. So you can all go take a flying fuck as far as I'm concerned. See you at the Grammys. I'll be the one up on stage, looking down on you bastards working as seat warmers." The message ended with an abrupt click.

"Charming," I said.

Keith rubbed the back of his neck. "Like I said, he didn't exactly leave the band by mutual consent." I could see he felt badly about it, but if I was him I wouldn't lose any sleep over it. Damian was what we call back in Australia a mongrel. You're better off without blokes like that in your life, and I told Keith just that.

"I guess you're right," he said.

I nodded at the phone. "Can you play the message again?"

"Sure." He hit play. This time I ignored Damian's diatribe, pushing it aside to concentrate on the cacophony of sound in the background. There was something familiar about it. The clickety-clack of a train running down the tracks; the shouts of a crowd; even some screaming. But happy screaming, not panicked or troubled.

I realized where Damian was.

Or at least where he was when he'd made that call.

21

"I'm sorry I snuck into your place," I said to Keith. "I'm just really desperate to get to the bottom of all this." Not to mention save my own behind.

"That's OK." Keith leaned back on his bed. "I shouldn't have jumped to conclusions. And I probably would have done the same thing as you if I was in your shoes. You'll let me know if you find out anything about Damian?"

"Sure," I said, even though I was surprised that he was still interested after the way Damian had spoken to him in that voicemail. "You don't have a photo of him, by any chance?"

He shook his head. "We haven't got around to doing publicity shots for the band yet." He grinned. "I guess that saved us a bunch of money."

I bade Keith farewell and hoofed it down Avenue A toward Houston, keeping a wary eye out for any slow-moving plumber's vans. I ditched the suitcase next to a homeless bloke on the corner of First and First, figuring he might able to put it to better use than me, then caught a downtown F at the Second Avenue stop that wound its way through lower Manhattan before slipping under the East River. The first Brooklyn stop was in Dumbo and I felt a pang of guilt for not contacting Hannah. Then I felt another pang of guilt for sleeping with Gina, and another pang of guilt for sleeping with Gina while Hannah was pregnant. It was a plethora of pangs and I thoroughly deserved each and every one of them. I resolved to call Hannah as soon as I could.

Twenty minutes later, the F train emerged above ground to traverse the industrial clusterfuck known as the Gowanus Canal. Ugly the area may be, marred by cement factories and abandoned manufacturing plants, but the extended view from the raised section of track is one of the most spectacular in a city full of incredible vistas. To the west, Red Hook, New York Harbor and the Statue of Liberty; to the north, the towers of Lower Manhattan, where work had recently started on the new Freedom Tower; to the south, Staten Island and its namesake bridge; to the east, the greenery and brownstones of Park Slope.

After two stops, the train returned underground, re-emerging twenty minutes later near Ditmas Park, where sprawling Victorian houses sit jammed together on tight suburban blocks and orthodox Jews wander the streets dressed in last century's garb while talking on this century's devices. I wondered whether their attire would ever become more appropriate for the times and the climate, or whether their common sense of cultural and religious identity would be strong enough to keep societal pressures at bay. If history was any guide, I voted for the latter.

When I smelled the sea air two stops out from Coney Island, my spirits lifted. Not even having a bloodthirsty Mexican cartel and a pregnant girlfriend on my ass, or a murdered mate lying on a mortuary slab, could nullify the pick-me-up effect of the ocean. The beach was the one thing about Australia that I truly missed — apart from my family and mates, of course. The perpetual undulation of the swells, the hypnotizing tubing of the waves, the constantly changing shape of the beach courtesy of the tides. From an early age, our old man had instilled a deep love of the ocean in my brother and me; so much so that the beach was the one place where I truly felt at peace.

Not that Coney Island was a beach in the Australian sense of the word. No one frequented Coney Island for the surf because there wasn't any to speak of, not unless you counted harbor-like ripples that not even a toddler could ride. Besides, the Rockaways were just an A train away if you wanted a real break. No, people went to Coney Island for the sheer spectacle of it all. Its dilapidated, last-century amusement park vibe that was slowly showing signs of refurbishment. Its freak shows, both on the boardwalk as the masses of New York mingled semi-clad and off the boardwalk as bearded ladies and two-headed babies performed at actual freak shows. In fact, a sideshow attraction called Shoot the Freak epitomized Coney Island: members of the public could roll up, roll up, and shoot paint balls at a costumed freak doing his best to hide in an exposed, fenced-in area.

I, however, was not visiting Coney Island to gun down freaks. I was there to visit The Cyclone. The railway sounds and the shouting I had heard in Damian's voicemail led me to believe that I was listening to New York City's one and only roller coaster. Hannah and I had once ridden it, the wooden structure so shaky that hurtling through its twists and turns felt like traveling in an open-topped subway car at sixty miles an hour.

I knew that finding Damian in Coney Island was a long shot, but at least I had an indication that he'd been there so it seemed like a logical place to start. I began my quest at The Cyclone's ticket box. A line of people snaked toward it, the late evening sunshine having drawn revelers from the city. I waited my turn and then asked the callow youth working the booth if he recalled an English bloke sporting a dragon tattoo. He shrugged his shoulders, shook his head and then reached for the money of the teenage girl behind me.

I thanked him and did the rounds of the other sideshow attractions — dodgem cars, air rifles, knock 'em downs — but came up empty-handed. Most of the carnies showed a natural aversion to my questions and I can't say I blamed them. The rest of society views them as little better than gypsies.

This wasn't going to be any stroll in the woods, I realized. But what did I expect? I didn't even have a photo of the bloke I was looking for, a bloke who may or may not have called Keith from somewhere near here twenty-four hours ago. Damian could be halfway to Alaska by now.

I tried to think like Damian, from what little I knew about him. He was into partying and football, I knew that much. I walked over to Surf Avenue, Coney Island's main drag, and entered the first bar I found. They'd never seen or heard of him. I tried a second bar, and a third. Ditto.

Just as I began to question the wisdom of my approach, I saw a bar catty-corner to the Coney Island Aquarium and tried one last roll of the dice. Sam's Sports was the biggest, brightest bar on the strip and kitted out like every other sports bar — framed baseball and football memorabilia of dubious value lined the walls, half a dozen flatscreen TVs were turned up just slightly too loud, and the expectation of excitement emanating from the punters was little to none.

The barman, a bloke with thick arms and an even thicker neck, was munching on a plate of Buffalo Wings at one end of the bar.

"Gidday, mate," I said.

He gave me a jock nod in response. He was wearing a weightlifting tank top sporting the logo of a Coney Island gym; the telltale acne of the steroid abuser dotted his shoulders.

"I'm looking for a bloke. Thought he might have been in here."

He cracked a chicken bone between his teeth.

"Little bloke. English accent. Dragon tattoo…" I added hopefully.

The barman put a splintered bone back on the plate and wiped his fingers with a red paper napkin. "He was in here yesterday," he said in a high-pitched voice and with a pronounced lisp. "Watched a replay of the Man U game."

I stifled a giggle. He was like Alvin the Chipmunk trapped in Arnold Schwarzenegger's body. "Really?"

"Nasty little motherfucker."

"What makes you say that?"

"He picked up a local girl and was slapping her around a bit. He was pissed that Man U lost."

"Local girl?"

"Charges by the hour, know what I'm sayin'?"

"Oh, that kind of local girl. Did they say where they were going when they left?"

"Didn't have to."

"What do you mean?"

"There's only one place around here that girls like her take guys like him."

My father's hotel on the north coast of New South Wales was nothing fancy — single-level brick construction, fifteen rooms, each room with a parking spot out front and a view of the Pacific out back — but the joint was neat and tidy and well maintained. In short, everything that the Hang Ten Hotel was not.

Located five blocks back from Coney Island beach, on Neptune between Twenty-First and Twenty-Second, the Hang Ten Hotel stood in permanent vacancy purgatory where Coney Island's tourism zone ended and its industrial zone began. To the left stood Brien's Auto Repairs, to the right Los Pollitos Rotisserie Chicken. Judging by its design, The Hang Ten dated from the Fifties, but a paintbrush had barely graced it since. The sea air had rusted all its metallic surfaces, including a neon sign that flashed *Vaca cy* every few seconds, as well as cheap wrought-iron railings that ran along its upper balcony. From twenty yards away, even in the pale light of dusk, I could see steel rods poking through the building's side walls where they wept with concrete cancer.

The hotel was rectangular in shape, two floors, ten rooms to a floor, their numbered cream doors facing out onto Neptune Avenue. It was anyone's guess which room, if any, Damian was in. The parking lot held one car, a beaten-up Jeep with its soft top removed. The hotel's occupancy rate probably stood in the single digits. My odds of finding Damian were good — if he was there.

I was trying to decide whether to smooth-talk whoever was working reception to get the information I needed or to conduct a random door-knock of all the rooms with their lights on when a car backfired.

It backfired again, followed by a man yelling and another bang.

Then I realized it wasn't a car backfiring.

It was gunshots.

22

Flashes of light burst from a hotel room window. Upper level, third from the right.

There was no way of knowing if Damian was in that room. But my gut told me he was. I considered playing the hero, running over to stop whatever the hell was going on, but even I knew that only an imbecile runs into gunfire. Especially in a confined space.

I ducked behind a lamppost, counted six shots. They sounded like they all came from the same weapon.

Then the shooting stopped.

I peered around the post. The door of the room cracked open, then closed again.

I stayed where I was. Watching.

Thirty seconds later, a fat bald bloke in his underwear poked his head out of a room two doors down.

I took that as my cue. I bolted across the street, bent low, then scaled the stairs to the balcony level two at a time.

I pounded on the door.

"Open up!" I shouted, then jumped aside in case any shots came through the door in response.

Two rooms down, underwear man slammed his door. Distant sirens pierced the silence.

I slipped my hand inside my T-shirt to avoid leaving fingerprints and then tested the doorknob. Locked. I decided to hell with it and kicked the door open, ducking to one side again to avoid any gunfire. When none came, I counted to five and went in.

The room smelled like my apartment on the night Ajax died. Gunpowder.

Damian lay on the bed, naked. Or what remained of Damian. His torso was leaky with bullet holes. Four of them. Somehow his face had remained untouched and he looked almost beatific, as though he were only sleeping. The traces of a tattoo that consumed his entire chest was visible through the blood: a Union Jack with some kind of crest.

He'd taken four bullets. I'd counted six shots. I saw that one had pierced a cheap print of Monet's *Water Lilies* hanging above the bed. I couldn't see where the sixth bullet went.

Nearby, an open duffle bag sat atop a chest of drawers. It was crammed with packets of white powder. Damian had sliced one of them open; a credit card and the remains of several lines lay on the dresser's glass top.

The front door creaked. I froze until billowing curtains at the rear of the room betrayed the wind as the culprit. I walked over and pulled back the curtains. A drainpipe that ran down the side of the building, its bolts loosened over the years, was swaying back and forth. I looked out into the rapidly dwindling light. The cover of descending dark had allowed whoever shimmied down the drainpipe to make their escape.

The sirens were closing in now, winding down as police cars screeched to a halt out front. I didn't fancy spending the night explaining my presence at a murder scene to the Coney Island coppers. I took one last look around. That's when I saw Damian's mobile sitting on a bedside table. Without thinking, without even considering whether it might be of any use or not, I grabbed it.

Then I climbed out the rear window and escaped down the drainpipe into the night just like the killer before me.

I skirted the banks of a creek that ran behind the hotel, climbing chain-link fences separating scrap metal yards and taxi depots as I followed my nose east toward the Stillwell Avenue subway stop. Somehow I made it to the station without incident and jumped on the first D train out of Coney Island.

After a few stops, my heartbeat returned to its resting rate and I noticed the bulge in my pocket. Damian's phone. I took it out. It was a cheap flip-top Nokia in the days before smartphones. It didn't lock and only performed rudimentary functions. But it did store a log of the most recent calls, both incoming and outgoing, as well as a list of contacts. I scrolled through them but didn't recognize any names except Keith's. I couldn't recall ever seeing Ajax with a mobile phone so it made sense to me that his name wasn't there.

The train was running on elevated tracks through Brooklyn so the phone had a signal. I hit re-dial on the last incoming call, just to see who might answer, but before the call could connect my own phone rang. I closed Damian's and answered mine.

"We've got a bit of a problem here, dude," Anchor said. He never was one for beating around the scrub.

"What's that? Some sheila got her left tit caught in the right pocket again?"

"Dude, I'm not fucking around."

"Sorry, mate." My poor excuse at humor was probably an attempt to laugh away the carnage I'd just seen. But I didn't bother trying to explain that to him. "What is it?"

"Two dudes just totally smashed up the bar."

"What do you mean, smashed up the bar?"

"I mean two Mexican dudes walked in with baseball bats and smashed up the bar."

Fuck. La Familia. "What, they just laid into the place?"

"Well, not quite. One of them demanded to speak to you first. I said I didn't know where you were, because I didn't, and then…" His voice trailed off. He sounded freaked out, which was not at all surprising but also not at all like Anchor. I couldn't blame him, though. Those Mexican bastards were hard-core.

"Shit."

"Yeah, shit is right. It was insane. They went ballistic. Smashed glasses, bottles, tables. The place is an absolute mess."

"Jesus. When did this happen?"

"About half an hour ago."

Right when Damian was becoming intimate with several bullets. I wondered if that was coincidence and then reckoned it had to be. I couldn't see the point of a synchronized assault, or any logic that could link them.

"Anyone get hurt?" I asked.

"Just Joe. He made the mistake of trying to stop them."

Typical Joe. Bouncers don't take shit from anyone. "Is he OK?"

"Just a swollen lip and dented ego. But they…well…"

"Well what?"

"They said he wouldn't be the only one that gets hurt next time."

"Next time."

"They said they'd come back every day until they find you."

"Did you call the coppers?"

"Not yet. I wanted to call you first."

"Good. Don't."

"Why?"

"I don't want them involved." The last thing I wanted was Malone and Lirianos knowing that someone had trashed my bar. Then they really would wonder what kind of business I was running, what extracurricular activities I was up to — and my silent partner, if they found out about Charlie.

"But what about the insurance?" Anchor said. "Who's gonna pay for all this?"

"Let me worry about that. All you need to do is tidy up as best you can and then close up."

"Closing up won't be hard. There are no punters left. They all ran for their lives when the bats started swinging."

"Can't say I blame them. Listen, sweep up the broken glass and then call it a night. I'll call you tomorrow and we'll work out a plan of action. About whether we should open up or not."

"I say we go for it. The bar should be fine once I straighten everything out."

"But there'll be no point opening up tomorrow night if they're just coming back for a repeat performance."

"Totally. I guess that's why you're the boss." He paused. "Luke?"

"Yeah?"

"Why the fuck would anyone do this to us?"

"Dunno…"

"Well, why are these Mexican douches looking for you?"

"I dunno, Anchor." The last thing I wanted was for him to know what was going on. If La Familia got wind of that, they'd have him strapped into a chair in no time to find out where I was. They'd be using baseball bats on him, not bottles of booze. I reckoned he was safer remaining in a state of blissful ignorance.

"Come on, Luke. I'm not a total idiot."

"I know," I said. "Listen — I owe some blokes some money, that's all. I'll sort it out."

"All this, over money?"

"Yep. I needed a deposit for the new bar and the banks knocked me back. I went to the next best thing."

"Charlie couldn't help?"

"Didn't ask. I wanted to stand on my own two legs for this one."

"Hopefully they won't get broken."

"Quite."

"I've got some dough socked away if you need it."

Good old Anchor. It was always the blokes who had the least to give who were the first to offer.

"Thanks, mate, but I'm all right. Just a bit of a cash flow problem. Overextended myself a little. I'll sort it out."

"Whatever you say, boss."

"Anchor, one other thing."

"What's that?"

"You got someone you can stay with tonight?"

"Chillax, dude. I'll be fine. It's you they're after, remember."

"Oh, I remember, don't you worry. Anchor, one other, other thing."

"Yeah?"

"Be fucking careful."

As the D train jiggled its way through outer Brooklyn towards Manhattan, I was at a loss. Yesterday I thought that 2Pay might be the perpetrator of Ajax's killing but now that someone had eliminated Damian I wasn't so sure. By my calculations, that someone couldn't be 2Pay, because (a) there seemed to be no torture involved, if you can call dying of four gunshot wounds in a squalid hotel room torture-less, and (b) it seemed highly unlikely that a drug kingpin like 2Pay would associate with a lowly muso like Damian, although I suppose anything was possible in the murky milieu of the criminal world.

That left the Mexicans. But they had been conducting batting practice at The Billabong around the time of Damian's murder and Coney Island is about an hour's drive from the Lower East Side. So unless Cheech and Chong had turbo-charged their van in the last twenty-hour hours, that pretty much ruled them out. Which left a third party responsible for Damian's murder, and presumably also involved in the drug war. I wondered if Malone, Lirianos and their ilk knew that. My head was on a wilder ride than The Cyclone trying to figure it all out.

One thing was certain, though. Not just me but also Anchor, the Billabong and anyone else who frequented the Billabong were now at risk, as well as any bar that I opened in the future. And how much longer before the danger spread further? To Charlie? Hannah? Or Gina? Perhaps Charlie had been right and I should have left well enough alone. But if I had turned the other way, Malone and Lirianos might be engraving my initials on a pair of handcuffs right now. I hadn't had any choice but to get involved, and now I needed to find my own way out. My hard work in making The Billabong a success, plus the well-being of everyone that I held near and dear, were all the motivation I needed.

The D train entered a tunnel not far from Green-Wood Cemetery and then pulled into the Thirty-Fifth Street station. Gina's stop. I sat there staring at the car's open doors, thinking of the love and compassion that had greeted me in her apartment last night. As bells chimed to warn of the carriage doors' imminent closure, I made a snap decision and pushed my way out of the crowded carriage. The lure of Gina was just too great. And perhaps the distraction of seeing her would clear my mind. At the very least, I could feel safe for a few hours.

It was a brisk five-minute walk to Gina's apartment — just enough time to make the phone call that I'd been avoiding for days. So while I was on the way to visit the sheila I was having an affair with, I called the sheila I might be having a baby with. I marveled, not for the first time, at the ability of the mind to compartmentalize.

Hannah surprised me by picking up on the first ring. "Gidday, stranger."

"How you doing?"

"Not too foul."

"Good to hear."

There was a long silence. Neither of us knew what to say about the eight-pound baby in the room.

"We're running out of time, Luke," she said finally.

"What do you mean, running out of time?" I passed a basketball court where a bunch of blokes were playing night hoops. The way they were swaggering, you'd have thought they were all Lebron.

"We can't just wait around forever. There's a certain point in every pregnancy where it becomes too late to do anything about the baby and it needs to be kept."

I knew that but I reckon I had conveniently forgotten. "Is that point soon?"

"Soon enough. A few weeks. But I'd rather not wait till…" Her voice broke and she stifled a sob.

"Hey, Han, it's gonna be all right."

She took a deep breath. "I know…it's just…well, it's really bloody hard. Not knowing whether I should be planning for a baby or not. And each day, it's getting bigger. Becoming a real person. I can feel it. Even if it's just my imagination, I can feel it."

A lump formed in my throat. "I need a few more days, Han."

"Are you getting closer to a decision?"

"Yeah," I said, but it was a lie. The truth was that I hadn't had time to give the matter much thought. But I couldn't very well tell her why. That I'd been too busy confronting a Harlem drug lord, getting kidnapped by a Mexican cartel and then escaping only to blunder into a murder scene out in Coney Island. Oh, and also having my bar trashed and sleeping with another sheila while I was at it. Let's not forget about those little distractions, either. Jesus.

"I think I'm getting closer, Han. I just need to think on it a bit longer."

She sniffed. "Two more days, Luke. But that's it. I can't live like this for much longer."

You and me both, babe, I thought. You and me both.

23

Passing a hole-in-the-wall on Fourth Avenue, I smelled chicken stew and realized that I hadn't eaten since breakfast. I'd slept through lunch in that armchair at Keith's place. I handed over eight bucks for a plateful of Caldo De Pollo served with yellow rice and black beans and smothered with hot sauce. I washed it down with Diet Coke, artificial carcinogens be damned as I sought caffeine to lift my energy levels.

Feeling semi-human again, the bump on my noggin now less an injury and more a reminder of the insanity that had become my life, I made my way to Gina's apartment. I rang her buzzer and waited until she let me in. She was standing in her doorway wearing her Blue Skies bathrobe, wet hair leaving dark patches on each shoulder.

"Luke, I've been worried sick about you since this morning."

"I'm fine. Did I get you at a bad time?"

"There is never a bad time with you. Come in." She closed the door behind me and fell into my arms. "I have some bad news."

"What is it?" I said, bracing myself. I didn't know how much more I could take.

"I am working the late shift tonight."

"Oh."

"But I do not have to leave for twenty minutes." She leaned in and nibbled my earlobe.

"Just enough time then."

"For what?" she asked innocently, already knowing the answer.

We didn't make it to the bedroom but the apartment had plenty of other shagging locations. In the time available we tried out the sofa, a kitchen chair and the kitchen counter. We finished up on the living room floor in a heaving, sweating heap. Hugh Hefner would have been proud.

"Wow," she said.

I let out an exhausted whistle. "Indeed."

She was lying underneath me. I rolled off her and she climbed unsteadily to her feet. "It is a good thing I have to work tonight."

"Why?"

"I am not sure how much more of that I could take."

"I'm sure you'd find a way."

She giggled and disappeared into the bedroom. I stood up to search the room for my clothes. I found my undies and jeans halfway between the front door and the sofa. I pulled them on, feeling a lump in the back pocket of my jeans. Damian's phone. I'd forgotten all about it. I pushed it back into my pocket as Gina came into the room dressed in a simple navy-blue uniform.

"My turn," I said.

"For what?"

"For bad news."

"What is it?" She fastened the clasp on the bracelet of a no-nonsense Timex. It looked like something a nurse would wear.

"A friend of Ajax's died."

"A friend?" she said, as she bent down to retrieve some comfortable cream loafers from the closet near the door. "I did not know he had many friends in New York."

"He had at least one. Actually, you might know him," I said, remembering where Damian worked. "He was a barman at the Blue Skies."

"Really? What was his name?"

"Damian. English bloke. Kinda small and scruffy."

"Damian. I do not remember anyone by that name."

"Really? It's not a very big hotel, is it?"

She looked at her watch. "It is big enough. Plus the cleaners are kept separate from the rest of the staff. We are low down in the…what do you call it?…pecking order?" She pushed a black lock of hair off her forehead. "I am sorry to hear about this Damian but I cannot talk about it right now. I am late for work. You can tell me everything in the morning."

"No worries." To be honest, I was relieved more than anything else. I didn't fancy reliving the carnage from that hotel room.

She sat down on the sofa to slip on her loafers. "You are going to stay tonight?"

"I'm not sure. Maybe. If that's OK with you. I really don't have anywhere else to go."

"Of course. There is beer and also left-overs in the refrigerator."

"I just ate," I said, still feeling the burn of hot sauce on the tip of my tongue.

"Yes, I tasted that…" She smiled.

"But I might take you up on that beer."

She stood up. "Make yourself at home."

"I feel like I already have."

"Do not go anywhere." She bent down to kiss me, running her tongue smoothly between my lips to touch mine. "I want you right there when I get back."

"That shouldn't be a problem. After that little performance, I'm too tired to move."

She walked out the door, the flat soles of her loafers causing her hips to gyrate a little less than normal. Then the door closed behind her and I was all alone. I did what any bloke would do after a hard day's detecting. I warmed the set and cooled the tinnies, cranking up the TV and cracking open a Pacifico from the fridge. A Yankees/Red Sox game at Fenway looked mildly interesting — scores tied, bottom of the fifth — so I settled in for some mindless sports viewing to switch off my mind. Then Alberto wandered over, leapt up beside me and snuggled against my side. It had become a boy's night in.

The first Pacifico barely touched the sides. I wandered back to the kitchen to grab another. In a cupboard above the fridge I found a mini tube of barbeque Pringles. They always remind me of ceiling tiles because of their unrelenting uniformity.

I took the pack back to the sofa. The Yankees had hit a leadoff single in the top of the Seventh. I shifted on the couch to get comfortable. When I put my feet up on the coffee table, I felt a hard lump under the right side of my bum.

I tilted sideways, taking care not to squash Alberto, and removed Damian's phone from my back pocket. As a batter took the full count, I scrolled through his contact list. When that again proved less than revelatory, I pulled up the record of incoming and outgoing calls. The last call had come in just a few hours before Damian died. It was from someone named Gabriela. I took a swig of Pacifico and hit the call button.

As the phone rang in my ear, I gradually became aware of a buzzing sound coming from somewhere in the apartment. I kept the phone to my ear and walked toward the bedroom, where it became louder. At first I thought it was the alarm, set to remind Gina about her shift. But the clock was silent. I moved around the bedroom, playing a version of hotter-colder, until I zeroed in on the sound. It was coming from a dresser beside the closet. I pulled open the top drawer and found the culprit hidden beneath a spare blanket.

It was a phone. A vibrating phone. And its caller ID was flashing one word. Damian.

24

I took Damian's phone away from my ear to check that it was still ringing Gabriela's number even though I could hear it loud and clear. I was having trouble comprehending the situation. Who was Gabriela? Why was her phone in Gina's bedroom? Why was she the last person to call Damian before he died? I didn't know the answers, and wouldn't for some time, but after visiting Doof-doof's apartment and now discovering this phone half-formed thoughts began brewing in my mind.

I hung up, took the phone out of the drawer and prised open the back. The SIM card was a pre-paid AT&T card. Probably untraceable. I slid the SIM card back in and returned the phone to its original spot. Then I spotted a stack of receipts shoved toward the back of the drawer. Western Union money transfers, all sent to an address in Juarez, Mexico.

The town that Doof-doof came from.

And the home of La Familia.

I mightn't have been certain about what it all meant but I knew one thing for sure. I needed to get the hell out of that apartment. I grabbed one of the Western Union receipts from the bottom of the pile, threw on the rest of my clothes and then bolted for the door.

I hurried up the street towards Fourth Avenue. I was back to square one. Actually, square zero, because I was still under the gun from the Mexicans but had now seemingly lost my only safe haven. I felt like I couldn't trust anyone. I thought about where to go, my head swimming faster than a surfer with a Great White Shark nibbling his bum. Then I remembered a punter at the bar mentioning that a Holiday Inn Express had recently opened on Houston Street next to the Second Avenue subway stop. I had my wallet; hopefully they had a room. I quickened my pace and caught the D train back to Chinatown, then stuck to the shadows of the tenements until I snuck into the hotel's overly lit lobby.

"Can I help you?" said the Indian bloke working the front desk. He was doing the *New York Times* crossword with a pen, not a pencil, as sure a sign of intellectual confidence as you'll ever see. He was probably an engineer or brain surgeon back home but had been reduced to working a minimum wage job by America's strict employment regulations. Just like Gina.

"Gidday, mate," I said, "I need a room for the night."

He held out his hand. "ID and credit card, please."

I took out my wallet and handed him my credit card. "I don't have any ID with me, I'm afraid." I never carried my green card because even though it was the law, it was too risky. Lose that and I would face a mountain of bureaucracy to replace it. And my passport was back at the apartment. I was buggered if I was going to risk going back to get it.

"No driver's license?"

I shook my head. I'd never seen the point in getting a New York license, given that I didn't own a car and bicycle or subway were my main modes of transport. My Australian license had expired a few years ago but I'd never bothered renewing it.

"State law prohibits me from renting a room to anyone without government-issued identification and a valid credit card."

"I understand that. But listen, mate, I'm here on my honeymoon." I made my Aussie drawl thinker than usual, laying it on with a trowel. "The missus and me...well, the honeymoon's not going so crash hot, I reckon. We just had a stand-up barney." I sounded like Paul Hogan after one too many beers.

"Barney?"

"A blue. A fight. She accused me of flirting with this other sheila, then threw an ashtray at my head." I showed him the lump on the back of my noggin. "Then she tossed me out of the digs where we're staying."

"I'm very sorry to hear that, sir, but —"

"Oh, it'll sort itself out," I said, as if those kinds of shenanigans happened all the time. "The missus has always been a bit of a firecracker, ready to go off at the slightest thing. It's what keeps it interesting, if you know what I mean." I winked at him, but he looked at me like he didn't have a clue what it means. "She just needs a little time to calm down. But in the meantime, I need somewhere to stay."

He studied me, breathing deeply through his nose. Then he swiped my credit card through a reader and handed it back to me, along with a key card. "Room 547. Fifth floor." He pointed to a bank of elevators to his right. "Not much of a view, I'm afraid."

"No problem. You don't happen to have a business center, do you?"

He nodded down the hallway to the left.

"And a phone charger?" I asked hopefully.

The business center was an airless room with grey wallpaper and a locked window facing onto a brick wall. It housed a Dell PC, a dot matrix printer and a fax machine with an out-of-order sign taped to it.

At that hour, the business center was understandably deserted. Given the hotel's location, its guests would be tourists intent on enjoying the downtown nightlife; most self-respecting businessmen would choose to stay closer to the centers of trade – Midtown or Wall Street.

I closed the door, plugged in the phone charger and connected my mobile. Then I called Bertha Oldfield, my journo mate from *The New York Post*. Her mobile rang several times before she picked up.

"Well, well, if it isn't Crocodile Dundee," she said, slurring her words.

"Gidday, Bertha." I could hear honky-tonk in the background. "Where are you?"

"The Rodeo Bar."

"Giddy-up." The Rodeo Bar, on Twenty-Seventh and Third, is New York City's longest running country music hangout. The joint does a roaring trade catering to a music genre that the city's other live venues largely ignore. Tourists, southern transplants and lovers of good old-fashioned twang pack the joint night in and night out to get their fix of pedal steel and boot scootin'.

"Oh yeah. I haven't had this much fun since I went horse-riding as a Daisy Scout."

"The music sounds good. Who's playing?"

"Who cares? Right now it's some four piece, three blokes in string ties and Stetsons backing a little lady with a big set of pipes and even bigger things in front of her."

"Well, they sound great, even over the phone," I said, ignoring her allusion to the singer's cup size. I could hear the drummer setting the pace with brushes while what sounded like a double bass and a rhythm guitar generated enough energy for twice the number of musicians, injecting new life into the old Patsy Cline hit "Walkin' After Midnight".

She took a slurp of her libation. "Why don't you come up here and take a look for yourself?"

"I'd love to, but I have something I need to take care of."

"At this hour?"

"You know what they say. No rest for the wicked."

"Must be why I'm so damn tired all the time."

"I don't want to keep you from all the fun. But I need some investigative tips."

"Oh, you do, do you?" She took another slurp. "Where was all this interest in talking to Bertha when I was trying to reach you about a certain rock star's untimely demise?"

"Sorry about that. It's just that things have been kinda crazy. I really did mean to get back to you but it slipped my mind."

"Enough with the heartfelt apologies. What can I help you with?"

"I was wondering what you know about tracking down missing persons."

She gulped another mouthful of whatever concoction she was drinking. If I knew Bertha, it was a cheap domestic drop — Bud or Coors Lite — accompanied by shots of Jack. "Are you looking for someone?"

"That's generally what one does with a missing person."

"Listen to Mister Snark."

"I need a list of people who might have gone missing from the Mexican border region over the past ten years or so."

"That would be one hell of a long list. Do you have any idea how many people that could be?"

"I can narrow it down to a specific region."

"Such as?"

"Juarez and El Paso."

"That's one of the most crime-ridden border areas. But sure, I guess that helps." She belched. "Back when I started clacking away at a typewriter, you would have had next to no chance of finding those names."

"When was that? Back in the Stone Age?"

"Just call me Wilma Flintstone. But these days, you should be able to find all that online."

"I figured as much." I looked at the clunky old PC. "But I thought you might be able to give me some pointers. You know, what sites to look at, that kinda stuff."

"Ever heard of Google?"

"Sure, but I could be googling all night before I find the right site. I thought this might be quicker."

"Tomzap dot com," she said, just as the song ended and the crowd erupted with applause.

"What was that?" I said, her words eluding me in the ruckus.

"Tomzap dot com," she repeated. "It's a site where Mexicans post about their missing loved ones. Straight from the mule's mouth, so to speak."

I reached for a hotel pad and pen. "Can you spell it out?"

She sighed and enunciated the letters.

"Sounds like as good a place to start as any," I said.

"Luke?"

"Yeah?"

"Are you gonna tell me what the hell this is all about?"

"I'm not sure yet. But this could help."

"Wouldn't have anything to do with those three murders next door, would it?"

"I'm not sure," I told her again.

"Well, can you do me one teensy weensy little favor?"

"What's that?"

"If you ever are sure and it becomes a fucking story, call me," she said, shouting the last two words to accentuate her point.

"I will." Although I knew that if I did discover anything, public disclosure was probably not going to be an option.

"Good luck. Hit me up," she said as she rang off. It took me a moment to realize that she was talking to the barman and not me.

Internet access on the hotel PC was ten bucks an hour but I was in too much of a bind to worry about super-highway robbery. I fired it up, entered my name and room number, and despite the unfamiliar PC operating system soon found Safari and the Tomzap site.

A well-meaning amateur web developer must have built the site because its light aqua background stood in marked contrast to the dire nature of the content. I clicked on a U.S. flag at the top of the page to switch from Spanish to English and went to work. At first glance, seemingly every type of person — young or old, Mexican or Caucasian, male or female — had disappeared from U.S.-Mexico border towns like Tijuana, Mexicali, Nogales, Juarez, Loredo and Brownsville. Families had posted photos and descriptions of their loved ones; each made for sober reading. An uncle who had gone fishing in Tijuana and didn't return with his catch of the day. A Loredo hairdresser who missed bowling night for the first time in eight years. A father of three who never clocked in at his construction site in Nogales, the only trace that something was amiss coming in the form of a late-night phone call from a stranger asking for money — and then no further contact for twenty-three years and counting. In desperation, some listings offered rewards, in one instance the Mexican equivalent of one hundred thousand U.S. dollars to find a grandmother who had vanished from Juarez.

Like most people, I heard about murders on a daily basis and so I'd probably become desensitized to them. But vanishing was a rarer and possibly even crueler fate because there was no closure for those left behind. The purgatory of endless anguish for these families must have been unbearable, and they could do little more than post items on blogs like this. With the police in the sway of the drug cartels, they really had nowhere else to turn.

The order of the listings was chronological, not alphabetical. I jumped back a few years and then continued scrolling backwards, skimming each listing but only reading the details of those persons missing from the Juarez and El Paso areas. The reading was unrelentingly bleak —occasionally I came across a listing marked Found, but for the most part the site was a litany of unanswered questions.

After about two hours, my energy and optimism sagged. A can of Diet Coke from a vending machine gave me a temporary lift.

Over the course of the next hour, my mobile rang three times. Each time I let it go to voicemail. It was Gina, on her dinner break, saying that she was worried about me. I was sure she was, but possibly not for the right reasons.

Then, as dawn began filtering through the room's only window, I found a posting from five years earlier.

Name: Gabriela Maria Marquez
Height: 5'5"
Weight: 140 lbs
Date of Birth: March 18, 1978
Last known location: Juarez
Our beloved daughter, Gabriela, went missing on December 23, 2001. Gabriela was last seen leaving home for her job as a schoolteacher. She never arrived at the school and has not been seen since. Her family has searched Juarez and El Paso with no result. Please help us reunite with Gabriela. Following the loss of her brother, her disappearance is more pain than one family can bear. If you think you have seen Gabriela, or know something about her disappearance, please call us.

No photo accompanied the text. But then I noticed that her name was highlighted in blue. It was a hyperlink. I rolled the cursor over the name and the words changed color. Then I clicked on it and a photo appeared in a pop-up window.

It was Gina, staring back at me from a previous life.

25

I probably should have been surprised that Gina and Gabriela were one and the same person. But if I was fair dinkum about it, I'd have to admit that so much insanity had happened over the past few days that nothing could surprise me anymore. After finding Gabriela's phone in Gina's closet, someone could have told me that the Pope had come out of the closet and I probably would have believed them.

Besides, while I hadn't known for sure that Gabriela was living under the name Gina, finding the second phone hidden in her bedroom had strongly suggested she was.

I had zeroed in on the who. Now I needed to figure out the why and the how.

But before that, I needed sleep.

I printed out the posting about Gabriela and slipped it into my back pocket. Then I logged out, unplugged my phone and charger, and killed the lights. I found my room and, fully clothed, collapsed into bed.

I woke a few short hours later, around nine thirty, my mind foggy but my body bristling with nervous energy. I needed some exercise to iron out the kinks but retrieving my bike from the bar's basement wasn't worth the risk. And I knew from experience that walking wouldn't hold the same rejuvenating effect no matter how far or fast I strode. I rang the front desk and was advised that The Holiday Inn, as convenient as it was to many local attractions, did not have a gym. But even if it did, I'm not sure I would have partaken. There was something about the pointless exercise of a bike machine that depressed the hell out of me.

Abandoning all thoughts of exercise, I conducted some rudimentary ablutions and then ducked downstairs to grab a coffee and knish from Yonah Schimmel's, an old school Jewish joint that had been in operation on Houston Street since the dawn of time. I took the tucker back to my room and watched the latest news on *New York 1* while I ate. The lead story was a townhouse collapse in the West Village that killed a homeless bloke sheltering in its shadows. The owners, however, were spared, ensconced in their upstate country house while extensive renovations were being undertaken. That's irony for you — a homeless bloke killed by some rich fucker's home falling on him. But I reckon when your digit's up, your digit's up, and there's nothing you can do about it. Especially in New York, where the city seems to invent new ways of killing people every day. Just last week, a bloke who dropped his mobile phone on the subway tracks in Queens was decapitated by a train while trying to retrieve it.

I swallowed the last bite of knish and pulled out the printout from the night before. Then I opened my wallet and took out the international calling card I used whenever I called home. The small print on the back listed the rate to Mexico at two cents a minute, which seemed more than reasonable to me. Not that price mattered much, because I reckoned the call wasn't going to last very long.

But not for the first time, I reckoned wrong.

"Ola," a man on the other end said.

"Ola," I said back, then abandoned all pretence of bilingualism. "Do you speak English?"

"Si, si. Yes, I speak English."

"Great. Who am I speaking to, please?"

"Jose. Jose Marquez."

"Just the man I want."

"What is this about?" he said, suspicion hardening his voice. I couldn't blame him, after what he'd been through.

"I saw your post on Tomzap."

"Yes?"

"I'm calling about your daughter."

"Gabriela?" His suspicion waned, softened by the hope that at long last someone might be able to tell him something, anything, about his missing daughter.

"That's right."

"You have news?"

"Yes, I have news."

I heard a woman in the background ask a question in Spanish. I listened as the man presumably explained to her that I was calling with news of Gabriela. The woman broke into sobs before she even knew what the news was.

The man spoke into the phone again. "What is it?" His voice had taken on another edge now. Stern. Bracing himself for the worst.

"I've found her."

"Is she...?" He was unable to finish the sentence.

"Alive," I said, finishing it for him. "Yes, she's alive."

"If this is some kind of joke—"

"It's not. I'm serious. Dead serious."

Something in my voice convinced him that I was genuine. There was a moment of silence as the news sunk in, then he started crying. But I could tell they were tears of joy. And so could his wife. She screamed something in Spanish and I heard him say, "Si, si," before he dropped the phone to embrace her.

Gabriela's father asked many questions. Understandable, given that their daughter had been missing for over five years. I did my best to answer them, but I hadn't known Gina for very long and she'd only shown me one side of herself. But I was able to relay that yes, Gabriela was healthy, yes, Gabriela was happy, and yes, Gabriela was gainfully employed, although no longer in the job of schoolteacher that she had loved so much.

The most important question, the one thing they absolutely wanted answered, I couldn't tell them. It wasn't my place to reveal where Gabriela was living. It was up to her to decide if she wanted them to know.

After their questions, I steered the conversation around to my questions. All in all, we talked for about an hour, and by the end of the call I had learned all that I needed to know.

Of course, I didn't know the whole story. There was only one way to learn that.

After I hung up, I pulled out Damian's phone and dialed the phone that I'd called the night before. Gabriela's phone. The one lying in the bottom of the drawer in Gina's bedroom.

Just when I thought it was going to ring out, Gina answered.

"Hello?" A question, not a statement.

"Don't worry, it's not Damian calling you from beyond the grave."

"Luke! I have been so worried about you, I —"

"Come off it, Gina. You can cut out the act."

"What do you mean?"

"I know about Gabriela."

There was silence. Then, "It is a second phone that I keep. Just for emergencies."

"And what kind of emergencies might those be?"

"Luke, please. Do not do this."

"You must know that someone knew, if you saw the missed call from Damian last night."

"I did notice that," she said softly.

"And yet you didn't bother to call back."

"I—"

"Didn't you wonder who had his phone, since you already knew he was dead?" I could hear her breathing as she thought through this turn of events. "I guess you were worried that it might be the coppers. Or worse still, La Familia."

"What are you going to do?"

"I don't know yet."

"Luke. Baby. Come over here. Let me explain everything to you in person."

"Why? So you can do to me what you did to Damian?"

"Luke, I would never do that."

I took a step back.

Did she realize what she'd just said?

She'd tacitly admitted that she played a part in Damian's death.

My heart sank, because even though I'd already figured as much, having it confirmed by her was another matter entirely. How had I not seen her for what she really was — a cold-hearted killer? Of course, I knew the answer to that. I'd been so infatuated with her since the night we met that she could have been Jeffrey Dahmer for all I cared. Love isn't just blind — it's deaf, dumb and mute.

"I want to see you and explain everything in my own words," she said.

It was my turn to think. "OK. But not at your place." We needed to meet somewhere public. Preferably highly populated, so she couldn't use the same gun on me that she'd used on Damian. Better to be safe than six feet under.

"What about Sunset Park?" she suggested. "There are always many people there."

"No," I said, not wanting to stray onto her home turf and give her some kind of advantage that I wasn't aware of. "I know somewhere better."

We agreed to meet in one hour. I hung up, checked out of the hotel and headed straight to the Second Avenue F stop. I rode the subway to York Street in Dumbo, pushing aside thoughts of Hannah's nearby apartment, and walked down York to Prospect and climbed the steps up to the Brooklyn Bridge. I'd arranged to meet Gina on the bridge's pedestrian walkway, at a viewing platform located at the Manhattan-side pylon, so that she would expect me to arrive from Manhattan. By approaching from Brooklyn, I would hold the element of surprise.

The bridge was crawling with tourists, cyclists, and runners, the day's clear skies and low humidity making for perfect outdoor conditions. Normally I would revel in a walk across the Brooklyn Bridge — it's one of the great New York experiences, offering views of the Statue of Liberty, Governor's Island, the Brooklyn and Manhattan skylines — but that day the journey held nothing but dread for what waited at the other end.

I spotted Gina from halfway across the bridge. The wooden pedestrian ramp hangs above the main level of the bridge; it sags after the Brooklyn pylon but then rises again in the middle, affording a clear line of sight down the walkway toward Manhattan. Through a line of vertical steel cables I could see Gina waiting at the first pylon. She was standing on the uptown side of the viewing deck, her back turned to me because, as I had hoped, she was expecting me to approach from the other direction. She was wearing a loose-fitting cream T-shirt over black jeans, perhaps to conceal a weapon. The purple handbag slung over her shoulder would barely hold a set of keys. I edged closer, studying her body shape. I couldn't discern any bulges around her waistline. Maybe she didn't have her gun, I thought, or had chosen to leave it at home.

I expected her to turn around at any moment and see me. But she didn't. I was able to walk right up to her and embrace her from behind like a long-lost lover.

"Sweetheart," I said, running my hands over her pockets and waistband as she spun around to face me.

"Luke! You surprised me."

"That was the general idea." I held her close and looked into her eyes. I'm not sure what I expected to see. The look of a stone-cold killer, perhaps. But the same Gina stared back, her dark pools peering into my soul. At that moment she looked like she couldn't hurt a blowfly. And maybe she couldn't. For a moment I thought that maybe I'd got the whole thing wrong. But I knew otherwise. After all, she'd admitted her role in Damian's demise during our phone call.

"So," I said.

"So," she said.

I released her. "Let's walk as we talk."

"Of course."

She got another surprise when I grabbed her hand and led her away from the city toward Brooklyn. A black teenager on a BMX swerved out of the bike lane to avoid a tourist taking a snapshot and almost collided with her; I tugged her hand to pull her out of the way.

"You need to be careful up here," I said. "Anything could happen."

"I can look after myself." She tried to pull her hand away but I held tight. To any passers-by, we looked like two lovebirds taking in the sights.

"I spoke to your father this morning," I said.

Her eyes stared straight ahead, looking down the walkway towards the towering granite pylon with a United States flag on top fluttering in the breeze.

"No, you did not."

"Yes, I did. Jose Marquez of Cuidad Juarez, Mexico."

"I do not know who you are talking about."

"Come on, Gina. I know all about Gabriela."

"Who?"

"You know — the person who owns that pre-paid phone in the bottom of your bedroom drawer?"

She continued to play dumb.

"OK," I said, "let me tell you all about her. Once upon a time, there was a beautiful little Mexican girl called Gabriela. She lived in Cuidad Juarez, the poorest of the poor border towns. But she was very happy. Her father was a carpenter and her mother the best cook in the neighborhood."

"Sounds too good to be true."

"She also had a twin brother who she loved very much. His name was Alberto and he was her hero. One day he was going to be a doctor."

"What a lucky girl," she said without emotion.

"Indeed. A lucky senorita. As a child, she herself dreamed of becoming a schoolteacher, and three years after finishing high school she achieved that dream. Everything was perfect." I paused. "Until the day her brother didn't come home." I glanced at her face to see if that registered but she remained impassive. "For days, Gabriela and her parents fretted over the fate of Alberto. And then late at night on the third day, the police came to their door." I stopped to see if she wanted me to go on. She kept staring straight ahead. "They had located Alberto. He had been delivering drugs for a cartel — voluntarily or involuntarily, to this day no one knows for sure. But either way, someone took a disliking to Alberto. Maybe he said something that he shouldn't have. Maybe he tried to short the transaction. Whatever the cause, he was killed and his body parts left scattered along the highway leading into Juarez as a warning to anyone else who might think of messing with La Familia."

I stopped and took her by the shoulders, turning her to face me. She didn't look up. So I put a finger under her chin to tilt her head back.

"Alberto was a good boy," she said, a fierce look in her eyes. "He was studying to be a doctor. He never would have worked with those animals."

"Perhaps not. But we both know that what happened happened. Then not long afterwards, Gabriela's parents suffered a second blow."

"Gabriela disappeared," she whispered.

"None of her family knew why. But I'm pretty sure I know. Everything in Juarez reminded her of Alberto and the fate he had met. It was too much. She needed to get away."

Gina didn't nod in agreement, but she didn't refute my claim, either. After all, she had told me as much when she claimed her brother had died in a car accident.

"So great was her anguish, Gabriela was able to put her parents' feelings aside. She snuck across the border like many an immigrant before her and ran as far away as she could." I looked at the city skyline. "She ended up in New York. A place where anyone can blend in, become anything they want to be. The perfect place for reinvention. Second starts." I thought of Ajax and his failed efforts. "Gabriela was smart, beautiful, and picked up English after only a few lessons." She was hanging on my every word now, like it was someone else's story that she was listening to. That's because she knew I was getting to the most interesting part. "Gabriela worked hard and she was clever. Soon she had steady employment, an apartment of her own. Even a cat. She was slowly recovering from the loss of her brother. But then two things happened that changed everything."

She looked at me. There was a hint of a smile on her lips.

"She saw Jesus Sanchez. I don't know where. In the street. Maybe at the hotel bar where she worked. But wherever it was, she followed him home so that she would know where he lived."

"And the second thing?" she said, not denying the allegation.

"The turf war."

26

"The turf war provided you with the perfect cover to take revenge against La Familia, didn't it?"

"I tried to forget what they had done to Alberto, but I could not." A steely look came into her eyes that I'd never seen before. "He was my brother and they treated him worse than a dog."

I wondered how I'd feel if someone treated my brother like that. Who knows how I would react. The bond of family is so strong, it can make people act in unexpected ways.

"You knew that if you could somehow get to Doof-doof, his death would be seen as another hit in the turf war. Another bloody piece of tit-for-tat."

"Tit-for-tat?"

"You know — payback for the deaths that had already happened. But first, you had to work out how to get to Doof-doof." We had now reached the pylon on the Brooklyn side of the bridge. I steered her into a corner of the viewing platform that faced south. The East River, Governor's Island and New York Harbor stretched out before us. "You needed help. That's where Damian came in."

"It was actually his idea."

"He didn't seem that smart to me."

"Oh, Damian, he is cunning."

"Was."

"Oh," she said, like she had just remembered. She dropped her head. I momentarily regretted my bluntness until I reminded myself that she was the one responsible.

"How did Damian get involved?" I said.

"I am a schoolteacher, a cleaner. I could not possibly do something like that on my own. I heard from another cleaner about how she had overheard Damian boasting to some of his co-workers about time he spent in the army. How he was trained to kill."

A gazillion-watt light bulb went off in my head. That tattoo that I had noticed on Damian's arm when we first met: Who Dares Wins. It was a military tattoo. The larger one on his chest, that I'd seen riddled with bullet holes and smeared with blood, no doubt had the same origin.

"You must have offered him a lot of incentive to get him involved in something so serious." I thought of Damian lying naked on that hotel room bed and wondered if some of the incentive was physical.

"Yes, I offered him money," she said stiffly, as if reading my mind. "The ten thousand dollars that I had saved up to do my bridging course. But that Damian, he was always scheming. After I approached him, he decided that killing Sanchez could also be a way to steal drugs and money from La Familia."

I had figured that out already. The empty safe at Doof-doof's apartment, the duffle bag full of blow in the hotel room. It didn't take Sherlock Holmes to put it all together. Not only did Gina pay Damian a fee for services rendered, he also collected a tidy bonus along the way.

"Greedy little bastard," I muttered.

She pushed a stray lock of black hair that had been loosened by the wind back behind her ear. "After we talked, Damian scouted Sanchez's apartment and saw that it would be almost impossible to force his way into. It was too heavily secured. But then he noticed your bar next door, so he had a few drinks there and learned from one of the customers that you lived upstairs. Then, when he met Ajax, he realized that an Australian connection might be just what he was looking for."

I thought Damian had looked familiar when I first met him. Now I knew why. He'd drunk at my bar, looking for ways to break into Doof-doof's apartment. Chances were I'd even served him a beer or two. Sneaky fucker. He'd set me up good and proper, right from the get-go. It was no coincidence that Ajax had wandered into my bar on that night after Cinco de Mayo. Damian had planned it all, right down to Ajax's obnoxious performance at the bar so that we'd kick him out and he could come back to start milking my sympathy. Gina, Damian and Ajax had all exploited my tendency towards common decency — to give Ajax, in Aussie parlance, a fair go — like it was some kind of character weakness, just to satisfy their ends. Jesus, human beings are capable of some cynical shit. It's a fucked-up world we live in, no doubt about it.

"Damian also thought that having someone on the inside to give him access to your apartment would leave less sign of where the killer had come from," she said. "And that coming through the kitchen window would give him the element of surprise."

"He was right there," I said, thinking of the three blokes laid to waste as they played Texas Holdem. I studied her. "But that left Ajax."

Her face darkened. "Ajax went crazy after you told him about what had happened next door. He realized what Damian had done. Ajax was a musician. He did not want to be a part of any murders. He started talking about going to the police." She looked me in the eye. "I did not know that Damian would kill Ajax, Luke. I swear."

"What — so Ajax didn't know everything that was going on?" She opened her mouth and then closed it again. "Come on, Gina. Spit it out. I know most of it anyway."

"All right," she sighed. "Damian had told Ajax that he merely wanted to rob Sanchez and promised Ajax high quality heroin and enough money to record his music if he helped him gain access to the apartment. So after Ajax began staying at your apartment, he cut Damian a copy of his key." She sighed, watching a seagull float in the wind currents over the East River. "Ajax, he was so desperate to record his music. That was all he ever wanted."

No wonder Ajax looked so shocked when I'd told him about the murders. He hadn't known until then that the reason Damian wanted to get into Doof-doof's apartment was to kill him.

I also remembered how he and I had talked about heroin powering Keith Richards' creativity. It sounded like Ajax had employed the same strategy; he'd sold his soul to the rock'n'roll devil by agreeing to help Damian in exchange for the heroin that would help fire his creativity. Bon Scott was right. It sure is a long way to the top if you want to rock'n'roll.

"So you blokes staged that whole cock and bull story about Ajax assaulting you just so he would have a reason to ask to stay at my place?"

"We knew that you wouldn't say no. You are too much of a...how do you say, good bloke?"

The epitome of a backhanded compliment.

"Did Ajax actually assault you? So he'd get arrested and I'd feel sorry for him and let him sleep on my sofa and all of that?"

She shook her head. "That was Damian. Ajax was unconscious at the time, still drunk after his performance at the Living Room. When I got him back to the hotel, Damian took one look at him and knew that it was time to act. He was the one who hit me. Several times." Her voice dropped off. "He looked like he enjoyed it."

"I'm sure he did, the bastard. But you got your revenge in the end."

She didn't say anything to that.

"It was you, wasn't it? That night out in Coney Island."

"I did not trust Damian. I could not. He had already killed Ajax to keep him quiet and I knew it was only a matter of time before he came after me. And then you."

"Me?"

"After you visited him at the Hotel Chelsea, he kept talking about you. He was worried about what you might find out. I managed to convince him that you were harmless. Just an amateur, digging around in something that you did not really understand, and that you would give up soon enough."

"That's not so far from the truth."

"But I was still worried. Damian could not be trusted. So I went out to Coney Island to warn him to leave me and you alone or else I might do something drastic. He laughed in my face, said that I would never have the courage to shoot him. When I protested, he handed me his gun and dared me to pull the trigger. I panicked and it went off. Once that happened, I couldn't stop firing." She turned to face me. "I swear, I have never killed anyone before in my life."

I thought of the spray of bullets in Damian's hotel room, the hole through the Monet print. Whoever fired the gun clearly didn't have much experience around weapons.

"I believe you, Gina. But the fact remains that you have killed a man and had a direct involvement in the death of four others. Almost five, if you include me."

"I'm sorry, Luke. I didn't mean for you to become involved."

"Maybe you should have thought of that before you decided to use my apartment as the starting point for murder." I looked out at the Statue of Liberty. Give me your tired, your poor, your Mexican schoolteachers hell-bent on revenge.

"What happens now?" she said.

"If this was a movie, a bunch of coppers would come running down the bridge right now, their weapons drawn, and march you off to the electric chair."

She looked around at the sea of pedestrians and cyclists. "You have called the police?"

"Not yet. And I'm not sure that I will."

"Why?"

"Partly because I'm motivated by trying to protect my own ass and the coppers can't really help me with that."

"Then who can?"

"Don't you worry. I'll work something out."

"So we can forget that all this ever happened?" She smiled and squeezed my hand.

"I didn't say that, Gina."

"Oh." She tugged at my hand and nodded at her shoe, where a strap had come undone. I let go of her hand and she bent down to tighten it.

When she stood back up, she was holding a gun. A revolver. Damian's, I reckoned, the one that he'd handed her to prove how weak she was and she'd killed him with. She must have had it strapped to her ankle, underneath the leg of her jeans.

She held the weapon close to her stomach where no one around us could see it. The barrel was trembling as she pointed it at me. She was nervous and frightened: not a good combination when someone is holding a gun on you.

"Put the gun away, Gina."

"I can not let you turn me into the authorities."

"So you're going to shoot me right here, in front of thousands of people?"

I could tell by the look on her face that she hadn't thought through that part of the equation. I held her eyes with mine, trying to ignore the shaking gun inches from my stomach.

"Let me explain to you how this is going to work," I said. "To save my own skin, I'll probably have to tell some people what really happened to Doof-doof. And those people are not going to like it. Which that means anyone involved should disappear toot sweet."

"Toot sweet?"

"Twelve hours toot sweet."

"You will give me twelve hours to leave?"

"I know, I must be fucking bonkers." I nodded at the gun. "Come on, Gina, put that thing away before someone gets hurt."

As she pondered that, she relaxed slightly and the gun barrel dropped. I clamped down on her wrist with my left hand and wrested the gun free with my right, then tucked it inside my waistband. A tourist beside us noticed the transaction but didn't say a word. She just shuffled away without looking back. If nothing else, it would give her a good New York story to tell when she got back to Italy or Poland or wherever the hell she was from.

"I am sorry, Luke." Gina started to cry. "I did not want to hurt you. I really did fall in love with you. That was not part of the plan."

"Twelve hours, Gina," I said, battling to stay firm. I knew that if I waivered, if I looked into those eyes for just one moment, I'd be a goner. With one look, she could convince me to do anything. Maybe even go with her. And while I might be stupid, I was pretty sure I wasn't that stupid.

"But where will I go?"

"I know two people who really want to see you."

Her eyes widened. "But what would I tell them?"

"You could always start with the truth."

"The truth?"

"That you love them."

As I watched Gina walk across the Brooklyn Bridge toward Manhattan, disappearing into the crowd and out of my life, I knew that I was bonkers for not calling the coppers. But I realized at that moment that I truly did love her — Gina, if not Gabriela — and for that reason I couldn't bring myself to turn her in. Every good person deserves a second chance and deep down Gina was a good person, with a good heart, motivated only by a desire to bring some sense of justice to the violence La Familia had wrought upon on her family. Who could blame her for that? Perhaps if more people stood up to the cartels, the drug mess south of the border might sort itself out. Unlikely, yes, but a bloke can dream.

Besides, when it came right down to it, Ajax was the only innocent victim in all of this. All he'd wanted to do was make music, albeit with the help of some ill-gotten chemical gains. The rest of the victims weren't so blameless. Doof-doof and his mates had, as Ajax pointed out, lived and died by the syringe. And Damian certainly wasn't free of guilt, no doubt making a conscious or unconscious decision at an early age to put his instincts as a killer to use in the army before using them on the streets.

And although I might have been post-rationalizing, I reckoned that Ajax's heroin addiction would have caught up with him sooner rather than later. He was like many a muso before him — including Bon Scott himself. Living on borrowed time. It was a minor miracle that he lasted for as long as he did.

I took one last look for Gina but she was gone. She hadn't really escaped, though. She would never be free, even if she didn't serve a single day in prison. I felt sure that what happened in New York City over those spring days would haunt her for the rest of her life.

She wasn't alone on that score.

I crossed over to the side of the bridge facing Dumbo. Hannah's building stood a few blocks away. I fantasized about hiding out there for a few days, just the two of us, the way things used to be before Ajax, before Gina, before everything.

But seeing Hannah would also give her an opportunity to press me for an answer about the baby. And while I was closer to making a decision — much closer, because Gina's story had made the stakes clearer — I wanted one more night to sleep on it.

I also had some unfinished business to attend to before I would feel safe. So I wandered back toward Manhattan, soaking up the sun and feeling glad to be alive for the first time in days. The dawdling tourists and life-threatening cyclists on the bridge's pedestrian path annoyed me but there are, as I had just learned, worse things in life. I stepped off the bridge and ambled through City Hall Park, pausing to empty the bullets from Damian's gun into a drain and then toss the gun into a garbage bin. The gun might have come in handy, but if I carried it then I had to be prepared to use it and I knew I wasn't. I would probably freeze at the moment of truth, even against the Mexicans. Then they would disarm me and use the gun against me. Better to take my chances unarmed, I reckoned.

I dawdled along the former Indian trail of Broadway to Soho in no particular hurry. When I hit Broome Street, I headed east to the Bowery to walk past the Blue Skies Hotel. The place where this sad, sorry story had its beginnings. If Gina, Damian and Ajax had never met there, I thought, a lot of people would probably still be alive.

In the bright afternoon sun, the hotel looked as harmless as any other hipster hotel, although it would never seem that way again to me. Strange how locations can take on the meaning of the events that happen there, even though the area itself obviously has no influence over what transpired. Dealey Plaza in Dallas, the site of JFK's assassination, springs to mind. The events of November 22nd, 1963 and the plaza are now synonymous with one another, even though the shooter (or shooters, depending on your disposition to conspiracy) could have targeted the president from any number of locations along the motorcade route. I sometimes felt sorry for the plaza's namesake. An intended honor to Mister Dealey had forever linked his name with the most infamous crime in American history.

I studied the hotel's front entrance and considered checking in for the night — I still needed somewhere to hide out until I had everything resolved

— but opted instead for the cheaper Holiday Inn. It was more my style and besides, I was familiar with it. I headed over to Houston where a different, more pragmatic Indian bloke than the night before occupied the front desk. He was having none of my dysfunctional honeymoon bullshit as I checked in.

"Save your sob story," he said, gesturing impatiently for my credit card. "I've heard it all before."

I'm pretty sure you haven't, I thought, as I handed over the card.

I had some time to kill because my next port of call was a nocturnal affair. So I napped for five hours — if one can call that a nap — and then called Anchor when I woke.

"Hi, dude." His voice sounded distant, in a cavernous space. He was on speakerphone.

"What's the John Dory?"

"Not much. Just prepping the bar to open up."

"You straightened out last night's mess already?"

"Yep." I heard the clink of glass as he stacked some stubbies in a fridge. "Just finished. Hopefully those dudes won't be back for a repeat performance."

"I don't think they'll be back period."

"I dunno, dude. They seemed totally pissed."

"I'm sure they were. But I think I know how to take care of that."

"You found the dough you need to pay them back?"

"Yeah, something like that."

"Well, be careful. Those dudes sounded like they wanted to string you up by the cajones."

Anchor didn't know how accurate his description was.

"I'll be careful. I was just thinking — how's the business course going?"

"Welllllllll…" he said, "it's not really—"

"Your cup of tea," I finished for him.

"Instant-coffee is more up my alley. Yeah, I'm finding it tough. But I'll hang in there and get it done."

"Atta boy," I said. "Although I reckon you know what you're doing without a little piece of paper hanging on the wall behind you."

"Thanks, dude." He thought about that. "I guess it's a little like marriage."

"Why's that?"

"What do they say? It's only a piece of paper."

"Yeah, I reckon they do," I said. But I knew from experience that it was a tad more complicated than that.

27

I made one more call and then took a long shower, setting the hotel's five-mode shower nozzle to massage and letting the water drill hard into the back of my neck. Afterwards, I dressed in the same ratty clobber that I'd been wearing for the past few days, consoling myself with the knowledge that if everything went according to plan I would soon be back in my apartment with all the clean T-shirts my armpits desired.

The breakfast knish from Yonah Schimmel's had been my only meal of the day and I needed fuel for what lay ahead. I caught a cab to the West Village and alighted on Bleecker. The area's Dylan-esque Bohemian vibe was now well and truly gone, its artists and writers replaced by investment bankers, advertising executives and celebrities — the only people who could afford the exorbitant real estate prices. My ex-wife Suzie was a case in point. When we first arrived in New York, my hotshot creative director on the rise just had to live in Greenwich Village. When she and Phoebe returned to Sydney post 9/11, I had been more than happy to head for the seedier and relatively cheaper pastures of the Lower East Side.

If I was fair dinkum about it, though, I would have to say that I had enjoyed living in Greenwich Village. The reasons were many, not least of which was that one of my favorite restaurants resides there. The Fisherman's Net has stood on the corner of Bleecker and Leroy for nearly fifty years. I parked my bum at a window table, all the better to people watch. I wasn't particularly worried that the Mexicans might spot me because I was a long way from home — in New York parlance, at least, where neighborhoods can change dramatically from one corner to the next.

A scruffy waiter who had many things on his mind but none of them customer service eventually paid me a visit. I ordered the bouillabaisse and a Brooklyn Lager, then ate my way through a basket of warm bread rolls while the chef prepared the meal. When the main course arrived — a steaming pile of clams, prawns, mussels and fish in a cast-iron pan — I pushed my troubles aside and attacked it with gusto. Extricating some of the clams from their shells proved challenging, but by meals end not one morsel had escaped my attention. I signed the credit card bill, leaving fifty bucks on forty-one, then pushed back my chair and stood up.

Belly full, it was time to step into the belly of the beast.

I had called the Calloway Club earlier to check that the owner would be in attendance that night and told the woman who answered to let him know that Bradman would be at the crease later. When she sounded confused, I told her that he would understand what that meant.

I entered the club warily, nodding at the same barman and getting a lazy eye back in return. The joint was nearly empty, with just one table occupied by a nattily dressed older couple enjoying dinner — he the fried chicken, she the grilled fish. The same clarinetist from my previous visit sat slouched on a stool to the right of the stage, drinking coffee as he skimmed the sports section of *The New York Post*.

I pulled up a pew at the bar and the barman brought me a Red Stripe unbidden. Then he picked up the phone and made a call, avoiding my eyes as he did so.

I was halfway through the beer when the door at the end of the bar opened. The Hulk filled the doorframe. He beckoned me forth with a nod.

I belted back the rest of the Red Stripe in a few gulps — false courage, to be sure, but better than no courage at all — and squeezed past him into the office.

The door clicked shut behind me.

2Pay was sitting at the Eisenhower desk, cleaning his fingernails with the tip of his silver letter opener. It still looked very shiny and very sharp.

"Bradman," 2Pay said.

"Lara," I said.

"I am surprised to find you back here after your last defeat."

"I figured I'd return for one more match."

"Your call. But don't be surprised if your innings comes to a swift close."

"I dunno," I said. "I feel like I could bat all day." I dropped into the seat in front of his desk with as much nonchalance as I could muster.

"Interesting. Word on the street is that your form is poor."

"Fair dinkum?" I wondered how much he knew about what I'd gone through. Perhaps he was bluffing, or perhaps one of his contacts on the street had heard a few whispers.

"From what I've heard, it could be only a matter of time before you play your last shot."

"Well, I'm still at the crease. And with your help, I might be able to survive a little longer."

He shifted in his seat. "Everyone needs a batting partner."

"I have some information that might be useful to you."

"What kind of information?"

"Who killed Jesus Sanchez."

Now he sat up straight. "I assume you want something from me in return for that information?"

"I want you to make it clear to the cartel that I had nothing to do with it."

His lips pursed as he studied the blade of the letter opener.

"What makes you think I know this cartel?"

"Come on, mate. Can we stop playing games?"

"All right. Let me put it another way. Why would I do what you're asking?"

"Information is power. If you know who killed Sanchez, I'm sure you can put it to good use."

"In what way?" he said, like he'd never had a devious idea in his life.

"Well, it might be useful if you were, say, involved in some kind of ongoing dispute that was beginning to prove costly on a human and financial level. If you wanted to find a way to sit down and talk with the other party about ending some kind of…I dunno…turf war?"

I held my breath as he thought about that. This was when things had turned pear-shaped last time. He hadn't wanted to concede that he was involved in any illegal activities.

But this time, he nodded. "Proceed."

I told him the story. How La Familia murdered a woman's brother in Juarez and she fled to New York City. How she saw an opportunity to seek revenge when the turf war erupted. How she and Damian faked Ajax's assault on her so that I would take pity on Ajax and let him stay in my apartment. How he in turn gave Damian access to my apartment so that he could climb into Sanchez's and commit the murders on her behalf, then also rob Sanchez while he was at it. And how Damian then killed Ajax to stop him from going to the coppers, and the woman then killed Damian — not out of spite but fear, and also because he taunted her — before running for her life. The only part I left out was that the woman and I were romantically involved.

He didn't speak a word until I finished my monologue.

"That's one hell of a story, Bradman," 2Pay said. "And one hell of a woman, if it's true."

"It's all true."

"But how do I know that?"

"Do you honestly think I could make that up? I'm a good bullshitter but I'm not that good."

"I don't doubt it. But I don't think you understand the dire nature of the circumstances, Bradman. For me to get anyone to leave you in peace, they must be absolutely sure that you were not directly involved in Sanchez's death. All you have given me is hearsay."

"It's not hearsay," I said.

"But there is no proof." He pounded the table with his fist to emphasize each word. "If I am to tell them, they will need to be certain so that they can report back to the head of the cartel."

"Alejandro Navas."

"Oh, so you are familiar with Navas?"

"We've never met, if that's what you mean. But I know of him, yes."

"I have never met him, either. But I know that he is a man of…how shall we say, exacting standards. A little like myself. He will need proof of your innocence. And there's only one way to achieve that, as far as I can see."

"What's that?"

"They will need the girl."

"Why?"

"According to you, she is the only one still alive who can support your story."

"Oh."

"What's her name?"

"Gina," I said, a little too quickly. But telling him her fake name couldn't do any harm. Even if La Familia used it to track down her workplace and home address, the trail would end there, assuming she was smart enough, and had had enough time before she fled, to remove all the traces of her past. The Western Union receipts and the like.

"Last name?" he demanded.

"Marks."

"That's her real name?"

"Yes."

"If it's not, the Mexicans will soon find out."

I stared at him. I could feel my face draining of color even as I willed it not to.

"Come on, Bradman. You can't tell me you unearthed all that information without finding out the girl's real name."

The Hulk made a move toward me and 2Pay didn't stop him.

"I really do think it's in your best interest to tell me," 2Pay said as The Hulk grabbed my left shoulder. "At this point, it's either you or her. Because if I know this cartel, they will need a bone to throw their boss and they won't care whose it is." The Hulk grabbed my other shoulder and pushed me further down into the chair until I was stuck firm.

"I'd tell you if I could," I said. "I really would. But I don't know her real name." My heart accelerated, like it was going to burst through my chest. I hadn't seen this coming at all. I had thought the whole saga so bonkers that

2Pay would accept my story at face value. I should have realized that a bloke like 2Pay would need to know everything, every angle, if he was going to use my information. Jesus, how naïve can a bloke get? I felt like such an idiot.

2Pay stood up and walked around the desk, twirling the letter opener between his fingers. The scene from *Reservoir Dogs* flashed through my mind: the one where an adversary taunts a bloke with a switchblade while "Stuck in The Middle with You" plays in the background. Not in a million years did I think that one day I'd be acting out that scene in real life.

"Come on, Bradman," 2Pay said. "Don't make me do this the hard way."

I searched for an answer. A way out. I came up blank.

2Pay placed his long fingers under my chin and tilted my head backwards. I tried to pull back from his hand but The Hulk held me firm.

"What does every great batsman need?" 2Pay asked, his voice quiet, gentle, like a doctor displaying his best bedside manner.

I shook my head, afraid of the answer.

"His eyes, Bradman." He raised the letter opener and ran the sharp end over my left eyelid. "His eyes. When a fast bowler is charging in, about to launch a rock-hard piece of leather at one hundred miles per hour, depth perception is critical to following the path of the ball." He touched the tip of the letter opener to my left pupil. My eye closed tight, involuntarily, like a sea anemone that has had a seashell dropped into it. The Hulk leaned over and forced my eye open with his pudgy fingers.

The letter opener loomed large as it again moved toward my pupil.

"You have three chances, Bradman. You've had one. Here's the second." 2Pay turned the letter opener around and applied the blunt handle to my left eyeball with slightly more force. My eye watered and my vision blurred.

He pulled back. "That's two."

He took a firmer grip of the letter opener and leaned in again. This time he steered the handle into the corner of my eye socket. I felt the cold metal against my skin, then in the very corner of my eye. God damn it, I thought, as the pressure slowly built. I can't give Gina up. I just can't. I would never be able to live with myself. I tried to ignore the pain, push it away, but then it returned tenfold. It was like nothing I'd ever felt before. A perfect storm of pain located in one epicenter with potential blindness waiting at the other end.

"What's her name?" 2Pay pressed.

I almost blurted out where she worked, just to give him something. But if I told him that, La Familia really would figure out where Gina lived. I wasn't going to make it that easy for them.

"I don't know," I cried.

"Her name, Bradman." He applied more pressure with the opener and I wondered how long it would be before my eyeball popped out.

"I. Don't. Know. I really don't," I said, surprised that through such agony I could still be embarrassed by my voice taking on a panicked, high-pitched tone. "Look, I like my eyes, OK? I don't want to lose them. If I knew, I'd tell you."

The pain was excruciating. Unbearable.

Until suddenly it was gone.

"Enough," 2Pay said to The Hulk.

He ran the handle of the letter opener over my cheekbone, leaving behind a cool streak of moisture, a mixture of tears and eye fluid. "If that doesn't make him tell us, nothing will. He obviously doesn't know what we are asking." He tapped the letter opener against his open palm, thinking, as I sat there blinking, trying to return my vision to normal. "Besides, I have no real wish to hurt him. He is not a competitor. Let him go."

"What?" The Hulk said.

"Let him go. He is an innocent bystander. He will not cause us any further problems."

"But he knows too much."

"He doesn't know anything. That much is clear. And I have told him nothing of substance. He doesn't pose any threat to us. Besides, we will always know where to find him should he try to cause us any trouble."

"He might run, like the girl."

"I doubt it. There will be no need, after I tell Navas that he had nothing to do with Sanchez's murder."

"You're going to tell him that? She-it."

"Of course. A gentleman always honors his agreements." He looked at me. "I'll do it right now, otherwise Mister Bradman here will not get much sleep." He smiled like we were the best of friends. Maybe he truly was a psychopath. But regardless, I was grateful for the moment of sanity that had led to my reprieve.

The Hulk let go of my shoulders. "Gawd dammit. I still don't trust his scrawny white ass. He could disappear forever once he leaves here."

"Understandable. But there's another reason why he won't run."

"What?"

"That bar of his. He would never leave it behind."

Fucking criminals. Say what you want about them, but the best ones sure do understand human nature.

28

Such was the incongruity of my life at that point that fifteen minutes after I had almost lost an eyeball to a letter opener wielding drug lord I was rattling home on a crowded B train like any other late-night commuter. A few riders took a double take at my ruffled appearance but mostly it didn't register. Quasimodo himself wouldn't attract many second glances on the New York City subway.

I didn't have much choice but to take 2Pay at his word and assume that he immediately called the Mexicans. I needed access to my apartment for what I wanted to do next. Still, I cased the joint from a car park across the street for half an hour just to be sure it was safe. Then when all seemed clear, I ducked into The Billabong.

Anchor took one look at my clothes and stopped mid-chinwag with a hipster dressed like Boy George.

"Jesus Christ. What the fuck happened to you, dude?"

"Tough ride on the subway." I checked myself in the mirror of the back bar and was surprised to see that I didn't look as shabby as I felt. Where I expected to see swelling around my eye I saw only redness. A shudder passed through me at how close I had been to losing an eye.

Anchor poured a glass of water and plonked it down in front of me. I drank half of it in one gulp, even though what I really craved was a cold tinnie from the fridge behind him. But I would need my faculties for what I needed to do next, so a beer would have to wait — a positively un-Australian sentiment, to be sure.

"The good news," I said, "is that I reckon those little Mexican bastards won't be coming back any time soon."

"Sweet. What happened? You paid them off?"

"Let's just say that their attention has shifted elsewhere."

"I pity the elsewhere."

"Hopefully they won't find it." I drained the glass of water. "Not if I can help it, anyway."

"Well, be careful," he shouted at my back as I took the stairs up to my apartment two at a time.

I unlocked the door and made a beeline for Ajax's music gear, ejecting the tape containing his recordings from the four-track recorder and slotting in a new cassette. Then I plugged in the microphone, took out Damian's mobile and called Gina on speakerphone.

After that morning's showdown, I had no idea whether she would answer or not. After all, she was probably kinda busy getting the fuck out of Dodge. And she didn't answer. The call rang out, ending in a dull lifeless tone that somehow seemed appropriate. I put the phone down and then picked it up again, determined to give it one last shot.

But before I could redial, it rang. Someone was trying to call Damian.

Gabriela.

I hit speakerphone, flicked the four-track to record and held the microphone close to the speaker.

"Luke?" she whispered, like someone she might be trying to avoid had gotten hold of Damian's phone. Which, granted, was a distinct possibility.

I could hear low conversations and the hum of an engine in the background.

"Where are you?" I said.

"I am on the bus. Heading south. I decided to follow your advice."

"Good. Stay on the bus. You'll be safer there, believe me."

"Have you spoken to them?"

"Yes."

"Are you OK?"

"Somewhat."

"What did you tell them?"

"That Gina Marks killed Sanchez. What else could I tell them?"

"But it was Damian."

"I know he pulled the trigger, but you were the person behind it. And then there's the small matter of you killing Damian."

"I told you why I had to do that," she said. "Did you tell them anything else?"

She wanted to know if I'd told them her name. The sixty-four-thousand-dollar question. "No."

"Luke, I don't know how to thank you."

"It wasn't easy." Understatement of the year. "These people play for keeps, Gina. I reckon you should give yourself up. Go to the coppers. Tell them about your brother, explain why you did what you felt you had to do."

"I cannot."

"Gina, jail is the safest place for you. You know that La Familia will track you down no matter where you go."

"They will find me much easier in jail. I will take my chances on the outside, thank you very much."

"Please. Gina. Give yourself up. The police can protect you."

She stifled a laugh. "I do not think so."

I sighed. The time for talk was over. Besides, I'd gotten what I wanted out of her. "Take good care of yourself, Gina."

"Thank you, Luke. I'm sorry for everything that happened. Maybe in another life we could have —"

"Goodbye, Gina." I hung up before my emotions came into play. There was no point torturing myself over what might have been.

I punched stop on the four-track, ejected the cassette and slipped it into my pocket. Her admission of involvement in the murder of Ajax and Damian was just the insurance I would need if and when Malone and Lirianos came gunning for me again. Hopefully it wouldn't come to that, because if I played them the tape then the NYPD and/or the DEA would track Gina down and extradite her from Mexico. That would result in a trial and all the media hoopla that goes with it. Everything would come out, possibly even my partnership with Charlie. At the very least, it would be a mess of titanic proportions.

Yes, best for all concerned if Gina just stayed disappeared.

The next morning I rose late and scooted down to the diner, sliding into a window booth under Cosmo's watchful eye. I must have eaten there five hundred times but he never acknowledged my status as a regular.

Unlike his daughter.

"Yo, Dundee," yelled Maria, flexing her hips as she walked over with a glass of iced water. "Long time no see. You been out wrestling crocodiles again?"

"You don't know how close that is."

"Hey, are you OK?"

"It's been a rough few days. But I'll muddle through."

"Women trouble?"

"Nothing that a little tucker won't fix."

"The usual?"

"Sure. And coffee. Thanks."

I pulled out my phone and saw two missed calls from Hannah. No voicemails. She must have been trying to reach me while I was sleeping the morning away. I almost pushed the button to call her back then I stopped, realizing that it would be much better to talk to her in person. I had finally made up my mind about the baby and wanted to tell her face-to-face. I put the phone away then wasted a few minutes staring out the window at the Williamsburg Bridge traffic, lost in thought.

Before I knew it, Maria was back with the tucker. She slid the plate in front of me. "That'll put hairs on your chest."

"I hope so. I've got a big day in front of me."

"Exploring the outback?"

"Something like that. Definitely stepping into uncharted territory."

I finished the spinach and mushroom omelet and left Maria a four-dollar tip on eight bucks. Then I hightailed it back to the apartment and hauled my bike up from the basement to tackle the trek out to Brooklyn. Midday mania clogged the streets of Chinatown so I was the fastest vehicle around, weaving and dodging in and out of stalled delivery trucks and apoplectic cab drivers as I sped down Chrystie Street toward the Manhattan Bridge. Once on the bridge's bike path, however, the city's insanity fell away; the sound of my own breathing was all I could hear. I felt the ride doing me good, replacing the events of the last few days with some much-needed optimism. Perhaps I had put the worst behind me, I thought.

I coasted down the other side of the bridge into Dumbo, bumping along on cobblestone streets past Civil War-era warehouses. At a bodega on the corner of Front and Jay Streets, I bought a bunch of mini roses and then headed to Hannah's. Some bloke moving out of her building monopolized the elevator with crates of artwork; it was fifteen minutes before I was able to roll my bike into the lift and ride up to the third floor.

I leaned my bike against the wall and raised my fist to knock on Hannah's door. Then I stopped. After this moment, there was no turning back. I would be in for the long haul. Stinky diapers, midnight feedings, collapsible strollers that only collapse when they're not supposed to collapse. I'd been there, done that, and knew that fatherhood is no picnic in Central Park. The first years feel like Groundhog Day, helping the baby perform the same functions day in and day out. Then one day, after the little buggers finally begin to stand on their own two feet, it's about seventeen more years of hard work, albeit the most rewarding work you can do. As a mate of mine once said, for ninety-nine-point nine percent of the population having kids is what life's all about. The reason we exist. They're the only legacy we leave behind, unless we're lucky enough to be a Picasso, a da Vinci or a Shakespeare.

Besides, if the last few days had taught me anything it was the power of familial love. One could definitely question the morality of what Gina had done, but to me her motives were rock solid. Her love of family had put her on a path to endangering the new life that she had built for herself, but still she felt compelled to go through with it because she had decided that avenging her brother's death was the right thing to do. She had put that ahead of her own needs and desires. I knew that when it came to Phoebe, I would do almost anything to protect her. Maybe not kill someone, but ...well, I reckon you never know what you're capable of until you have to make that choice.

Who was I to deny Hannah the opportunity to experience that kind of unconditional love for someone else?

I rapped on her door three times. Then, after thirty seconds, I knocked three more times. I pulled out my mobile and called her; when she didn't answer, I left a voicemail explaining that I was waiting outside.

I was standing there with a bunch of rapidly expiring roses in my hand, trying to figure out what to do next, when the tumblers of the lock clicked and her door swung open.

29

Hannah wore an over-sized T-shirt and her hair was pressed flat against one side of her head. Dark hollows anchored her eyes, contrasting with her pale skin.

"Han? Are you OK?"

"Come in," she mumbled, her eyes on the floor. She shuffled sideways to let me through the door. I walked into the kitchen and waited while she fastened the deadlock.

"Morning sickness?" I remembered the roses in my hand and held them out to her.

She took them from me and laid them on the table. "Thanks."

"Jesus, Han, I hate to say it but you look terrible. Is there anything I can get you? Some Tylenol or something?"

She shook her head. "I did it." She placed both hands on the kitchen table to ease herself into a seat.

"Did what?"

"What we talked about."

"What we talked about? I don't understand." A sick feeling was brewing in my stomach.

"The baby." Her bottom lip trembled. "I did what we talked about."

"You…"

She nodded, crying now.

"But Han. You said you'd decide after you knew if I'd support you. I came here to tell you that I think you should keep it. That I'll do whatever I can to help you and the baby."

"I tried to call you!" she shouted. The outburst jolted me, made me recoil. "You never answered your fucking phone!"

"Oh, Jesus, Han. I've…well, I've been busy." That sounded lame, even to me.

"So have I," she yelled. Normally she was so calm and controlled but right now she was like a wild animal. "Busy thinking about the baby, and whether I had time in my life for it when my partner clearly does not." She made air quotes with her fingers around the word partner.

"What? So you just went ahead and did it without me?"

She glared at me. "What the fuck was I supposed to do? Stand idly by and wait until you found the time to discuss it, wait until it would be too late to do anything about it? I told you I was running out of time and that didn't make one fucking difference to you, you selfish prick. So yeah, I went ahead and did it." She bowed her head and started to cry again.

I stood there looking down at her. I was angry. Fuming. But not with her. With myself. Too busy with my own problems, and infatuated with Gina, I'd ignored the one thing that really mattered. But I couldn't tell her any of that. And even if I could, there was no point trying to explain it. After what she'd just been through, on her own, I could have told her that I'd been wrestling with the fate of the entire western world and it wouldn't have made any difference. And rightly so. My behavior was indefensible. I realized that as much as I liked to kid myself that I'd invented a new, more successful Luke Bales when I opened The Billabong, the truth was that I still had the capacity to fuck up big-time. It's hardwired into our DNA and no matter how hard we try, if we're fuck ups, we're fuck ups. Me and Ajax both, I reckoned.

"Is there anything I can do?" I said, already knowing the answer.

She shook her head. "Just go."

"Han. We can work this out."

"Maybe. But not today."

"Han." I put my hand on hers and squeezed it.

"Just go. Please."

I left her at the kitchen table, her head in her hands.

I hopped on my bike and meandered south through Brooklyn, feeling the lowest of the low. It was one thing for me to pay a price for my mistakes. But Hannah? That was completely unfair.

Then there was the unborn baby, who had paid the highest price of all.

I reached Sunset Park just as the schools came out, releasing a flood of jubilant children onto the streets. I locked my bike to a fence half a block down from Gina's apartment and watched the building for ten minutes; the only signs of life were teenage kids flirting with each other as they walked by. I put my head down and walked briskly up to the building, then rang the super's buzzer.

"UPS," I mumbled into the intercom. He buzzed me through.

The lobby was empty. I put my ear to Gina's door and didn't hear a thing. I took one last look around and then thought to hell with it. This was no time to stand on ceremony. I kicked the door, hard, right below where the lock met the jam. The old timber split and the door swung wide open.

I slipped inside and shut the door. I needed to work quickly before someone came to investigate what all the noise was about.

Then I heard a meow.

"Alberto?"

He stuck his head out from underneath the sofa. I went into the kitchen and he followed. I refilled his bowls, then while he ate I went into the bedroom to do what I had come to do. I found an old backpack in the bottom of the closet and then opened the top drawer. The Western Union receipts were still there. Gina must have gone straight from our rendezvous on the Brooklyn Bridge to the Port Authority, not even taking time to return and clear out her apartment before jumping on a bus. Maybe it wasn't necessary, but for my own peace of mind I had to be sure that there was nothing left behind that La Familia could use to trace her. I stuffed the receipts into the backpack, along with the photo of her brother. Then I quickly scoured the apartment for anything else that might lead to Gabriela. I found nothing.

I returned to the kitchen. Alberto rubbed up against my legs and purred. I reached down to scratch his head, realizing that there would be no one here to feed him tomorrow. Or the next day. I considered letting him out the door but I wasn't sure how long he would survive on the streets.

I stroked his back a few times then opened the backpack and put it on the floor. To my surprise, he jumped right in, like he already knew exactly what was expected. He had more gumption than I gave him credit for. I zipped the backpack three-quarters closed, leaving just enough room for his head to poke out the top, and that's how we rode all the way back to the Lower East Side, garnering quite a few looks and cheers of encouragement along the way.

I needed something to keep my mind off all the bad karma swirling around me so I told Anchor to take the night off and worked The Billabong solo that night. Anchor didn't take much urging. He'd been working a lot lately due to my absences, and the destruction wrought by the Mexicans still weighed heavily on him. He agreed that he needed some R&R. And by that he meant rock'n'roll, in the shape of heavy metal karaoke at Arlene's Grocery.

Alberto immediately made himself at home behind the bar and the punters took to him like he'd always been there. The Billabong now had an official bar cat. I went about doling out the booze, lost in the rhythm of the hustle and bustle until the last punters left at about two in the morning. I closed up and grabbed a six-pack from the fridge, leaving Alberto asleep on the bar, a bowl of water beside him for when he woke. As I climbed the stairs that I'd climbed a thousand times before, I recalled the night I had done just that only to find Ajax dead on my living room floor. A matter of just weeks had passed but it seemed like an awfully long time ago.

I cracked open a stubbie and slipped the cassette of Ajax's recordings back into the four-track. Maybe I felt like hearing his voice again, maybe I just wanted to hear any voice other than the one inside my head.

There was an album's worth of songs on the tape so I'd polished off three stubbies by the time the last chord rang out, an acoustic cover of "It's a Long Way to the Top". Every song was at least a solid album track, with probably two or three worthy of release as singles. Perhaps the high quality of the music was a result of the stash of high-grade heroin that Damian secured for Ajax. Or maybe he had just been on a song-writing roll and hit a prolific purple patch. I reckoned I'd never know for sure one way or the other.

But as I cracked open a fourth stubbie, I was sure of what to do with the tape.

Tompkins Square Park is a wasteland at seven o'clock in the morning, or at the very least severely wasted, casualties of both the night before and life in general sprawled across its wooden benches. I bought a bottle of water from a corner store and picked a spot near a dog run across from Keith's apartment building where I could keep an eye on his front door.

He appeared at seven fifteen, wearing his pinstripe suit over a bright orange shirt and lime green tie. If this was Gotham City, he could have passed for The Joker.

"Keith!" I shouted, but my words were lost on him, his ears blocked by iPod earbuds.

I looked both ways and then darted across Avenue A. I caught up with him on the corner of Fifth Street.

"Keith," I said, grabbing his elbow.

He spun around, fist primed. That's what living in New York does to you – puts you permanently on guard, ready to lash out at any hint of a threat.

Keith saw it was me and pulled his punch. He took out his earbuds. "Luke?"

"Yeah. Sorry to surprise you, mate."

"That's cool." He looked around, as if confused about where he was. "You live around here?"

"Nah. Above my bar, on Essex."

"Oh. That's right."

"You got time for a coffee?"

He checked his watch. A Rolex, probably a copy bought on Canal Street. "A quick one, I guess, if I can grab a cab after. I start at eight."

"I'll pay for the cab."

We found a diner a block downtown. The joint was humming. We took the last two seats at the counter. I ordered two coffees from a clearly hungover waitress and then turned to him. His aftershave was strong at close quarters.

"So you heard about Damian?"

"Yeah." He shook his head. "He was a right little bastard but no one deserves to die like that. In a shithole, with no one around."

"Live by the sword, die by the sword," I said, paraphrasing Ajax. It was harsh, but there had been a lot of dying going on and Damian had played no small part in it.

The coffee arrived, black swill in shallow cups. I added some milk to mine but Keith left his black.

"I'm not really here to talk about Damian," I said, and Keith raised his eyebrows. "I want to talk about Ajax."

"What about him?"

"You know he was working on some new tracks when he died, right?"

"Damian mentioned something about them. Said they were pretty good."

"Not were." I pulled the cassette of his songs out of my back pocket. "Are."

"That's them?"

"The one and only copy. Four-track. Haven't been bounced down yet."

He looked at the cassette for a long moment. Then he took a sip of coffee. "What's it got to do with me?"

"You've got a band, don't you?"

"Yeah."

"So I've got the material."

His coffee cup froze halfway to his mouth. "You want us to record that?"

"Why not?"

"Because we have our own material, that's why. Some pretty good stuff, too."

"OK. But just humor me. Listen to these songs and tell me they're not worth laying down." He looked skeptical but I pressed on. "Damian told me that you blokes were going to help Ajax record them."

"That was different. We were just going to be his backing band. It was still his thing."

"Is it different, though? Now you lay them down and if they're any good you get the kudos. I'm sure all Ajax would have wanted is a song-writing credit."

"I dunno. Like I said, we have our own material. And besides, recording studios cost money. We're still scraping together enough dough to lay down our own stuff."

I put the cassette on the counter between us. "Just take a listen. That's all I ask. If there's anything in there that you think could work for you blokes, let me know. I'll cover the cost."

"Seriously?"

"Seriously," I said, thinking about how badly Ajax had wanted his music to be heard.

On a sunny afternoon two days later, as I was biking in Red Hook in a bid to escape my troubles, my mobile rang. I screeched to a halt at the end of a dead-end street overlooking Buttermilk Channel. Governor's Island was straight ahead across the narrow channel of water; a half block to my left, a Snapple distribution center hummed with delivery trucks.

"Luke? It's me, Bertha. You got a moment?"

"Sure." I could tell by her voice that something was up.

"I'm working on a piece about this drug war that's been going on."

"OK."

"There's this stiff that turned up in Coney Island that's got me thinking." I could hear computer keyboards clacking away in the background. She was no doubt ensconced in the Rockefeller Center offices of the *New York Post*, where NBC and a bunch of other high-falutin' media companies resided.

"Why's that?"

"There's a link to your buddy."

"Which buddy?"

"Farmer. Seems this stiff worked at the same hotel Farmer was staying at when he first arrived in New York."

"Really?"

"Uh huh."

"That's a coincidence."

"Might be more than that. I was ringing to see if you'd heard Farmer mention the stiff's name. Ellis. Damian John Ellis. English fella. Ring any bells?"

"Damian? Nope, doesn't sound familiar."

"Interesting background, this Damian character."

"How so?"

"U.K. records show that he was in the British armed forces. SAS."

"Crikey."

"Uh huh." She slurped some coffee. "They're hard bastards. He joined straight out of high school and did two tours of duty in Afghanistan. Unfortunately he picked up a love of all things powdery while he was there. Was given an early dishonorable discharge for consorting one too many times with drug dealers in Kabul."

"Interesting."

"I've also learned that the bullet that killed Farmer was altered to cause maximum damage. An ex-military guy would know how to do that."

"I guess they would."

She coughed. "Anyway, I thought you might be able to confirm a connection between this Damian character and Farmer. But apparently not. I guess anything else would just be pure speculation at this point."

"I reckon it would. Sorry I can't be of any more help."

"Oh — one more thing," she said. "Did you ever find that person you were looking for in Juarez? You know, the one you called me about?"

"Nah. That was a total dead end."

"Sorry to hear it. Well, I guess I'll just keep plugging away then."

"Good luck," I said, then mumbled goodbye, unable to get off the phone fast enough.

30

Ever since we started our partnership, Charlie and I met each Sunday for a weekly chat at his hotdog company, a semi-respectable enterprise that he ran with a bunch of his Hell's Kitchen mates from back in the day. The warehouse was conveniently located just a few minutes from St. Malachy's, the Catholic church near Times Square where Charlie worshipped the good Lord each Sunday morning before the local media duly worshipped him at a curbside press conference conducted upon his exit from the abbey.

When we talked that Sunday, he made it clear in his own inimitable fashion that I had done the right thing with Bertha. I should not, under any circumstances, tell her anything about what had transpired, because the blowback could ruin both of us. As usual, he was right. While he lusted after the mayoralty, I lusted after that second bar out in Red Hook, and any smell of a scandal could ruin both our dreams. For me, it was more than a dream: it was also the one chance I had to prove to myself that I could do something right after letting down Hannah.

So as much as I wanted to set the record straight with Bertha and clear Ajax's name in the process, I knew I couldn't. It would have been simple: just point out that a certain Gina Marks, who worked at the same hotel as Damian and where Ajax stayed, had disappeared immediately following Damian's death, and then let Bertha follow the trail from there. She knew that I had been looking into missing persons from Juarez so it wouldn't take her long to put two and two together.

I could have also told her that Forensics should look at the bullets that killed Damian. Tests should prove that the bullets came from the same weapon used in the Doof-doof and Ajax deaths, providing another link between Damian and the killings.

But since Charlie's sources told him that Malone and Lirianos had gone cold on me, that they'd found nothing that proved that I was in any way involved in the murders, Charlie was adamant that I let sleeping dingoes lie. He was right, of course, so even though I desperately wanted to clear Ajax's name, circumstances snookered me. Sure, Ajax had brought about his own demise by trying to trick me, but I reckoned he didn't deserve to go down in history as a bloke who would top himself when in fact he was doing the opposite, fighting hard to be the very best he could. It just didn't seem fair to me. Plus, well, you know, once a boyhood hero, always a boyhood hero. I wanted to keep him up on that pedestal.

My inability to do that — not to mention the termination of Hannah's pregnancy — left me at a particularly low ebb. Not just because they were both in no small part my responsibility, but also because, not for the first time in my life, I felt like a complete and utter failure. People had died, lives had changed, and yet despite what I'd learned the world still believed that Ajax Farmer had committed suicide. To top it all off, I had let down Hannah, the one person in the world I absolutely did not want to do that to.

I coped with these depressing realizations the only way I knew how: by burying myself in my work, drinking as little alcohol as possible and cycling mile after mile after mile. When the state of New York returned Ajax's bail money, I used it for its original purpose — as a deposit on a new bar. I signed the lease on the Red Hook butcher's shop without really thinking about it, just trying to place one foot in front of the other, the process of thinking through the interior design and locating contractors for the renovations that lay ahead helping to keep my mind off darker thoughts. Then when Anchor aced the first real exam of his life, I celebrated with him as if he'd passed the bar, just happy to rejoice in a moment of positivity. And why not? Anchor had come a long way since he'd wandered in off the Bowery to ask for a job. There was no telling how far he might go, and I told him just that.

As for Hannah, I left her to recover in her own way, leaving a voicemail to explain that I was there for her if she needed me and then waiting patiently for her to reach out. I completely understood why she might never want to see me again but I held out hope that one day she would.

Over time, my affair with Gina felt increasingly like a dream that made a swift U-turn into a nightmare. Never much of a pants man in the first place, she had left me warier and much less trusting of women. In my darkest moments, as I surveyed different sheilas cavorting around the bar, I thought that there was only one woman in the world who I could ever trust again: the one I had so badly disappointed. But I also knew that that was grossly unfair to the female race and I had only myself to blame.

I was still waiting for Hannah's call as August turned into September. Then one humid Wednesday night, as Anchor and I were working a moderately manic Billabong, I felt my mobile vibrating in my back pocket. I hurriedly stuffed the two bucks I was holding into Fort Knox and took out my phone.

But it wasn't Hannah.

"Keith," I said, "how the fuck are ya?"

I'd met with Little Drummer Boy a few times since that morning at the diner when I'd asked him to listen to Ajax's music. He and the other members of The Knock had subsequently decided to record all of the tracks, as I had thought they would because they were bloody great songs. I had fronted the money for the session, as promised, and last I heard the band had gone into Blue Million Miles studios to start recording.

"I'm great," he said. "Where are you?"

"Where else would I be? The Billabong." Alberto smooched against my arm as I leaned on the bar.

"Have you got a radio handy?"

"Radio? Sure." I kept a crappy old AM/FM radio around for when I was working after hours, doing a stock take or some such other mindless activity. It gave me a chance to keep up with what was new in the world of music, a goal that was proving more elusive the older I got.

"Tune it to 105.6 FM," he said.

I killed the music on the jukebox; a couple of punters groaned. Then I powered up the radio. A baseball game blared from its tinny speakers before I switched it from AM to FM. I thumbed the tuner to the right frequency.

And then stood there, dumbfounded.

The last time I'd heard the song, it had been playing on a four-track recorder in my living room. Now, here it was on the radio in all its glory: meaty guitars, full drum sound, classic glam rock vocals. The groove was T-Rex with a modern bent.

"That's you blokes?" I said.

"It most certainly is."

"But how —"

"When we were recording Ajax's stuff, an A&R guy came to visit the band in the studio next door. I managed to slip him a copy of what we'd recorded so far and he liked what he heard. The rest, as they say, is history."

"Let me listen to the song," I said. But truth was, I was having trouble talking. A lump the size of an emu egg had formed in my throat. After years of disappointment and rejection, Ajax had finally made it onto U.S. airwaves.

The song ended in a flurry of guitars and then the announcer said, "That was The Knock with their brand new single, *Fly*. It's from their debut album, *Ajax*, which I'm told is the result of a collaboration with Ajax Farmer, the legendary Australian rocker who sadly committed suicide in New York earlier this year. The album launches the week after next, and something tells me these boys are going to go far."

I turned off the radio. "Congratulations, mate."

"Well, it's not like we've hit mainstream radio or high rotation or anything. That's just an upstate college station. But it's a start."

"It sure is."

"Luke, we couldn't have done it without you. I don't know how to thank you for bringing me that tape."

"I can think of something."

"All you have to do is ask."

"Drop a copy of that CD around here. I want to put it on the jukebox." Having part of Ajax residing permanently at the bar was an appealing thought. Even though The Knock weren't Australian like the other artists on the jukebox, Ajax and the compositions were and that was good enough for me.

"Of course. I'll swing by tomorrow after work."

"Thanks, mate. See you then."

I hung up and Anchor sidled over. "What was that all about, dude?"

"That song on the radio — it was written by Ajax."

"Really? It was sick."

"Like I said when he first walked in here — that Ajax Farmer was really something."

"Still is, by the sounds of it. But how did his song end up on the radio?"

"It's a long story." I hadn't explained the ins and outs of Ajax's death to Anchor. I reckoned the less he knew the better.

"Then give me the short version, dude."

"OK." I took a dollar note out of the till and walked over to the jukebox. "It's like they say."

"What's that?"

I fed the note into the slot, found the right song and hit play. A barrage of guitars filled the room. I walked back behind the bar, cranked the volume up to eleven, and then climbed onto the bar.

Then, when the chorus kicked in, I threw my arms out and sang at the top of my lungs, "It's a long way to the shop if you wanna sausage roll!"

By Simon Foster

Wanderlust – Luke Bales
Mysteries Book 1

The Diary of Lee Harvey Oswald

Lazarus – Luke Bales
Mysteries Book 2

About the Author

Simon Foster hails from Sydney, Australia, but has called New York home for many years. He holds a degree in writing and pays the bills by working as an ad man: a job that, whilst ranking just above car salesman in the credibility stakes, has helped him hone his writing skills and seen him walk the red carpet at the Emmys. Married with two daughters, he spends his time working, writing and chasing errant children around the house. He cycles, reads and visits pubs for relaxation — not necessarily in that order.

To get the latest news about Simon's writing, subscribe at
www.simonfosterauthor.com.

Whether you loved or hated Lazarus, please consider leaving a review where you purchased the book. Thank you.